KARI ROBINS

THE LOST WOLSTEINCROFT
BOOK 1

ALMOST TRAGIC MAGIC

Table of Contents

One 1

Two 10

Three 24

Four 29

Five 36

Six 44

Seven 50

Eight 55

Nine 69

Ten 79

Eleven 92

Twelve 104

Thirteen 115

Fourteen 128

Fifteen 137

Sixteen 147

Seventeen	155
Eighteen	164
Ninteen	170
Twenty	177
Twenty-One	185
Twenty-Two	193
Twenty-Three	202
Twenty-Four	207
Twenty-Five	212
Twenty-Six	219
Twenty-Seven	225
Twenty-Eight	229
Twenty-Nine	235
Thirty	241
Thirty-One	247
Thirty-Two	252
Thirty-Three	257
Thirty-Four	265

Thirty-Five	269
Thirty-Six	275
Thirty-Seven	279
Thirty-Eight	287
Thirty-Nine	293
Forty	299
Forty-One	306
Forty-Two	311
Forty-Three	316
Afterword	320
Acknowledgments	321
About the Author	322

Other Books

The Lost Wolsteincroft Series

Almost Tragic Magic

Almost Tragic Alliance - Coming Soon

Anything For Magic - Coming Soon

Almost Tragic Vampire - Coming Soon

Anything for the Pack - Coming Soon

Almost Tragic Fae - Coming Soon

Almost Anything for our World - Coming Soon

The Vörður of Yggdrasil Series

The Rise of the Vörður

The Battle for Yggdrasil

The Luna Sage Series

Scarlet

Ivory

Luna

This book wouldn't have seen the light of day if not for my friend, Jamie. When I was ready to toss it to the cutting room floor she read it and gave me hope

One

Josie

nother Friday night, and what was I doing? Sitting at my desk, grading tests, and planning out next week's practice schedule. Sectionals were coming up soon and scouts would be watching. Living in a small town had its benefits, but knowing many of these kids would never get out of here because of finances kept me up at night. And then there was Caleb. He had controlled my every move, making sure I did everything he'd deemed worthy of being a perfect wife. After years of being under his thumb, I was finally free to do what I wanted. Despite that, I sat here at work after dark. At least the silence was a pleasant change of pace to the noise that echoed the halls throughout the day.

My phone chimed from inside my desk drawer, bringing me out of the multitude of thoughts running through my head and back to the wonderful world of education. I dug around the cold metal drawer until my fingers wrapped around the hard plastic case of my phone and I pulled it out.

"Hey," I answered, not bothering to look at the caller ID—Vanessa was the only person who would call me so late.

"Don't tell me you're still at the school?" the voice on the other end asked. My best friend and the closest thing to a big sister I ever had didn't even bother to say hello.

"Of course not, Nessa," I lied.

"You can't lie to me. I know the echo of your office. Girl, seriously, they don't pay you enough to be there this late. You're a P.E. teacher, not the principal. Why are you still there?"

"I was just scheduling next week's practices. But I'm heading home now, I promise." I raised three fingers in a scout salute.

"Liar. Whatever. I'll be at your place at nine tomorrow morning. No arguing. I'm taking you out for the day. So, you better get home right now and get some sleep. You hear me, young lady?"

"Yes, Mother." I rolled my eyes but stood up anyway. After shutting off my computer monitor and grabbing my purse, I headed for the door. "But why? You know I hate being away from home all day."

"After being married to that bastard for twenty years, don't you think you should cut loose a little?"

"Hey now, I bought a new house and a car."

"True, but that's the only thing you've done for yourself since freshman year at BSU, and that's about to change! My mom's taking the kids for the weekend, and Clinton's on his way to the airport for a conference. So, you and I have the day and night to ourselves. I know it's only been six months since the divorce's been official, but you really need to get out, and my goal is to get you laid, so we're going to Indy to a new bar called Rogue, and there's nothing you can do about it."

"I'll call the cops if you kidnap me." My empty threat did nothing to her resolve.

"Josefina Marie, my husband is a detective. Do you really think that would stop me?" Her voice was all serious. "Now, get your butt home right now or so help me, I will come and find you. You know I will. Love you!"

"Love you too." I hung up, grabbed my coat from the rack, and turned off the lights, locking the door behind me. I walked through the musty stench of both locker rooms, doing one last check before I left. Deer Run might be a small farming town, but kids still snuck things into the school they didn't want their parents finding.

The telltale sound of squeaking tennis shoes and a rubber ball on the hardwood of my gym floor piqued my interest. I had been the only one in the building when I locked the outer doors to the gym. I cracked open the locker room door to see a few kids shuffling down the court.

I stepped out into the gym, pulled a whistle from my pocket, and blew three quick blows. The boys all yelped, and a few even jumped.

"Son of a—, Miss C, you nearly gave me a heart attack," Rocky said. He was the tallest of the boys and my point guard on the varsity team. His golden-brown skin and long dreads set him apart from the rest of the pale boys of the Midwest, but his loyalty kept a large group of friends around him. He was one of the few kids who had a real chance of getting a scholarship and getting the hell out of this one-horse town.

"Watch your mouth, Rocky, or I'll make sure you sit your butt on the bench Monday night." We both knew better than to take me seriously, but he saluted me just the same.

"Yes, ma'am."

"Now, what the hell are you boys doing here? How'd you even get in?"

"Well, Rock's got a way with—ouch," one of the other boys, Keith, started before getting an elbow to the ribs. He was nearly as tall as Rocky and stick skinny. His bright orange hair hung low around his eyes and his cheeks reddened as I eyed him.

"We were just bored, ma'am. Not much else to do around here on a cold Friday night," Rocky said.

"Yeah, I get it, reasons I'm still here too, but you gotta get out of here. I'm heading out, and I'll be setting the alarm, so if you break in again, you'll have Old Tom to deal with." Old Tom was what passed for a chief of police in a town that had zero crime.

The boys all laughed but pulled their sweats over their shorts anyway and headed toward the doors with me.

"Rocky!" I called after them.

"What's up, Coach?" He trailed behind his friends.

"Just wanted to check in with you. Why are you really here?" I pulled him aside and looked him in the eyes. Well, as best as I could; he was a foot taller than me.

"Miss C, it's nothing." He studied the gym floor like describing it would be worth half his grade.

"Bull," I huffed and crossed my arms as I narrowed my eyes at him. "I know better. What happened?"

He sighed heavily. "He's drunk again. I can't be there when he's like that or else I might kill him. Sarah's back with her birth parents, and Beth married that drunken bastard, so she's on her own." Rocky's been a foster kid since his mother died a few years back, and his current home wasn't the best environment for his short temper. I'd called CPS on his foster dad, but they said they were too understaffed to come out and investigate a kid who was about to age out.

"Do you have somewhere else to go?"

He shrugged. "I'll probably just hang with Brian until his parents kick me out. No biggie."

"Do you have gas money to get out there or whatever else you need?"

"I'll manage."

I sighed and dug into my purse. Making sure his friends weren't watching, I shoved a couple twenty-dollar bills into his hand. "Just take care of yourself, okay?" I walked toward the outer doors, pulling my coat on.

"Yeah, I do. Thanks, I'll pay you back for everything, Coach."

"Pay me back by getting outta this town and making something of yourself, okay?"

"Sure, I'll make it into the NBA, and I'll buy you something shiny with my first check!" He laughed.

"That's a deal." I offered my hand to him, and he shook it loosely.

After flipping off the gym lights and setting the alarm, I walked out into the cool night air.

Rocky slid into the driver's seat as his friends piled into the bed of his pickup, and they headed out of the parking lot. I slid into my brand-new Tesla and headed out to my new cottage, settled in a large thicket of woods off rural Route 52. The house was small, but the grounds had a nice sized barn for the animals I wished to have someday.

Another Friday night alone with Netflix and fast food.

My stomach protested at the meager meal I'd had hours ago, so I steered my car to the only drive-thru in town. The line stretched around the building. Each car no doubt held teens, as everything else closed down at nine o'clock, sending most of the adults home.

I turned up the local country station and relaxed against my seat, waiting for the line to move. Car by car, I finally reached the speaker and ordered a greasy cheeseburger, fries, and a large non-caffeinated drink. The Charlie Brown adult voice cracked over the speaker, telling me a total that I couldn't understand. I rolled up my window and waited for the car ahead of me to move.

Another five minutes, and I was at the window. I blinked at the kid taking my money and nearly dropped it to the ground. Her skin and hair were so pale it looked as if someone had drained all the color from her. Even her eyes were the lightest of grays. She tucked a strand of hair behind her pointy ear, and I audibly gasped. The girl's eyes widened as she quickly grabbed my money and closed the window behind her. She looked over her shoulder at me as she counted my change.

I watched the other workers as they packed my food. They all had the same white-gray skin and blindingly white hair. Gulping down the lump in my throat, I closed my eyes, trying to clear the image from my mind.

"Ma'am?" the girl's voice called, and I forced my eyes open again. She leaned out the window to hand me my change. She tucked her pale yellow hair under her red hat and her blue eyes looked at me with concern. "You okay, ma'am?"

I shook my head and reached for the money. "Just exhausted, I guess. Glad I skipped the caffeine."

"No worries," the girl said, now handing me my drink. "I get that all the time working the late shift." She ducked back inside, grabbed my bag, and leaned back through the window, handing me my food. "Have a good night."

"Th-thanks, you too." Setting my food on the seat next to me, I put the car back into gear and headed home.

I pulled into my driveway ten minutes later.

My English Tudor cottage was something straight out of a fairytale. It sat nestled in a thicket of trees with wildflowers sprouting all over the place. I had painted rocks with glow in the dark paint over the summer and sprinkled them up the walkway to the door, making it look like fireflies were welcoming me home. Inside was small but cozy. I kicked off my shoes at the door. The cool hardwood floors soothed my aching feet. I dropped my bags on my old cast-iron stove that never got used and walked toward the back hall.

My room was just big enough for my king-sized bed, but the bathroom and closet were luxurious. I stripped out of my school clothes and into a pair of sweats and a hoodie.

I walked back through the kitchen and grabbed my food before heading to the living room, where I dropped into my favorite oversized loveseat and curled up with the quilt my great-grandmother had made me.

I flicked on Netflix and scrolled through, looking for something new. Sappy love stories were my go-to any given night, so I cocked my head at the suggestions my TV was showing me. Things like *Bright*, *Stardust*, *Beautiful Creatures*, and *The Chilling Adventures of Sabrina* popped up on my "to watch" list. I went to the search bar and found *The Kissing Booth* instead.

My cheeseburger and fries were surprisingly still hot and tasted better than any steak I'd ever made for myself. I devoured my meal as the movie played.

A faint, mournful cry stirred me from the depths of sleep, tugging me toward consciousness. My eyelids fluttered, heavy and reluctant to open, as the sound grew louder; insistent. It was my cat, his cries sharp and pitiful, coming from somewhere outside.

I stretched, my movements sluggish and weighted by the lingering fog of an unplanned nap. The dim light in the living room cast long shadows, and for a moment, I was disoriented, unsure of where I was. Then the quilt draped over me registered, the soft cocoon of its warmth now an anchor keeping me rooted in place.

Another wail from my cat broke through the haze, more demanding this time. I forced myself to sit up, rubbing my eyes and stifling a yawn as I tried to shake off the grogginess. My body protested, my limbs stiff from dozing off in the awkward sprawl of the couch.

With a low groan, I pushed the quilt aside and shuffled to my feet, my bare toes curling against the cool floor. The cries intensified as I made my way to the back door, my movements slow and deliberate, still half-asleep.

As soon as I slid the glass door open, my orange cat shot inside like a streak of flame. His bright fur gleamed in the light, and he twisted around my legs, purring loudly as though scolding and thanking me at the same time. I sighed, still groggy, and headed toward the kitchen with him dancing at my heels, his tail brushing against my calves with every step.

"Alright, Ollie, I'll give you some food, then I'm off to bed. It has been a very long day."

I scooped out some food for him before heading back to my room and climbing under the covers. The exhaustion of the day hit me faster than I'd expected. I didn't even set an alarm before I fell asleep.

Two

Josie

I told myself this was a day for me, something I hadn't done in years. Caleb would have scoffed at the very idea of a salon day, calling it frivolous or selfish. My mind wandered, unearthing the familiar ache of regret. We'd met my junior year of high school, and I'd fallen so hard, so fast, swept up in his charm. Back then, I would've done anything to please him, bending myself into whatever shape he required.

The weight of his control had been insidious, creeping in slowly over time. It wasn't until years later that I realized how entangled I'd become. Despite that one rebellious night when I'd dared to enter the college tattoo shop, I'd lived entirely by his rules, my own wants buried beneath the weight of his expectations.

A sudden prickle ran down my spine, sharp and uncomfortable, cutting through the nostalgia. I glanced toward the mirrored wall ahead of me, trying to shake the feeling. The reflection showed only the usual buzz of the salon—stylists chatting, customers scrolling on their phones—but something felt... off.

"Jo?" Nessa called, causing me to jerk my unfocused eyes up to her wide, green ones.

"Huh?" I asked.

"She asked if you want a refill."

I finally noticed the girl from the front desk standing in front of me. She pointed down to my nearly empty coffee cup. I nodded, handing her the mug.

"Long night?" Nessa asked. She sat in the chair beside me with her long, dark brown locks under a dryer.

"Weird night." Images of my dreams flooded back to me. "I had all kinds of strange dreams. They felt so real that it was super creepy." I stared at the magazine I hadn't been reading.

"What kinda dreams?" Nessa urged me on.

I raised an eyebrow at her. "Just dreams."

"Oh, come on, Jo. We haven't really talked in a long time. Caleb kept you locked up in that house like a tiger at the zoo. Talk to me. I can tell something's bothering you, so spill it."

The dreams haunted me: Monsters of fairy tales chased me while I fought them off with a fireballs shooting from my hands. I shivered at the memory, but Nessa's eyes pressed me into speaking.

"Remember the books I was obsessed with freshman year?"

"Do I ever? I can still hear your mother screaming at you for reading about magic and how dangerous it was. She acted like magic was real. She really freaked out."

My mother had been pretty extreme when I was a kid, and any mention of magic would send her into a frenzy.

"Well, my dreams last night were like I'd fallen into one of those books." I looked around to where our hair stylists were. They were both busy with other clients, so I leaned over and lowered my voice before I spoke again. "I was being chased by a tall vampire woman in a red dress down a dark alley, and some tall man did something to her. One minute she was behind me and then the next she flew, slamming into the brick wall in front of me."

"Oh, a Prince Charming dream? Did you get a good look at him? Was he handsome?" Nessa turned in her chair, staring at me.

"Seriously? I said I was being chased by a vampire and all you care about is if the guy was cute? You're pathetic." I threw the towel in my lap at her.

"Sorry, Clinton's been really busy at the department, so I've been a little lonely."

"Busy? Why? What's been happening?" I asked, my voice a little too quick, betraying my nerves. The lingering feeling of being watched clung to me, a phantom weight pressing at the edges of my awareness. I reached for anything—any topic—that could steer the conversation away from my unsettling dreams and distract me from the unease crawling under my skin.

"There's been a rash of missing street kids in Indy; a few days after they go missing, they turn up dead. He's spent several nights in his office. The conference he's going to this weekend is on forensic science. These poor kids..." She twisted the towel with her slender fingers. "No one can figure out how they're dying. And you know Clint; it's been keeping him awake at night." She turned her gaze to me with a painted-on smile. She tried to hide her fear and worry, but I'd known her too long to believe it. "You don't need to be hearing about this. I'm sorry. Today is all about you."

"Hey, sis, it's okay if you need to talk too, ya know?" I reached out my hand and clasped hers.

"It's just... He's been acting so strange lately, so I snuck into his briefcase the other night thinking I might find evidence of a mistress or something." She paused and ran her hands over her arms. "But I saw pictures... crime scene pictures. All I could see was one of my rug rats laying there on the asphalt. These kids had no one to worry about them, no one who protected them. Just breaks my heart."

"And you ask me why I stay late at the school on a Friday night? Guess what happened after I hung up with you? A few boys had broken into the gym and were playing ball. Even our little town has issues of bad parenting and drugs. I mean, I guess having them break into the school to shoot hoops is better than them shooting up somewhere." The thought of losing any one of my kids to drugs clutched at my heart, and I wiped the single tear from my eye before it could fall.

"I get it, I really do, but you gotta take care of yourself too before you burn out."

"Yes, ma'am." I laughed.

"I mean it! After we're done here, I'm taking your skinny butt shopping."

I rolled my eyes at her but squealed silently at the thought of new clothes. Again, Caleb probably would have thought it excessive.

My stylist pulled off the tinfoil, rinsed it out, dried my hair, and started the color process. It was nearly three o'clock by the time Nessa and I walked out the door. Me with my wildly colorful hair and her with mild highlights and a trim.

We hopped into my electric car and buckled up. Before I headed to the closest mall thirty minutes away, she spoke.

"I've been meaning to ask you..." Nessa glanced down at her feet before finally looking me in the eyes. I cocked my head at her. She'd never been afraid to ask me anything. "Where'd you get the money for this car? And your house... I mean, the house is small, but the property is huge. I know Caleb wasn't that great with money."

"My grandparents." I shrugged. "They were always good with money. Gran had an accountant and set up a large inheritance for me. Honestly, I didn't even know about it until after the divorce."

"Does Caleb know about the money?"

I shook my head. "Haven't talked to him since the hearing."

"He's such a tool," she said, her laughter bubbling up like it couldn't be contained. The sound was light, carefree, and it reminded me exactly why we'd stayed friends despite the years and distance between us. For a moment, her joy pulled me out of my head, and I found myself smiling, the tension in my chest easing just a little.

It had been so long since I'd heard that laugh. Too long. Caleb had made sure of that. He never outright forbade me from talking to Nessa, but his disapproval had been palpable: subtle comments, derisive looks, a cold distance that made every call feel like a battle I wasn't strong enough to fight. Slowly, without even realizing it, I'd let her slip away.

But when I finally found the courage to file for divorce, Nessa was the first person I'd thought of. My hands had trembled dialing her number, my voice shaky as I stammered through an apology for the silence, for the years I'd let him control me.

Nessa hadn't hesitated. She'd cut through my babbling with her usual bluntness, her voice steady and warm. "You're here now," she'd said. "That's what matters."

Now, sitting across from her, I felt a pang of regret for all the lost time, but it was mixed with gratitude—a deep, overwhelming relief that she'd been waiting, ready to catch me when I needed her most.

"Yeah, I think Gran thought so too. She was pretty sick for a while and every time I'd visit, she'd ask about Caleb and then get upset when I said I was still with him. When I told her about the divorce, she smiled." I shrugged. "That's when she told me about the inheritance. She said she didn't want him getting any of her money."

"I always did like that lady."

"Yeah, she was pretty great."

The afternoon flew by in a whirlwind of dresses, shoes, and Nessa's relentless enthusiasm. After a quick stop at the food court to refuel, we dove headfirst into the stores, trying on what felt like a thousand outfits. Nessa's energy was infectious, and before long, I found myself laughing at her over-the-top suggestions and even agreeing to let her drag me into a beauty supply shop.

There, she practically ordered me to stock up on new makeup. I protested half-heartedly, knowing I was more of a jeans-and-t-shirt kind of girl, but I had to admit—there was something fun about indulging in a little glamour every now and then.

By the time we left the mall, the sun was dipping low, and we were loaded down with bags brimming with goodies. It was just before seven, and neither of us had the energy to sit down for dinner, so we grabbed some fast food on the way back to her place.

As we unpacked and started getting ready, a flicker of nerves bubbled up inside me. Nessa hadn't given me much detail about her plans for the evening, and I wasn't entirely sure what to expect. It had been at least a decade since I'd set foot in a bar, and even longer since I'd done it without Caleb hovering at my side. The thought was equal parts thrilling and terrifying, but as I caught sight of Nessa's determined grin, I decided to roll with it. Tonight was about breaking free—and maybe rediscovering a piece of myself I'd almost forgotten.

Nessa fell asleep the second I pulled onto the interstate, and the gentle hum of rubber on asphalt threatened to drag me under as well. I turned the volume of my radio up just enough to keep me awake, but not so loud to wake Nessa. Keeping her kids from killing each other was a full-time job in itself.

I was tapping my thumb on the steering wheel in stop and go traffic when I heard a bike engine roaring behind me. Looking into the rear-view mirror, I squinted to see him properly. My jaw dropped. There was no bike, just a winged man flying between cars. The semi beside me inched closer to the line, blocking the man's path. He slammed his fist into the side of the truck as he stopped mid-flight beside me.

"What the hell!" I shouted, startling Nessa awake. The man turned, glaring at me. His golden skin shimmered in the evening sun. I angled my head to look behind him. He had real life, honest to God wings. Giant, dragonfly-like wings. His eyes widened.

"What?" Nessa asked, bringing me back to the car.

"That guy..." I trailed off.

"Ugh... Assholes on bikes piss me off. Just because you're small enough to thread through traffic doesn't mean you should."

I shook my head and looked back at him. I really needed to sleep. He straddled his black bike and wore a black leather jacket. No wings in sight. His eyes released mine and turned back to the truck in front of him.

"I think I'm going to need some coffee to make it through this night." I sighed.

"Me too," Nessa agreed. "And you definitely need a shower."

I shot her a glare. "Shut it!" I tossed a French fry in her direction, missing on purpose. "But seriously, I need a shower." The faint sting of sweat mixed with flowery shampoo clung to me, making my skin crawl. "I reek of mall air and overpriced shampoo."

Walking into Nessa's house would have been terrifying if you didn't know that there were three children, all under six years old, living there. I had to kick my way through the toys that littered the floor toward the couch, but that was a fruitless effort as a pile of clean clothes took up much of the seating.

I rerouted to the dining room and set the food and my bags down on the table, where we ate our cheap hamburgers in silence. Once Nessa finished, she threw her trash away and told me she was going to take a quick shower.

I finished my food and stood looking around her living room. She'd put up new photos on her walls. Her sharp-looking husband had his arms wrapped around her waist and rested his chin on her shoulder. The picture next to Clint and her held their three children suspiciously loving on one another. Someone must have bribed them to look so sweet.

"Jo!" she called from upstairs. I grabbed my bags off the table and headed up.

I tossed my stuff on her bed as I walked into her room. She stepped out of the bathroom in nothing but a towel, rubbing another through her hair.

"God, I always hate the way they style my hair. I know you're not supposed to wash your hair right after getting it done but I just had to wash out that stupid style," Nessa said, running her fingers through her freshly trimmed and overly styled locks, grimacing at the stiff, unnatural feel of the product. She turned her attention to me, a teasing smirk lighting up her face. "Your turn. You've got a very distinct gym teacher scent about you. Love you, but you stink."

She burst into laughter, and I rolled my eyes, throwing a mock punch in her direction. "Hey! I showered last night!"

Nessa raised an eyebrow, leaning back dramatically as if the air itself were offensive. "Did you use any soap?" she quipped, her laughter bubbling up again, filling the room with a playful energy that was impossible to resist.

"Ha, ha," I said dryly, crossing my arms and giving her a mock glare, though I couldn't keep the grin from tugging at the corners of my mouth. She always knew how to push my buttons in just the right way to lighten the mood.

Exhaustion from the day of shopping mixed with a jittery swirl of nerves and excitement as I grabbed my bags and headed to the bathroom. Nessa's teasing still lingered in my mind, a small smile tugging at my lips despite the restless energy bubbling in my chest.

Once inside, I flipped on the shower. The sound of rushing water filled the small space. My jeans clung uncomfortably as I tugged them off and let them drop, shrugging out of my t-shirt and hoodie before tossing them carelessly to the floor. For a moment, my eyes caught my reflection in the mirror. I looked tired, sure—exhaustion was etched into every line of my face—but there was something else there, something I couldn't quite name, flickering just beneath the surface. A flicker of anticipation. It had been so long since I'd done anything like this, so long since I'd felt a spark of freedom.

The steam filled the room as I stepped under the spray. The hot water hit my skin, melting away the day's chill and soothing the tension in my muscles. For a moment, I let myself linger, eyes closed, enveloped in the warmth like a protective cocoon. I kept my freshly colored hair out of the stream, mindful of the pastel hues Nessa had been so thrilled about.

The soap was unscented, simple, but as I lathered it over my skin, it felt like more than just a cleansing ritual—it was a small, symbolic act of shedding the old; the weight of everything I'd been carrying. Standing there under the water, I felt something begin to stir inside me. A tentative hope.

Finally, I turned off the water, reluctant to leave the safe bubble of the shower but eager to see what the night would bring. I glanced back at the mirror and caught my own gaze.

For the first time in a long time, I felt like maybe I was looking at someone ready to step into the unknown.

The fresh towel Nessa had left on the sink was still warm from the dryer as I wrapped it around my body. I dried off quickly and slipped into my new dress, then wrapped the towel around my hair. Nessa sat on the edge of her bed buckling her shoes as I stepped out into her room.

Nessa had always been the prettier one, even in high school, even after her babies were born. She stood at least six inches taller than me. She wore a light pink silky dress that hugged her body in all the right places. The simple black strap wedge sandals completed her elegant look. She looked up from the mirror where she was finishing her makeup.

"That dress is super-hot, Jo."

"Thanks." I reached for the black, off-the-shoulder, long-sleeve dress, my fingers lingering on the soft, stretchy fabric. After slipping it on, I adjusted the neckline, the smooth material sliding over my skin like a second layer.

The dress hugged my curves, the snug fit accentuating my waist and skimming over my hips in a way that made me pause. I tugged the top of the dress up, the low cut design exposing just enough collarbone and shoulder to feel daring without being over the top.

For the first time in years, I didn't just feel dressed—I felt powerful, even a little sexy. The reflection in the mirror was almost unfamiliar. The woman staring back at me had a spark, a confidence I hadn't seen in so long I'd almost forgotten what it looked like.

I smoothed my hands down the sides of the dress, taking a deep breath as a smile tugged at the corners of my lips.

Tonight, I wasn't just hiding in the background. Tonight, I was stepping forward, and I liked the way it felt.

"Leave it, girl. Show off that butt God gave you." She smacked at my hands. "Now, sit. Let's do your hair and make-up and get going."

Twenty minutes later, I was sliding into my knee-high red suede boots with three-inch heels and being dragged to the door.

"Are you sure you want to go all the way downtown? That's like... an hour away," I whined as we got into my car.

"Yes. Just drive." She laughed and cranked up my radio.

The nightclub had earned a reputation deserving of its name: Rogue, and the line to get in wrapped around the building. I glared at Nessa as we took our spot at the end. She wrapped her arms around my chest, covering my bare shoulders.

"Shoulda bought a whole dress," she mocked.

"Shoulda worn something other than underwear," I jabbed back.

"But I brought my coat like a smart lady."

"Oh, shut up!" I barked a little harsher than I meant to, but Nessa knew I was only playing.

We stood there for half an hour and only moved a few spots.

"I heard this place was hard to get into. You sure you want to try?" I shifted on my weight. "God, it's so dark out. I can't believe it's ten o'clock at night and I'm not at home."

"Crap, Jo, we're thirty-nine, not dead. Don't ruin my one free night by acting like an old lady!"

I watched as a tall, broad-shouldered guy—built like a bodybuilder—walked past us. His presence was undeniable, exuding an air of quiet power. He glanced our way, his eyes briefly meeting mine before he spoke into his wrist, his words low and purposeful. *He must be a bouncer,* I thought. He moved with such controlled confidence.

He nodded once, then started walking toward us, each step purposeful, like he was used to commanding attention without even trying.

"Evening, ladies." His deep voice rumbled through the air, making the hairs on the back of my neck stand up.

I felt an unexpected rush of unease as his gaze settled on me. There was something about his size, his presence, that made me instinctively take a step back. My breath caught slightly, a nervous flutter in my chest, and I couldn't quite place why. His voice was smooth, but his commanding stature made me feel small in comparison.

"Hello," I said, my own voice a little quieter than usual. I retreated just a step more, as if that small distance would ease the unfamiliar tension swirling in my stomach.

"What brings you two lovely women out tonight?"

"We're celebrating my friend's divorce from a jackass of a man."

I jabbed Nessa in the ribs before she could continue.

"Too bad for him." He stepped closer, reaching for the velvet ropes separating us. With one hand, he unclipped it from the post and offered me his other hand. "Might I speed the evening along for you, then? First drinks on the house. Tell the bartender Boss said so." He winked. "A beautiful lady like you should never pay for your drinks." The bouncer never took his eyes off me.

"Th-Thanks," I muttered, grasping his hand. He led the way to the front of the line and ushered us to the door.

"These gorgeous women are free to enter," he told the greeter. She stamped our hands, and the bouncer opened the door for us. "Have an exciting night."

Three

Warren

The security cameras flickered to life, casting a cold glow over my office as the split-screen angles filled the monitor. It was a routine I had perfected over the years—surveying the bar from the comfort of my desk, ensuring everything ran smoothly. The rhythmic thrum of the crowd filtered faintly through the walls, blending with the low hum of the equipment. Business was good, as usual. Outside, the line of patrons stretched down the block, their eager faces illuminated by neon signs and the occasional flash of headlights.

I sipped my drink, eyes scanning each quadrant of the screen, when she appeared.

She stood near the end of the line, her arms crossed tightly against the cool night air, shifting her weight from foot to foot. The streetlight above bathed her in a soft, golden glow, turning her hair into a delicate halo. She wasn't dressed to stand out—no sequins, no flashy jewelry, no attempt to blend into the glittering nightlife crowd. But the black dress hugged her every curve. Simple. Elegant. Breathtaking.

I leaned forward, the chair creaking under me, my focus narrowing entirely on her. Her face was soft, framed by loose strands of hair that danced in the breeze. She glanced toward the door, hesitation clear in the way she shifted her weight, as though she wasn't sure this was where she wanted to be. A friend beside her said something, nudging her shoulder, and a faint smile flickered across her lips, reluctant but genuine.

I couldn't look away. There was an unspoken gravity, a quiet presence that demanded my attention. I'd watched thousands of people come and go through these doors, but no one had ever made my chest tighten like this.

I didn't understand it—this sudden, overwhelming pull—but I knew I couldn't let her slip away into the night.

"Danny," I said, pressing the intercom button, my voice steadier than I felt.

"Yeah, boss?" Danny's reply crackled through the speaker, accompanied by the muffled sound of the crowd outside.

"There's a woman at the end of the line in a black dress. Let her and her friend in. Free drinks, no cover."

"You got it."

Danny never questioned my instructions, and tonight, I was grateful for it. My finger hovered over the camera controls as I watched him approach her. The way she glanced up at him, cautious but polite, tugged at something in me. She hesitated when he gestured toward the door, and her friend practically dragged her forward. For a moment, I thought she might turn and leave, but then she took a step, and another, until she was inside.

I switched to the interior feed, tracking her as she entered. The warm, dim lighting softened her edges, but even the shadows couldn't hide the quiet strength in the way she moved. Her gaze swept across the bar, taking everything in, her lips curving into a faint smile as her friend spoke animatedly beside her.

I leaned back in my chair, exhaling a breath I hadn't realized I was holding. What was it about her? She wasn't the loudest or the boldest person in the room, yet she was all I could see. The drinks, the crowd, the noise—it all faded into the background.

For the first time in years, I felt like something had shifted in my carefully constructed world, and I didn't know if I was ready for it.

I couldn't stay in my office. It was impossible. The pull was too strong, the curiosity too overwhelming. I had to see her with my own eyes.

The chair scraped against the floor as I pushed it back and stood, adrenaline thrumming in my veins. My steps were brisk, purposeful, as I left the office to stand just outside, on the balcony that overlooked the main floor. The instant I stepped into the open air, the noise of the club hit me—a relentless bass line vibrating through my chest, the mingling voices of a hundred conversations—but it was all a distant hum.

I scanned the crowd below, skimming over clusters of people until I found her.

She stood by the bar, her friend gesturing animatedly, clearly in the middle of some story. Her expression was polite but distracted, her gaze flitting around the room. She was taking it all in, the atmosphere, the energy, like she was trying to decide where she fit.

Then it happened.

As if sensing me, she tilted her head and looked up. Her eyes locked onto mine.

Time stilled.

The pounding music faded, the lights blurred into a hazy glow, and the crowd dissolved into nothingness. It was just her and me, our gazes locked in a moment that felt suspended in eternity. My chest tightened, my breath caught.

In her eyes, I saw something I couldn't put into words—a spark, a tether, a connection I hadn't known I'd been searching for until now. It was familiar, yet entirely foreign, like a melody I'd never heard but somehow knew by heart.

The sensation was overwhelming.

For a fleeting moment, a wild thought crossed my mind: Could she be my match?

The idea was absurd. Matches were almost a myth among my kind, whispered about in old tales and rare accounts. A magical soulmate, someone destined to complement your very existence, wasn't something people like me stumbled upon in crowded bars.

And yet, the thought clung to me.

I shifted back into the shadows of the balcony, pressing my back against the cool railing as I tried to steady myself. My pulse was erratic, each beat a reminder of the unexplainable pull I felt toward her.

It couldn't be real. I couldn't let myself believe it, not based on a fleeting glance. My life wasn't a fairytale; it was a maze of responsibilities, decisions, and guarded emotions.

Despite my best efforts to ground myself in logic, my eyes remained fixed on her. Her every movement fascinated me—the way she brushed a strand of hair behind her ear, the faint curve of her lips as she responded to her friend, the way she adjusted the top of her dress as if trying to shrink into herself yet failing to diminish her quiet radiance.

It wasn't just attraction. It was something deeper, more primal: a pull that felt as ancient as the blood running through my veins.

I leaned forward slightly, my hand gripping the railing as I watched her from the shadows. In that moment, I wasn't Warren the businessman, Warren the owner of this bar, or Warren the man who had seen and endured too much.

I was just someone inexplicably, irrevocably drawn to her.

Four

Josie

A grand stone archway loomed across the small foyer leading into the club. Stepping through it felt like crossing a threshold into another era. The stone walls stretched upward, towering at least three stories high, while massive columns lined the mahogany floors, supporting an intricately arched ceiling. Above, circular, multi-tiered iron chandeliers hung from the lofty heights, casting soft light over the room. The ceiling itself was a masterpiece—stone tracery spiraled upward from the cone-shaped tops of the columns, weaving a delicate web across the expanse. Outside, the glow of streetlights filtered through stained-glass windows, casting vibrant pools of color across the floor, adding an ethereal touch to the already stunning scene.

We pushed our way through the crowd and headed for the thick wooden bar. A tall, muscular man hustled from one end of the bar to the other, slinging drinks. We waited patiently for him to serve us, and I perched on an empty barstool, mesmerized as he worked with inhuman speed. His long, thick fingers twirled bottles faster than my eyes could follow. "You the 'beautiful ladies' the bouncer sent?" His wide jaw and bright eyes held my gaze.

"Yeah," I muttered. I looked back at him and nearly fell out of my chair when I saw a red-eyed, fanged monster instead of the handsome man with ocean blue eyes and a half-cocked smile that sent flutters through my stomach moments before. He stepped back, staring at me. I rubbed my eyes, wondering if the rumors that Vampyres—ordinary humans who paid for fang implants to become "real" vampires to drink blood—frequented this club were true.

Nessa elbowed me. I looked at her, then back to the bartender, who looked as shocked as I was.

"What, um, what can I get you?" he faltered.

"Oh, sorry. I thought I... never mind. Can I get a whiskey sour straight up? With Jameson? And a splash of grenadine?"

"Sure," he said sharply and bustled off to start our drinks.

"What's with you? He asked you like three times."

I shrugged. "He was... I don't know." I looked at him, and his blue eyes glanced back at me. "For a minute, I thought he... Never mind."

Nessa looked back at the bartender. "If I wasn't married, I'd totally bang him!"

I tilted my head and looked again. She was right. His tight clothes showed every inch of his rock-hard body. His features were so beautiful he could have been on the cover of a magazine.

I shook it off as he came back with our drinks.

"One good whisky sour with grenadine, and an appletini for the lightweight." He set them down and darted off before we could say thanks.

Nessa lifted her glass to me. "To the end of a crappy relationship."

"Amen." I clinked my glass to hers and took a long sip.

I peered over the rim of my glass to a wrought-iron balcony at the far end of the bar. The silhouette of a man leaned foward on the railing, watching over the club. I couldn't help but feel he was staring at me, even though I couldn't see his face.

I cocked my head and focused harder. The man stepped back into the light behind him and leaned against the wall. I laughed out loud at the audacity of his clothing. He was actually wearing a three-piece pinstripe gray suit, complete with a vest and handkerchief. Even his shoes were wingtips. He had his hair neatly combed back in a sideswipe. He could have stepped onto the set of a 1920s gangster movie and fit right in. His eyes seemed to flash with a golden glow, but he looked away so fast I couldn't be sure.

The buzz of the alcohol burned through me as I finished my first glass and turned to Nessa, laughing. "He musta given me the best whisky in the house." Flipping the glass on its rim, I laid it on the edge of the bar.

We took our second and third drinks to the only empty table against the far wall. Sipping on my whiskey sour, I looked around; I enjoyed watching people. There were a few like us hugging the walls, unsure of what to do, but most of the patrons were on the dance floor or sitting around tables with friends.

The massive crowd on the dance floor moved as one to the rhythm of the music. Bodies pressed into one another as if no one was watching. Women raised their skirts ever higher as their partner's hands slid up their thighs. Men danced bare chested, having discarded their shirts long ago. I watched as several couples entangled their bodies as much as their clothing would let them. It wasn't just men with women, or even two to a pairing. It seemed the longer they danced, the larger the crowd grew. My pulse raced, watching them. I felt a flush of embarrassment at the way my body reacted, and I had to turn away.

The tables held various groups of people enjoying their night. Some sat quietly, sipping their drinks. A few were puffing on their vapes. There was even one extremely loud table, all members focused on the girl with a "Bride" sash and tiara. The poor girl staggered on her feet as she took yet another shot.

"This place is crazy busy," I shouted at Nessa.

"I know, right? That bride over there is going to regret this in the morning."

I watched her suck down a shot off the shirtless boy's stomach who now lay across her table. "God, remember the last time we took body shots?" I laughed. It had been college after we took our last finals, and that was about all I remembered from that night.

"No, not really," she said, taking another drink. "I remember the next day wishing for death to take me."

The hair on the back of my neck stood up. I shivered at the feeling and looked around. Mr. Pinstripe was gliding down the metal stairs, looking right at me. The crowd parted for him, creating a path straight to our table. He never turned or looked away, even when the bartender called out to him. I gulped down the rest of my drink in one quick swig.

"Good evening, ladies." His husky voice spoke with an air of confidence. "I hear you're out in celebration tonight?"

"She—This is her first night out since her divorce." Nessa spoke for me, since my voice seemed to be missing.

"He's an imbecile for letting you slip away." He reached out and took my hand, brushing his soft lips over my fingers. "But it's lucky for me."

Heat flushed my face as a fire ignited deep within my core. I dragged my hand out of his grasp, never taking my eyes from his golden-brown ones that drank me in and looked hungry for more. His lips curled into a deviously sexy smile. Up close, those features I had laughed at now made my heart quicken.

"Anything you need, just let Sam, my bartender, know. Tonight, you drink for free." He bowed his head and strode off to the bar.

"Holy crap," Nessa breathed when he walked away. "He's hotter up close, for sure!"

I turned to look at the table next to us, trying to ignore the pull I felt toward the attractive stranger. A group of four men were playing poker; they silently laid down cards and picked up others, never even looking at each other.

Somewhere in the back of my mind, I heard Nessa speak, but I couldn't make out what she was saying. Keeping my eyes on the hand of the nearest man, I watched as his low cards changed to face cards. He slammed them down on the table and reached for the cash in the center.

The man next to him grabbed his wrist and shouted, "Cheat!"

The first man only laughed in response. Before I could react, the accused man came hurtling forward, slamming into me with such force that he knocked me from my chair and pinned me against the wall. My skull cracked against the cold stones, sending a shooting pain down my spine. My heart raced as I tried to push the man off me, but it was as if a magnet had stuck him in place.

Then, without warning, a force pulled him away. I tried to stand, but my knees buckled and I went crashing into the table face first before hitting the floor again. Warm blood trickled down both the back of my neck and over my eyebrow. *Great. Just what I need. Head wounds.*

I knelt on all fours, glancing up, and shivered at the sight in front of me.

Time seemed to stretch and blur, each second dragging like an eternity. My head throbbed, and the room tilted slightly as I struggled to make sense of what I was seeing. The man hung in the air, suspended three feet above the floor, his limbs twitching as though some invisible force held him in place.

I blinked, certain my vision was playing tricks on me. No one was touching him. The crowd around us seemed frozen, their faces a mix of shock and confusion, yet no one moved to help or question what was happening.

Then, as if by magic—or madness—Mr. Pinstripe appeared between the two men. One moment he was across the room, and the next, he was there, standing calmly as if he had always been in that spot.

My pulse quickened; a cold sweat prickled my skin. Maybe it was the drinks. Maybe it was the head wound. Or maybe my sanity had finally cracked under the weight of this surreal moment. There was no humanly possible way for him to move like that, no explanation for the man floating midair. My thoughts spiraled: desperate for logic yet coming up empty. This wasn't real. It couldn't be real.

I closed my eyes for a brief moment, hoping when I opened them again, the scene would resolve itself into something rational. But the eerie stillness and impossible tableau remained, leaving me more disoriented than ever.

"Enough!" Mr. Pinstripe growled in his deep voice. The man crumpled to the floor. Mr. Pinstripe's head snapped to me, huddled on the floor in a very unladylike position. His eyes never left mine as he snarled, "Leave," to the table of card players who stood and headed for the door without argument. He knelt before me, cupping my chin in his hand. "I apologize for their behavior, Miss..."

"J-Josefina... Jo."

"Miss Josefina, I can clean this up for you if you'd like?" He offered me his hand.

Turning my face to Nessa, she looked green but said, "Go on, you need to get that taken care of." Nessa looked away from me and the man—she never could stand the sight of blood. "I can take her to the ER if it needs stitches."

"I'm sure she will be fine, but I will pay for the visit if she needs it," he informed Nessa, his outstretched hand waiting for my response.

Nodding once, I accepted his hand, and he helped me to my feet. Wrapping his arm behind my back, he guided me toward the stairs and the balcony where I'd first noticed him.

I turned my head to look back at Nessa. She gave me a thumbs-up with a wide grin. I mouthed "Shut up" before heading up the steps.

Five

Josie

$\mathcal{H}$e closed the door to the office softly behind me. At the far end stood a solid oak desk with a wall to wall built-in bookshelf behind it. He gestured to the large ottoman on my right and gently pushed on my shoulders, guiding me down to the cushion. He sat on the edge of the couch and pulled me closer to him. "May I inspect that?" he asked before leaning in to look at my face.

I pulled away. "Don't you need gloves or something? A towel, at least?"

He laughed. "If it would make you feel better." He stood, walked over to his desk, and pulled a red box from the drawer.

"It would. I don't even know you."

"Sorry, Miss Josefina, I'm only trying to help."

"I'm sorry. You're right. And you can drop the Miss, please?"

"Very well. Josefina." He placed a hand on his chest and bowed. "I am Warren Harris, proprietor of this establishment."

I gaped at him. "You own this bar?" I rubbed my head. "Sorry, I should've known that. I musta hit my head harder than I thought."

"I understand. Yes, this is one of my businesses in town. Which is why I am so appalled at your treatment. May I look at your wounds now?" He hadn't moved, yet he wore gloves and held a cleaning rag.

"How..." My head was killing me. I nodded and raised my chin as he stepped in front of me so he could see the cut over my eye. His fingers brushed my hair away and dabbed my brow. I winced at his touch.

"Oh, it's not too bad. Should heal nicely." He gently wiped the blood from my face and applied a band-aid over the cut. "Now, let's see the back of your head." I stared into those bright eyes of his. He placed his hand on my back as he walked around and sat on the couch behind me.

My eyes followed him, but it only caused the room to spin, and I clasped my head in my hands.

"Easy now." He stood and leaned over me. He hesitated a moment and made a noise that sounded a lot like a cat's purr. "I'm afraid your new hairdo will take a bit of washing to save."

"New? How can you tell?" I couldn't even look up.

"I can smell the chemicals. Just stay there and let me have a look at it."

I did as he asked, and when his hands gently parted my hair, a wave of warmth radiated from his touch, sending a shiver down my spine. His fingers moved lower, brushing against the base of my neck, light and deliberate, igniting a flutter of unexpected sensation.

He pressed the cold cloth to my head, dabbing up the blood. Pain shot through my skull, causing me to yelp and pull away, but his large hand gripped my bare shoulder and pulled me back. "Hush now." His voice flooded my brain, easing the pain. He finished cleaning my head with the towel, then set it aside.

A spark of electricity jolted me as he lightly touched my wound with his fingertips. My scalp itched madly for a moment before settling down.

"You should be fine. Might have a headache for a few days, but you will be fine."

I heard the snapping of him removing the gloves. The room was spinning, so I rested my head in my hands again. I jumped as his fingers brushed aside my hair and traced the firebird tattoo on my back. His touch sent a warmth through me, easing the pain in my head.

He pulled away quickly. "My apologies, Miss."

The moment he pulled away, it ached again. My instincts told me to walk away, but my pounding head begged for reprieve. "No, don't stop. It makes my head feel better."

His hands returned to my exposed shoulders, gently rubbing them. His thumbs swirled at the base of my neck. The strange shock of electricity zapped me again, but this time, I didn't pull away. The pulse in my head slowed, and it no longer ached. His hands lingered, even as I stood. He dropped them to his sides as I turned to face him.

"How... how'd you do that?" My voice shook. I reached my hand up and felt where the cut should have been, but only found a normal scalp.

Before he spoke softly, he looked away and said, "'There are more things in Heaven and Earth, Horatio, than are dreamt of in your philosophy.'"

"Shakespeare..."

He shrugged nonchalantly, his gaze fixed on me like he wasn't quite seeing me. "He was a friend of mine."

I stared at him, blinking in disbelief, my mind struggling to process the words. "I... Wait... What? Shakespeare?" I shook my head in confusion, thinking he couldn't mean that literally. "That doesn't answer my question." I stumbled over the words, my brain feeling foggy, like I was trapped in some bizarre dream.

He only smiled faintly, unbothered by my disbelief. "Yes, it does. What do you know of your parents?"

I felt a strange tension knot in my stomach at the mention of them. The warmth of the moment, the lingering confusion from the past few minutes, made it all seem surreal. I shifted uncomfortably. "How does Shakespeare connect to my parents? And how does he answer how you fixed my head?"

He stared at me, unblinking.

"My mother has always been there for me. What does that matter?"

His eyes never wavered from mine, his expression unreadable. "And your father?"

I felt a flicker of irritation spark inside me, a mix of confusion and frustration building as he pressed on. "What's with all the questions?" My voice was sharper than I intended, my patience thinning.

He leaned forward, his eyes growing more intense. "You don't know, do you?"

I blinked, taken aback by his words. I didn't know what he was talking about, and that irritated me more than anything. His riddles were starting to push me toward the edge of something I didn't want to understand.

I crossed my arms tightly, the anger simmering beneath my skin. I turned my gaze away from his cool eyes, walking a few paces to collect myself. "Know what?" I snapped, my tone sharp as I stood there, trying to ignore the unsettling feeling spreading through me.

His silence only made my frustration grow. The more he said, the more I felt like he was toying with me. But there was something else there, too—a strange connection I couldn't shake, like he knew something I couldn't remember; something that I'd once known but long forgotten.

I paused mid-step, my breath catching as the weight of the moment settled on me. His presence felt both unnerving and magnetic, like I was teetering on the edge of something monumental.

"Come here, Josie." His voice was a soft, almost melodic whisper, my name rolling off his tongue like a secret meant only for me. The sound sent a shiver down my spine, and before I could stop myself, I obeyed, stepping closer as if pulled by an invisible thread.

His hands cupped my face—warm and commanding, yet gentle—and the world seemed to narrow to just him. My pulse quickened, my skin tingling where his fingers touched. Something about him felt almost magical, like he was drawing out pieces of me I didn't know existed.

And yet, deep inside, warning bells clanged.

This man—this stranger—was dangerous, though I couldn't pinpoint why. I wanted to pull away, to break free from whatever spell his presence had cast, but my body betrayed me, rooted in place as his eyes fluttered closed.

Then, as if a switch had been flipped, the strange, disjointed images I'd been seeing for weeks burst to life behind my eyelids. Flashes of people, places, things I didn't understand. But this time, they sharpened, settling on Caleb. His eyes—those cold, calculating eyes—burned into me as clearly as if he were standing right there.

I gasped, wrenching myself from the man's grasp, my heart hammering in my chest. "What the hell?" I demanded, stumbling back a step.

"These things you've seen are real," he said, his tone calm but heavy with meaning. His gaze locked on mine, filled with something that felt both tender and terrifying. "Your ex-husband is more than what he appears to be, and he blocked you from seeing the world around you for what it truly is. I can feel your power."

My power? What power? His words rattled me, clashing with the rational part of my brain that screamed to run, to get as far away from this man as possible.

Before I could respond, his hand slid through my hair, his fingers brushing against my scalp in a way that sent heat flooding through my body. He leaned in closer, his nose skimming the side of mine, his breath warm against my skin. "Josie," he breathed, his voice low and filled with something I couldn't name. His lips hovered so close that I could feel their presence, a whisper away from mine.

The air around us crackled, charged with an unnamed energy. My heart raced, not from fear but from an inexplicable desire that made my stomach twist in knots. Images of him—bare, vulnerable, raw—flooded my mind unbidden, and I clenched my fists, desperate to push them away.

I gulped hard, the intensity too much to bear, and shoved him back with all the strength I could muster. My purse tumbled from my hands, but I barely noticed.

"I'm sorry," I stammered, my voice shaky as I bent to snatch my bag. My fingers fumbled, clumsy with adrenaline. "Th-thanks." Without waiting for a response, I turned and stormed out, my heels clicking against the polished floor as I pushed back into the thrum of the bar.

Nessa found me almost immediately, her eyes wide with shock. "Do you know who that was?"

"The owner of the bar," I said quickly, my voice sharper than I intended. "Let's get out of here."

Grabbing her arm, I pulled her toward the exit, my legs trembling beneath me. The night air would help clear my head, but the weight of his touch, his words, and those haunting images lingered like a brand on my soul.

"Not just the owner of this bar. Jo, he owns like half of downtown! And you were just alone in his office! What the hell happened?" she shouted from behind me.

"Nothing." I dragged her outside and back to my car.

She broke the silence once I pulled onto the highway and slammed my foot down on the gas. "Jo, what happened up there? You look really unsettled."

"I... I don't really want to talk about it." My fingers tightened against the wheel.

"Did he make a move on you? I would sooo call the news station and burn him publicly if he did anything to you!" She tried to make a joke of it, but her voice broke mid-sentence.

I scoffed, "God, no! Nothing like that at all." I glanced over at her. "It was just... never mind. It's not a big deal. He just said some weird things." I shook my head. His words made no sense. "My head is throbbing, and I can't think straight. What happened? When I got slammed into the wall?"

Nessa's jaw dropped. "Two big thugs got into it over a card game. One shoved the other into you. The one that slammed into you grabbed the other by the throat. It was lucky the owner stepped in and stopped it."

"I—God, this night's been a blur." I rubbed at my temple, remembering clearly that neither man had laid a hand on the other. My brain tried to process what I'd seen. Nothing made sense anymore. I pressed my foot into the pedal and drove.

We arrived at her house twenty minutes faster than normal thanks to my lead foot, and I waited for Nessa to close the door behind her before heading to my house, hoping to find some shred of sanity in this crazy night.

Six

Warren

*A*ll the air seemed to suck out of my office the moment the door slammed behind her. The absence of Josefina's magic left me breathless, a hollow ache settling in my chest. Her energy lingered in the room, faint but undeniable, like the echo of a song that refuses to leave your head. I sank onto the couch and ran a hand through my hair, exhaling deeply as if trying to purge her from my system. But it was no use—I could still feel her, even now.

Her blood had told me what she didn't yet understand about herself. My blood magic wasn't just a tool; it was an extension of me, a sense as sharp as sight or smell. When I'd felt her magic, tasted it through our connection, I knew there was more to her than met the eye. Something ancient and untamed pulsed within her, something even she wasn't aware of.

And then there was the pull, that maddening, unshakable draw to her. *My match.* The idea crept in like a thief, and I slammed the door on it just as quickly. It couldn't be true. I had searched for centuries, and nothing, no one, had ever come close to matching me. Why now? Why her? It didn't make sense, and the thought of it left me reeling.

Her ex-husband had been a cambion, masking truths with charm and lies, and now that he was out of her life, the veil was beginning to lift. But what would she uncover? What was buried in her blood, calling out to me like a whisper I couldn't ignore? It wasn't just her power; it was something deeper, more primal—a resonance that vibrated through my very being.

I leaned back and stared at the ceiling, trying to push the thoughts away, but the connection was too strong. Her magic, her essence, was woven into mine now, a tether I wasn't sure I could sever even if I wanted to. And truth be told, I didn't want to. That was the most dangerous part of all.

A knock at my door brought me out of my thoughts.

"Enter," I said sharply, my voice cutting through the quiet hum of my office.

The door creaked open, and Sam, my bartender and oldest friend, stepped inside. His shoulders sagged, and his head hung low as he approached, a clear sign that whatever he had to say wasn't good.

"Warren?" His voice wavered, a rare crack in his usually composed demeanor.

"What is it, Sam?" I asked, narrowing my eyes as I took in his pallor. He looked pale—even for a vampire—and his unease was written across every inch of him.

"That woman who just left..." He trailed off, his hands fidgeting with the hem of his shirt. "I thought you should know—she saw me. I mean, she saw the *real* me." His voice dropped into an almost whisper. "I don't know how, but she did. I'm sorry."

I stood, crossed the room in two swift strides, and grasped his shoulders firmly. His avoidance of my gaze wasn't going to cut it. "Look at me, Sam."

Reluctantly, he lifted his eyes; a storm of guilt swirled within them.

"I know," I said, my tone firm but not unkind. "It's not your fault. She's been seeing a lot more of us lately." I dropped my hands and turned away, pacing a few steps as my thoughts raced.

"Warren?" Sam pressed, his voice tinged with both concern and confusion.

"I looked into her memories," I said, my tone sharper than intended. "She's been seeing a lot of *Figli Del Mito* lately."

Sam stiffened. "Why? How?" The tremor in his voice was more pronounced now.

"Because." I turned back to him, forcing a small, knowing smile onto my face. "She's like me, Sam. She's a warlock. She just doesn't know it yet."

"But—" He faltered, clearly trying to process what I'd just revealed. "She's far past the age of maturity for a warlock's powers to manifest. She should've known already. How is it even possible for her to not know?"

"That's not for you to worry about," I said, my tone decisive as I waved off his concern. "Let *me* handle it."

Sam hesitated, his worry etched deeply into his expression, but he finally nodded. "If you're sure..."

"I am," I replied, gesturing toward the door. "Now go. Entertain the masses. I'll be down shortly."

He left reluctantly, his footsteps fading as he descended the stairs to the club.

She was a mystery, one I hadn't even begun to unravel. A warlock without awareness of her own power. A woman whose magic flared with wild, untamed energy. And now, she was tangled up in a world she barely understood, a world I wasn't sure she was ready for.

But ready or not, it was coming for her, and I had a feeling she would play a larger role in it than either of us could imagine.

I let out a slow breath and sat down on the edge of the couch, my fingers brushing against the phone Josie had dropped in her rush to leave. Picking it up, I tapped the screen. The device lit up with a photo of a large group of kids wearing jerseys, all grinning at the camera and holding up a massive trophy. I placed the phone into my pocket and strode down to the club floor, locking my door with a wave of my hand.

The soft click of the lock echoed in the stillness, but it did little to quiet the storm in my head. I descended the stairs toward the club floor, my steps deliberate but weighted with the pull of restless thoughts.

Josie.

Her name lingered on the edge of my mind, refusing to fade no matter how hard I tried to redirect my focus. Her magic clung faintly to my senses, like the memory of a touch I couldn't quite shake. It wasn't just its intensity—it was its familiarity, as though I'd encountered it in some distant, fragmented memory.

I wove through the early crowd on the club floor, nodding distractedly to a few regulars. The room hummed with life, laughter mingling with the low thrum of music, but I felt detached from it all. My blood magic, usually quiet, stirred whenever I thought of Josie. It was unsettling, how her fiery essence had latched onto me, binding us through something deeper than mere coincidence.

I took a seat at the bar, rubbing the back of my neck and forcing myself to focus on the mundane tasks ahead. Yet every attempt to push her from my thoughts only brought her sharper into focus: her defiance, her strength, the haunted vulnerability that lurked beneath.

With a sigh, I reached for my phone, hoping to drown myself in something mindless, when it hit me.

A sharp, searing jolt ripped through me, a sensation so sudden and visceral that I doubled over for a moment. It wasn't pain, exactly—it was something worse. A warning.

My breath hitched, and my blood magic surged, reaching instinctively for the connection that had inexplicably formed between Josie and me. The tether blazed to life, and what I felt on the other end made my chest tighten.

Fear. Pain.

"Josie," I whispered, her name slipping from my lips like a prayer.

I straightened, heart pounding in a furious rhythm. My senses honed on her magic, which spiked wildly and erratically like a flare in the night. She was in danger; her emotions battered against the tether between us.

Panic clawed at me as I made my way back up to my office, my mind racing with possibilities. Before her fear choked me I reached the locked door. With a wave of my hand, the door swung open and I slumped to the couch pulling her phone from my pocket. With a sharp gesture, I summoned a thread of magic, coaxing the device to unlock.

My fingers moved quickly, scrolling through her contacts until I found what I was looking for—a landline number. Without hesitation, I dialed it, pressing the phone to my ear as I walked the length of the room. The first call rang out into an empty void, as did the second, then the third. Each unanswered ring only tightened the knot in my chest. "Come on, Josie," I muttered, gripping the phone tighter as I tried again, the growing silence on the other end sending dread crawling up my spine. Something wasn't right, and I could feel it in the very depths of my magic.

Seven

Warren

My heart still raced as I put the car in park and took slow, deep breaths, trying to calm my nerves. My hands had clutched the wheel so hard as I drove that when I released it, my fingers hurt. I opened my door and swiveled in my seat, hanging my feet out of the car. I yanked my boots off and threw them in the passenger's seat.

The concrete was cold against my bare feet. I looked up, a dark shadow sat in front of my barn. My heart stopped for a moment before realizing the shadow was just a car.

"Crap. Nessa's car," I breathed. I'd have to call her, but my mind kept racing back to Warren's office. Why had he asked about my father? I never met the man and never wanted to. What did he mean by Caleb had blocked me? Blocked me from what?

I reached into the car, grabbing my purse. Panic raced over me as I dumped the whole thing out.

"Crap! Where the is my phone?" I groaned, realizing I must have dropped it in the club. I rolled my eyes at myself. "That's just great."

I slammed my door and walked toward the backyard, needing a moment. The hard earth pressed against my feet as I walked, and the cold air bit at my skin, sending shivers down my spine. The young girl at the drive-thru flashed into my mind. She really had had pointed ears. It wasn't my exhaustion; they were real. And the biker today... he was... fae. They weren't human. If that were true, then the vamp wannabe at the bar tonight wasn't a wannabe.

Air caught in my throat and hot tears blurred my vision as sobs wracked my body, dropping me to the ground. Somewhere deep in my mind, I knew Warren was right— that there was more to this world than I could understand— but the idea felt like a weight too heavy to lift. The knowledge, hazy and overwhelming, swirled around me, and I couldn't grasp it, couldn't make sense of it. Frustration and fear tangled together, choking me from the inside as I cried out in helplessness.

A loud howl emanating from the edge of my property shifted my tears into cold silence as my eyes slid up toward the field behind my land. Shadows crept closer. Slowly, I stood. The full moon lit up the night's sky behind the animals as they stepped into the view of my barn's motion sensor light, flicking it on. If a German Shepard was big, these dogs were colossal.

My feet inched backward until my back slammed into the post of my basketball hoop.

"Crap," I whispered to myself. My shotgun was just inside the back door, doing me no good. Wolves were shy creatures. Why would they be stalking me? Besides, wolves in the Midwest were rare, if not unheard of. Coyotes, sure, but not wolves, and these guys were far too big to be coyotes.

Warren had told me the things I had seen were real. If fae and vampires really existed, then why not...

"No, it's not real." I closed my eyes and prayed when I opened them I'd be back in my room.

No such luck. The wolves were closing in.

I can feel your power. Warren's rough voice rang in my mind. Every nerve in my body buzzed. My brain quickly did the math, and there was no way I could outrun them. I looked up. The wolves were massive—easily as tall as me when they were on all fours, their thick, muscular frames dwarfing any creature I had ever seen. Even if I managed to scramble to the top of my basketball post, they could rise up on their hind legs with terrifying ease, their powerful limbs stretching higher than I could ever hope to climb. I could already picture the sheer force of their strength; the weight of their presence; how effortlessly they could close the distance between us. There would be nowhere to run, nowhere to hide.

Fear gripped me so tightly I couldn't breathe. My knees buckled, and I sank to the ground, instinctively shielding my face with my arms as if that could protect me from whatever was coming. My whole body trembled, bracing for the impact I was sure would follow. Instead, heat surged from my palms, so intense it felt like they were on fire. The warmth spread, radiating out of me in waves, and before I could make sense of it, a blinding light erupted from my hands, so bright it lit up the entire yard. I flinched, blinking against the glare, and peered through the gap in my arms.

When the light faded, everything was still. The air was thick with silence, save for the faint retreating yips of the wolves, now nowhere to be seen. My breath came in ragged gasps, my pulse pounding in my ears as I stayed frozen, my mind scrambling to make sense of the unreal. I was alone in the yard, the echoes of what had just happened ringing in my head. "What in the actual fudge?" The words were barely more than a whisper from my trembling voice.

I pushed myself to my feet, my legs unsteady, and stumbled back toward my car. I grabbed my keys, leaving everything else behind, my mind a whirlwind of confusion and disbelief. My body moved on autopilot as I headed inside, flicking on every light in my small house to cut through the dark.

I made my way to the kitchen, and as I passed the old landline, I noticed the blinking light signaling new messages. The only person who had my number was Nessa, so I figured it was her asking about her car. But when I saw more than one message, a chill ran down my spine. I grabbed the phone, my fingers trembling as I checked. The first message was from Nessa, but the second one... I hesitated, my heart sinking as I heard his voice. "You dropped your phone. I can bring it to you or you can come and get it. You know how to find me."

I melted into the barstool.

Then again, "Josie!" His voice sounded panicked. "Josie! Please call me back. I need to know you got home safe!"

I had just missed that call. I was too tired to deal with it, but the phone rang again.

"Yes, I'm fine," I said into the receiver without asking who it was.

Warren breathed a sigh of relief. "Thank God. I was worried. I thought..."

"You thought there might have been a pack of werewolves at my house?" I finished.

"I…" He didn't speak for a moment. "How did you know what they were?"

"I'm going to ignore the fact that, one, you know my landline, and two, you were aware those things were even here, because frankly, I'm too tired to deal with that little nugget of craziness," I said, pushing myself to my feet. "I don't know what was in my drink at your bar or what the hell is happening, but I've had enough. My head's pounding, and I'm completely drained. I'm going to bed."

"How'd you escape?" he asked before I could hang up.

"Don't know, don't really care. I'm just hoping to wake up in the hospital with a concussion. I'm going to bed."

"What about your phone?"

"I. Do. Not. Care," I drawled. "I'll buy a new one."

"Josie, don't be—"

"Good night, Warren." I hung up before he could say another word.

I stripped out of my dress, leaving a trail to my bedroom, then slid into my pajamas before crawling into bed.

Oh, how I prayed this was all just a comatose nightmare.

Eight
Josie

The next day, aside from a quick trip to get Nessa's car back to her, I ignored everything. I unplugged my landline and internet service and curled up in my chair with a good, cheesy romance novel until it was time for bed that night.

Monday morning, however, brought fresh worry into my normally quiet life. My first period of the day comprised most of my JV basketball team and a few of the younger varsity boys. As I walked around the court, the kids piling in before the bell rang, an eerie sensation of being watched crept down my spine, instinctively drawing my eyes to the balcony.

The bell rang, snapping me out of my thoughts. The kids all stood patiently in their spots for me. I walked between the lines, checking off all those present, then stopped at an empty spot. It took me a minute to register who was missing. When I did, I moved back and found Keith, the boy who had broken into the gym with Rocky on Friday night.

"Where's Rocky?" I asked.

He shrugged but wouldn't look me in the eyes.

"Where'd you guys go after you left here Friday?"

"We stayed the night at Brian's house," he said, almost as if he had rehearsed it all weekend.

"Then where?"

Again, he shrugged, his lips tight.

Glaring at him for a long moment didn't encourage him to elaborate. Kids lied. Most didn't do it to be intentionally deceitful; they were just scared. Keith reeked of fear. A bead of sweat dripped down his face, but he didn't break. He just stood there and stared straight ahead.

Left with no other choice, I marked Rocky absent and moved on with the morning. Going about my everyday life felt forced after the weekend I'd had. If Warren were to be believed, I had faced a pack of werewolves, hadn't I? And now I was watching a pack of teen boys hunt their prey in a violent display of dodgeball.

The bell finally rang, signaling my prep period. Out of habit, I reached for my cell in my pocket before remembering Warren had it. I walked back to my office and closed the door just as the phone on my desk rang.

"This is Miss Collins."

"Hey Jo, there's a surprise at the office for you! Some hot guy just dropped it off," Maranda, the school's receptionist, told me.

Great, I assumed "really hot guy" translated to Warren. Shaking his image from my head, I forced a response. "Thanks. Has anyone called in for Rocky? He wasn't in homeroom, and I'm a little worried about him."

"Um, I don't think so. Let me check with Mrs. Wells." Her muffled voice spoke to someone I couldn't hear before returning to me. "Nope. No one called in for him. You want me to call his house?"

"No, I'll try them. I-I saw him Friday night, so I was just a little worried. I'm sure it's nothing. Thanks, Maranda."

"Jo, what about your stuff?" she asked before I could hang up.

"I'll be down in a bit to get it. Thanks." I clicked the phone off and back on with my finger then dialed Rocky's home line—a number I knew by heart—and waited for someone to pick up. When it went to voicemail, I left a quick message and dialed his cell—getting the same thing. Feeling defeated, I hung up the phone and headed for the administration office.

Maranda stood behind the counter, her blonde hair pulled back in a messy ponytail, a few stray strands falling around her face. She looked a little tired, her posture slouched as she absently twirled a pen between her fingers. Her eyes brightened as soon as I walked in, and a smile spread across her face, wide and genuine, as if I were the first bit of excitement she'd had all day. It was the kind of smile that made you feel like you were the only person in the room, even though the place was far from empty. She stood up, setting a stack of chocolate bars tied with a bow onto the counter. My cell phone sat on top. Yep, Warren had been here. Well, at least I didn't have to deal with the hassle of getting a new phone.

"Seriously, Jo, that guy was hot. He drove up in a Ferrari. He isn't that billionaire from Indy, is he?" she asked, oblivious to the scowl on my face. "I've seen his picture in magazines, but they don't do him justice."

"My phone accidentally fell out of my purse in his—office." I stopped myself from telling my co-worker that I had visited one of the most notorious nightclubs in the city over the weekend. "I told him I'd just get a new one."

"But he brought you candy." Her grin was infectious.

"You wouldn't be smiling if you knew him," I said flatly, taking the pile from her.

"What do you mean?" she asked, dramatically pouting as if I were shattering her fantasies of some secret affair with the world's most attractive man.

"Well, first off, I never told him my last name or where I worked."

"Creepy! How'd he know?"

"Not sure I want to know. Thanks." I took my phone, which was completely dead now, and the chocolate back to my office.

I set everything down on my desk and pulled my phone out from under the ribbon. A white envelope lay under it. Opening it, I took in his handwriting: A blocky script laid out like a stencil.

Josie,

Please accept my apologies again for the incident at my club Saturday night. I'm grateful you weren't seriously injured. I screwed up in looking through your phone to find where you worked. It was chintzy of me, and I'm sorry. I hope I didn't get you into hot water with your partner. He's called several times. Again, please forgive any intrusion I might have made. If you are ever in need of anything, please give me a ring.

Warren

A chill ran down my spine. He'd broken into my phone. All my pictures. My notes. My TBR list. I shuddered and reread his note. *What man?* Not even my ex would've called me. I threw my dead cell and his note in my purse and set it in my desk drawer before heading back to the gym to prep for my next class.

I tried calling Rocky's house and cell several times throughout the day and got nothing. He'd be here tonight, at least. He never missed a game.

After my last class, I ran home to grab my charger. My phone lit up before I got back for the game. Unlocking it as I pulled back into the school's lot, I noticed fourteen missed calls: all from Rocky.

My fingers quickly dialed his cell, but it went straight to voicemail.

"Dang it!"

I tried his house one last time. Finally, someone picked up.

"Yeah?" his foster father's gruff voice answered.

"This is Miss Collins, Rocky's coach. He never showed up for school and I can't get ahold of him. The game's about to start. Have you seen him?"

"Look, lady, Rocky's a big boy. He can take care of himself. He'll be eighteen soon and not my problem."

Deep breaths, I told myself, trying to keep from screaming. "When was the last time you saw him?" I asked as calmly as I could.

"Hey, Beth! When was the last time you saw that boy?" he shouted, not moving the phone away from his mouth.

"What boy?" I heard her shout back.

Deep breaths, deep breaths.

"Rocky, you moron."

"Oh, I don't know. Friday?"

"Friday," he said, presumably to me.

"Nothing since then? Did he tell you where he went?"

"Lady, that boy's nothing but trouble. I don't ask where he goes when he leaves." The man hung up before I could say another word. How I wished I'd called from a hard line so I could slam the phone down. Throwing my touch screen that I just got back wasn't the best idea.

Rocky didn't show up for the game that night, or practice the next evening. At first, I brushed it off as nothing serious—maybe he had something personal to deal with. But when he didn't show up for school the next day, then the day after that, panic started to take root. I couldn't ignore the knot in my stomach or the creeping feeling that something was terribly wrong.

I continued calling, but his phone went straight to voicemail each time. That's when I started going through every avenue I could think of. The police were my next step, but "Old Tom," the town chief of police, barely gave me the time of day. He'd grown tired of my calls, dismissing each one with a wave of his hand, mumbling something about Rocky probably skipping town to do "his own thing" again. I knew better, but I was powerless to convince anyone.

My desperation grew with each passing day. The empty spot in our circle at school, the absence in the halls where he should have been—every minute he wasn't there made it feel like the ground beneath me was slipping away.

Rocky was almost eighteen, living in a bad foster home. As far as anyone was concerned, he'd run away and was probably better off. I kept thinking about the note Warren had left me. My fingers had dialed his number but never hit send several times. I didn't know where else to turn, I barely knew the guy, but still, I needed help.

Warren

MY LIFE WAS FAR TOO COMPLICATED TO WORRY ABOUT A single warlock who had yet to awaken to her powers who'd happened to walk into my bar one night. Yet I paced my penthouse floor, thinking about her. The tie around my neck felt like a noose, so I yanked on the knot and pulled it over my head. It had been a few days since I'd dropped her phone off at work, and I couldn't get her out of my head. After the fifth day of not hearing anything from her, I broke down and sent her a text.

> It's Warren. I just wanted to make sure you got your phone and my note. Again, I apologize for everything.

I set phone back down on the nightstand beside my bed and walked to the edge of the balcony in my downtown house. The iron railing ran across three of the massive brick walls. The setting sun poured through the east wall of windows, shining dancing color on the oak floor. I nearly jumped when my phone chirped and ran back to the bed to pick it up.

> I should be mad at you for finding out where I work.

> But ...

> Thanks for bringing me my
> phone.

> ...

> Rocky isn't my boyfriend. The guy
> that kept calling. He's a student
> and he ...

> I think he's in trouble, but no one
> believes me.

I read her texts over and over until the three little dots stopped flashing. *I can't get involved.* Setting the phone down, I walked back out to the balcony. *Human affairs need to stay in the human realm. I can't get involved again.* Turning back to my room, I stared at my phone. *No. But then again...* I flicked my wrist and called the phone to me. She isn't human.

> Why do you think he's in trouble?

> He's my star basketball player.
> He'd never miss a game without
> telling me, and I haven't seen him
> since Friday, and no one can get a
> hold of him.

> Why tell me?

> I'm telling you because you
> believe in werewolves and
> vampires, so maybe you'd believe

> me. I don't know who else to turn to.

A smile curled my lips, knowing she trusted me enough to ask for my help.

> Have you called the police?

> Yes, and they won't do anything because I'm not family. His "family" won't do anything because he's about to age out of the system.

> What do you expect me to do?

> ...

My words likely came across harsher than I'd meant. I typed out "I'm sorry" and deleted it several times.

Her rage seeped through the phone. She never replied, but I knew she was angry with me. This connection we seemed to have was like a direct link to her emotions, and I felt every bit of her anger. She had every right to be mad, but she didn't need me to help her. I had spent a lifetime—several lifetimes—learning to control my temper. If I got involved, the house of cards I called my life would fall. It was better this way.

In a desperate attempt to forget about her, I put my cell on my nightstand and kicked off my shoes. The cold tiles bit at my feet as I walked into the bathroom. After flipping on the shower, I stripped out of my suit, waiting for the water to heat up before stepping in. I entered, then leaned against the tile wall and let the water flow over me.

My breath caught in my throat as a tingle of magic sparked through my body, magic that hadn't come from me.

Her face flashed through my mind. Her anger subsided, leaving only anguish. She sat curled up in a chair, sobbing. I clenched my fist, muscles burning to punch something. Her tie to me was strong, and it scared the crap out of me. I unclenched and tried to shake off the torrent of emotions coming from her. She was angry and frustrated, but beneath it all, she was scared: So desperately afraid I trembled with my own fear.

There was more to this Rocky kid than just being her student. Her pain continued to tear through me, and I needed to know more.

She vanished from me as quickly as she had come. I crouched on the shower floor, gasping for breath. Her fear raked through me as deeply as if it were my own. I didn't know if she'd meant to, but she'd reached out to me at her lowest moment. Leaning with my back against the wall, I stood, clenching and unclenching my fists as I fought the urge to help her.

I reluctantly turned off the shower and walked over to my laptop, the steam from my body still lingering in the air. My hands shook slightly as I opened the browser, searching for her school's basketball team. It didn't take long to find Rocky's last name, and I started digging deeper. My fingers moved faster across the keyboard than my mind could keep up with as I searched for every shred of information on him.

Leaning back in my chair, I let out a slow breath and narrowed my eyes at the screen. The data on Rocky was scarce—nothing useful, just random social media posts— but Rocky wasn't just another lost soul I could write off. He meant something to Josie, and by proxy, he meant something to me too.

A growing unease gnawed at me, the sensation slipping under my skin like a cold draft in a room that had once felt secure. I couldn't shake the feeling that I was missing something crucial, something dangerously important waited just beyond my grasp. Every instinct told me there was something bigger going on than I realized—something I couldn't ignore.

The usual confidence I wore like a second skin felt thin, like glass ready to shatter at the slightest pressure. The calm certainty that had always guided me through the chaos of this world now felt fragile, as if it might crack under the weight of what I was about to uncover.

Rocky's disappearance was no simple case. He wasn't the first kid to go missing in the city. There were dozens missing, and I just knew they were connected. There was too much at play, too many unanswered questions. And that feeling... it was like the world was quietly shifting, something was just out of sight, waiting for the moment to reveal itself.

I couldn't just sit here, twiddling my thumbs and hoping the right person would show up with the right answer. I didn't trust anyone to do the work for me, not this time. I couldn't risk owing favors to people who dealt in shadows or would demand something in return. They always wanted something. Information, power, or worse—something personal. No, I couldn't afford that.

I exhaled sharply, my gaze narrowing as I turned back to my laptop. The screen was a sea of open tabs, each one a potential lead. I wasn't willing to let someone else dig through this mess for me, to pick apart the clues in a way that would leave me exposed. No, this was mine to unravel.

Every click of the keyboard felt like a step deeper into the rabbit hole, but it was the only way. I had to take matters into my own hands.

I typed faster, my fingers moving in a rhythm that matched the growing urgency in my chest. Every search, every site I scrolled through, felt like it was leading me down a darkened path, one that I had no intention of backing away from. Rocky's name never popped up in the sea of missing children and their paths never crossed. It was as if he'd just vanished.

My eyes flicked back and forth across the screen as I sifted through search results, looking for any information that could lead me to him. Nothing. I clicked on encrypted databases, trying to find something hidden deeper, something that the average search engine couldn't reach. Still, nothing. Every lead felt like it was going cold before I could even grasp it.

A pulse of frustration tightened my chest. I leaned forward, tapping at the keys, my gaze sharp as I dug deeper, into places where most would never go; dark corners of the digital world only a few knew how to navigate. It wasn't pretty, but it was effective. And I wasn't afraid of what I might uncover.

But even as I plowed through every available resource, that nagging feeling persisted, gnawing at me from the inside. There had to be something I was missing. Some small piece of the puzzle that, if found, could change everything. I had no doubt whatever I was about to uncover was more than just a missing person's case. It was something bigger. Something dangerous.

I clenched my jaw, my fingers gripping the mouse harder than necessary. The longer I searched, the deeper that gnawing unease grew. I wasn't finding answers, and the silence that followed felt like it was closing in on me. Every click on the keyboard echoed through the room, amplifying the growing dread in my chest.

What am I missing? What am I not seeing?

Through normal human channels, Rocky Sanchez didn't exist. He was a ghost in the human realm. With A few more clicks, I was searching for him in a database exclusively for warlocks, and the results sent a shiver down my spine. I had to talk to Josie.

I pushed away from my desk and moved to the nightstand where I'd left my phone.

This wasn't just about one missing kid... it was about the safety of my people—those who had been forgotten and ignored. The Figli Del Mito. I'd spent too long staying on the periphery, convincing myself I was above it all. But this was different. My world had always been right in front of me, but I hadn't seen it. Now, I was forced to. And I wasn't about to let it go unanswered. Not this time.

It was barely daybreak when I dialed her number.

"H-hello?" her groggy voice answered on the fifth ring.

"I'm sorry to wake you so early, Josie, but we need to talk. Can you meet me at my bar this morning?"

There was a long pause on the other end, and I wondered if she was still there.

"Who is this?" she mumbled.

"It's Warren." Silence, but I could feel her irritation. "I know you're pissed at me, and you have every right to be. My apologies. I did a little digging last night, and there are things you need to know. It's about Rocky, but there's so much more."

She didn't speak for some time, but when she did, her voice was cold. "Go on."

"Not over the phone. We need to talk face to face." I fought the urge to tell her I needed to see her again. "Please, it's important or else I wouldn't have bothered you."

"Fine," she snapped. "I'll have to get a sub for school and coffee... lots of coffee. What time is it, anyway?" The rustle of her blankets through the line sent goosebumps down my spine, and images of her in my bed flooded my mind.

"F-four a.m.," I stuttered like a dimwit. My body tingled again as the sudden image of her soft body lying naked next to mine had me acting like a fool.

"I haven't been up this early in a long time. I can be there around six. Will that work?"

"Y-yeah." Words weren't forming in my mouth correctly.

She huffed. "Sounds like you need some coffee as well." Then she hung up before I could respond.

Nine

Josie

The streets of downtown were eerily quiet as I drove back to the bar. The school wasn't happy I'd taken the day off at the last minute, but after ten years of never missing a single day, they had nothing to complain about. I parked right in front of Rogue and walked to the front.

The solid oak door swung in before I'd reached it. Cautiously, I stepped through. No one was in sight. The bar was a desert wasteland compared to Saturday night, and the stone walls felt warmer as the morning sun peeked through the stained glass windows.

"Hello?" I called out.

"Up here," Warren answered from his office.

My hands brushed over the massive redwood bar as I walked toward the spiral staircase. The last time I was here, people had covered the intricate wood. Today, I saw it for all its glory. It was thicker than even the front door, and each panel had a different picture carved into it. Stepping back to take it all in, it was like looking at a comic strip with no words. It told a story: one of monsters and magic. This bar had each creature I'd seen carved into it: vampires, fae, werewolves. As the panels grew darker, the last had several creatures alongside humans, all fighting against an unseen force. My breath caught in my throat.

"It's magnificent, isn't it?" His voice rang out over the empty bar.

"Is there truth in it?" I asked without looking away.

"Many years ago, a seer gave it to me as a gift. She told me the events would come to pass and that if we, the Figli Del Mito, didn't come together with the humans, we will destroy our world."

I cocked my head. "Figli Del Mito?"

"Children of Myth: A name we gave our kind after the humans stopped believing in us and we became fiction. But we are very much real, Josie." He disappeared from the spot where he was standing and reappeared right in front of me.

I slammed back into the bar with a yelp. "Holy crap!"

"Pardon me, I forget you don't fully understand." He took a step back and bowed in apology.

"Don't do that to me!" I rubbed my eyes, trying to catch my breath. "I... I thought... I prayed it was all a nightmare."

"I'm sorry, Josie, but it is all real." He looked at me with sorrow in his eyes.

"So," I started slowly, putting the pieces together. "If faeries have normal jobs and vampires work your bar..." I turned my back to him so he couldn't see the tears welling up in my eyes, "and werewolves wanted me dead, then you..." Thinking back to the books I'd treasured as a kid, werewolves and vampires had their obvious traits. The fae and wizards were harder to spot. I wiped my eyes, put on a brave face, and turned back to him. "Are you fae or a wizard?"

His laugh startled me, rich and deep, echoing off the high ceilings. It was genuine, unrestrained, and it hit me like a warm wave, cutting through the tension I hadn't realized I was holding in my shoulders. I blinked, caught off guard by the sound of it.

It wasn't the kind of laugh you faked to fill awkward silences or soften a blow; it was real, and something about it made my chest tighten. I didn't want to admit it, but it was the kind of laugh that made you want to laugh along, even if you didn't know why.

But I didn't. Instead, I crossed my arms tighter over my chest and looked away, pretending to find something fascinating in the scuff marks on the floor. My face felt hot, and I hated how easily he could disarm me like that, as if my walls weren't even there.

"We prefer the term warlock. There are no wizard schools for young magic users to harness their powers. And no, vampires don't sparkle in the sunlight. They only burn."

My younger self cried inwardly at the crush of dreams he'd spoken in one statement. I laughed a little at my ridiculousness and shook my head, trying to focus on the situation before me.

"Wait!" I had a sudden realization. "Is there some truth in novels?"

He shrugged. "Somewhat, depends on who wrote it."

"In those stories, humans can't see past the glamour. Is that true?"

He nodded and took a step forward.

"But why can I?" I murmured, my head spinning as the room tilted.

"Because there's more to you," he said softly, his voice close.

My knees buckled, the world blurring, but his strong arms caught me, lifting me effortlessly as he stepped toward the stairs.

"Oh, Josie, I'm so sorry," he whispered in my ear.

Everything went black. When I next opened my eyes, I stared at a dark ceiling. Blinking rapidly, I looked around without moving my head. The walls were a mix of dark wood, Gothic wainscoting, and dark teal paint. My hands felt the soft mattress I laid on. I turned my head to see Warren walking in from a bathroom, holding a washcloth. He sat in a chair beside me and laid the cool cloth over my forehead.

"I am sorry you weren't told the truth years ago." He looked down at his hands.

"I... I still don't understand. Not exactly. How can I see this world? I'm human, my mother's human... but I never knew my father. Is he not human? Am I not human?" I didn't want the answer, but I had to hear it.

"I wish someone else had told you. I've never been too good at being gentle." He didn't look up from fidgeting with his hands.

I sat up, letting the washcloth fall. "Then don't be. I need to know. My student is missing, and I'm worried something's happened to him. I'm the only one who cares about the kid, and I'm wasting time here." I threw my feet over the side of the bed, preparing to stand. "If I have some advantage to help him, don't hide it from me. Tell me the truth already."

His eyes widened, and he sat frozen for a moment. He shook his head before speaking. "You're like me, Josie. You're a warlock. Your father is a warlock as well. There's a database for Figli Del Mito, and I did some research. Your mother probably didn't even know what he was."

"I'm a—"

He waved his hand. "You wanted the whole truth, so let me finish."

"There's more?"

He nodded. "Your ex-husband is a cambion—a half-demon. He's the reason you are only now seeing our world. I looked into your memories—I'm sorry—but when I did, I saw you met him about the time you should have come into your powers, and his power blocked you. I'm not sure if he did it on purpose or not, but you can't trust the cambion. You should have known a long time ago." He looked into my eyes with such softness.

I leaned over and rested my head in my hands, feeling queasy. His shadow moved as if to touch me, but I never felt it.

"I—" I stood, running to the bathroom just in time to make it to the toilet. The six-dollar bagel I'd had for breakfast came up in chunks. The sink faucet turned on, then he knelt beside me and pulled my hair back, laying a cold cloth on the back of my neck. His hands worked delicately in my hair until it fell into a braid. "I'm sorry." My voice echoed in the bowl. I reached up and flushed the toilet, then slowly raised my head. I took the washcloth and wiped my face before turning away from him.

His fingers grazed my back so quickly, I hardly noticed them. "No, Josie, none of this is your fault."

I spun around on the floor, leaned against the wall, and looked at him fully. Goosebumps rippled over my skin. His fiery gaze tore into me, and I had to look away. My head was spinning with everything he'd just told me. Closing my eyes, I took a deep breath and steadied my breathing, then my eyes flew open as I remembered why I was here.

"Rocky!" I nearly shouted as I sat up. My head was pounding. I wasn't sure it could take much more bad news, but I had to understand it.

Warren stood, offering me a hand, and I let him help me up but quickly let go. He led me back into his bedroom, and looking around, I noticed there was no door to the outside world. Panic gripped my chest.

"How..." I looked around frantically.

"Easy." Warren faced me. "Breathe, I'll get us out of here. I just need you to breathe first, and I'll explain."

I forced air into my lungs. He offered me his hand again and grinned. The smile felt disarming despite the storm of doubt in my mind. I eyed his extended hand skeptically.

"Trust me," he said, his tone warm and steady, as though he carried all the assurance in the world.

Something about him—his calm presence, the steadiness in his gaze—silenced the warning bells in my head. I couldn't explain it, but I felt a pull, a quiet certainty buried beneath my confusion and fear. Against all reason, I placed my hand in his.

His fingers closed around mine, firm yet gentle, as he led me toward a nearby wall. My heart thudded in my chest, but it wasn't from fear. An unshakable sense of security that I couldn't understand settled within me. Somehow, I knew he wouldn't let anything happen to me. And for now, that was enough.

His hand reached out for something I couldn't see as he walked forward, pulling me into the darkness. I shut my eyes tightly at the icy feeling washing over me. When I opened them again, we stood in his office. "What? How?"

He smiled. "We were just in my bedroom here at the bar. I don't use it often, but sometimes it's easier to sleep here than to go home. I pride myself on being a private person, so very few know it's even there." He pointed to the bookshelves behind him. "That includes you, now. Magic is the only way in."

"Why would you tell me?" I walked up to the wall of books and ran my hand over the wood. Nothing betrayed the secrets this wall held. I stared at it for a long moment until I saw it: a shimmer at the center. It was like looking at the heat radiating off a fire. The book *The Tempest* sat in the heart of the fire. I stepped closer and grazed my hand over the spine and an invisible force pulled me back through the wall and into his room again. Warren appeared right behind me.

"That is why I told you. You can see it." He stepped closer to me. "I felt your power the moment you walked up to my bar. That's why I had my bouncer let you in. Few mundanes get in, and I knew you weren't human." He reached for me but pulled away before he touched me.

"Did I... Did I just do magic?" I looked at my hands.

"Yes." He said it simply.

"Well, that makes more sense now."

He cocked his head in question.

"The wolves," I said flatly. "I never told you how I escaped them. I was curled up in a ball with my hands shielding my face, and some bright light lit up the sky, and they went running."

He grinned, looking impressed. "Yep, magic." He took a step back, his body tense, and twirled his thumbs around each other. "Josie, I... Never mind." His lips moved, but no sound came out like he was having an internal conversation.

I looked down at my own hands uncomfortably. "What happened to Rocky?" I whispered, half hoping he didn't hear.

He looked up. "It's more than just him. There are a lot of kids missing."

"Street kids?" I looked up, suddenly remembering the conversation I'd had with Nessa on Saturday.

"Maybe that's how it looks to most people, but they are all Figli Del Mito. The police assume they're street kids because they go missing at night."

"Nessa said they've all ended up dead." Ice froze my veins, and I shivered. "Wait? Figli Del Mito? Rocky's not human?" I knew I had locked the doors to the gym on Friday night. Had he unlocked them by some other means?

Warren shook his head. "There's more I haven't told you yet. Maybe you should sit?" He gestured to the chair next to him where he'd been sitting in.

My heart was racing. I didn't need to faint again in front of him, so I sat and waited for him to continue.

"That database I mentioned before. I looked into him as well, and his parents weren't human. They were warlocks. So is Rocky. I don't know who is taking them or why, but someone is taking our people's children. By the looks of what they've found of them, they are experimenting on these kids." He sat on the edge of the bed and faced me.

"We have to find him. No one else will." I let a few tears fall as anger boiled inside me. How could anyone harm a child? The thought of Rocky being hurt right now and there being nothing I could do to stop it had me pacing the floor.

I couldn't think of what would happen if I were too late to save him.

"We will. I promise." He crossed his arms over his chest, holding them tight. "There's more, though. Rocky's father..."

I pulled legs up in the chair hugging my knees to my chest and wrapped my arms around them. Warren looked everywhere but at my face.

"What about his father?" I questioned.

"No easy way to say it. His father is your father."

His words blurred together; my heart sank into my stomach.

"What? How do you know?"

"The database. It is compulsory. Any time a warlock's mating produces a child, it shows up in the database. When I looked up Rocky and his parents, there was another child for his father. One Josefina Marie Collins. Rocky's your half-brother." He moved and knelt in front of me.

"What am I going to do now? I know nothing about this world. How can I save him if I don't even know what I am?" I sucked my lower lip into my mouth, sniffling as I tried to keep my tears at bay.

One side of his lips raised in a half grin. "I'll help you. I'm a sucker for a damsel in distress, so your wish is my command."

I was no one's damsel, so I stood, heading for the "door" in the wall behind him. I could feel his eyes on me, and I paused before walking through the magic. His chest pressed into my back the moment I stepped into his room, and I pulled away.

"Nessa's husband—the girl I was with Saturday—is a detective here in town working on this case. She told me they don't know how these kids are dying. I think we should try to talk to him. He'll understand. Well, maybe not the magic part, but he'll understand my concern." I looked at my feet and whispered to myself, "Especially now."

"Why didn't you go to him first?"

"It's complicated. But now that I know it's connected to his case, he might believe me." I turned to look back at him.

He nodded and walked up to me. "Which station? Is he there now?"

I checked my watch. "Should be there soon. He's on the east side."

"Let's get you cleaned up and grab some coffee, then we can head that way." He produced a new toothbrush out of nowhere and smiled at me.

Ten

Warren

When Josie came back into the bedroom, I walked her over to the far corner and pressed a finger to my lips. She raised an eyebrow, then her eyes followed mine to the floor. I waited for her to see it, but her colorful braid fell over her shoulder, blocking her face from view and forcing me to shift around to watch her eyes widen.

Her hand reached down to grab the rope that lay coiled up on the floor, and she yanked the trapdoor open. She gasped at the spiral stairs that lay underneath, and her gaze snapped up to mine.

"What? Do you think I'd walk through that crowd just to get to my room? I might own the bar, but it's not my style." I shrugged, offering her a hand. In her excitement, she didn't hesitate to take it, allowing me to help her down the steps until her slender fingers grasped the railing.

Following behind her, I froze the moment I cleared the opening, watching her sashay down the stairs. Her jeans hugged her tightly, showcasing her dainty body. My heart raced as she reached the concrete floor and turned to look back at me with those hazel eyes, a frown tugging at her lips.

"Are you coming?" she teased. I hesitated, her words tugging at the fragile thread of my restraint. As if sensing my internal war, she gave me a quick, disappointed glance before concealing it with another smile.

Josie's energy filled the space between us, and I could feel her emotions humming—mirroring my own desire. It was intoxicating, overwhelming, and utterly dangerous. Her magic was a siren's call, wrapping around me, pulling me closer with every moment.

I fought for control, knowing that crossing this line now would change everything. My rational mind, the part of me that clung to centuries of discipline, forced me to raise a shield between us, blocking the raw power of her magic before it consumed me. Even so, my fingers itched to touch her, to close the space that separated us.

I took the final steps to the bottom, joining her at her side. Her warmth seeped through my skin, and I nearly let the shield drop. Every part of me ached to be closer, to let the barrier between us fall, but I couldn't. Not yet.

The mudroom seemed even smaller than it normally did, closing us in with her scent, her presence, her everything. That grin she'd given me earlier replayed in my mind, and my resistance crumbled completely.

"Miss Josie," I said, my voice rough and low as I took her hand. Her fingers fit so perfectly into mine it felt like they belonged there. I hesitated; the warmth of her skin seeped into my palm and stirred a dangerous yearning inside me. Her breath hitched, her wide eyes meeting mine, and for a moment, I let my mind wander.

What would it feel like to close the space between us, to lean in and taste the magic on her lips? I could almost feel it—the soft press of her mouth against mine, her magic sparking like wildfire under my skin, setting every nerve alight. I imagined her stepping closer, her arms sliding around my neck, pulling me into a kiss that would shatter every wall I'd spent centuries building. She would awaken parts of me I'd long thought dead, make me forget the weight of my responsibilities, if only for a fleeting moment.

But the vision wasn't real, and I snapped back into myself, my chest tightening with the realization of how far I'd let my thoughts drift. I couldn't cross that line—not now, maybe not ever. It wasn't just about me; it was about her, about what this would mean for both of us.

Clearing my throat, I released her hand gently, my gaze lingering on her face for a second longer than it should have. "Come on," I said, my tone softer, more controlled now, as I guided her toward the door to the garage. Josie's silence was heavy, filled with unspoken words and emotions I didn't dare name. For now, all I could do was hold my ground, trying to ignore the part of me that wanted nothing more than to pull her back into my arms. Her eyes brightened slightly, and she nodded.

The air felt heavier, charged with unspoken emotions, but I forced myself to stay grounded, to ignore the part of me that still ached to close the distance between us.

We stood there in awkward silence for a moment before I moved hesitantly around her to the door. "Are you ready to leave?" I asked.

She nodded and followed me.

I paused at the door before I opened it. "This is my private garage. I don't trust my cars out on the streets."

She rolled her eyes. "Boys and their cars."

"Hey, when you spend as much as I do on a car, you wouldn't want it on the street, either."

Her eyes widened before I even opened the door.

"What?"

"I might not have spent as much as you on my car, but..." She looked toward the front of the club. "A nice new Tesla is sitting in front of your bar."

I laughed as I opened the door. "No, not as much as mine, but still too nice to leave out front. I'll move it for you."

She sucked in a breath as she stepped inside. I was a bit of a collector. The cars were nice, but fast cars were better. Here at the club, I had a Ferrari F12 Berlinetta and a Porsche 918 Spyder. But my favorite was my Bugatti Veyron. The matte black paint and tinted windows held just enough mystery to keep people interested but at arm's length.

She sighed. "Yeah, my little electric car will be outta place in this garage." I pointed over to the left of my Bugatti. There was a box attached to the wall with "Tesla" written on it. "I own one too. It's just not here at the moment."

She raised her brows. "How many cars do you own?"

"I have three residences and two or three cars at each one. At least here in Indiana."

She gaped at me now. "Three residences?"

I shrugged. "I like to travel." Pulling out the key fob, I unlocked the Bugatti. "Wanna drive?"

She backed away like I held a copperhead snake, making me laugh as I led her toward the passenger side. I opened the door and coaxed her into the seat, ignoring the "my jeans will scratch the leather" complaints. After opening the garage door, I pulled around to the front of the building, parking behind the Tesla. Josie handed me the keys without looking at me. I left my car running as I pulled hers in. She looked so small sitting in the seat when I returned; her arms wrapped tight around her chest and her feet tucked in close to the chair. I slid into the driver's seat and looked over at her.

"What's wrong, Josie?"

"This car, it's worth more than I could make in a lifetime." She sighed, turning to look out the window.

"And?"

"And I'm just wondering why you'd take me in it? Why would you be willing to help me at all?"

"Josie, first, you need to understand when I told you I was friends with Shakespeare I wasn't joking."

Her head snapped back to me, and her jaw dropped.

I nodded. "Yes, I was born in the early 1400s. So, money isn't an issue for me. Collecting cars over the years has been possible for me. My investments have paid me well and I live off the interest and I give any proceeds from my companies to charity. So I'm not worried about you hurting this car. You're going to be sore if you keep sitting so tight." I let my hand rest on the center console as close to her as I dared to get. "Second, you are mesmerizing to me. I don't know why, but I'd help you even if Rocky wasn't one of us." I looked down at my hand as she placed hers next to it, barely touching me. Electricity buzzed through me at the brief contact.

"I'm so worried about him. He's got no one." She dropped her eyes. "No one but me now."

"I promised we'd find him, and I keep my promises. Now, buckle up, and tell me where I'm going."

※

Josefina

I GRIPPED THE 'OH SHIT HANDLE' OF THE DOOR AS WARREN sped away from the bar. I'd never been in a sports car before, but this was faster than I expected. It was smoother than any car I'd ever been in, too. The only hint of how fast we were going was the buildings whizzing past my window.

His hand rested on the console, an open invitation, but I fought the urge to grip his fingers. I had felt his thoughts back in the mudroom as if they were my own. Images of him pressing his lips into mine had made my knees weak, but he'd never leaned in and made those visions a reality. I hadn't bothered to attempt to explain to myself how I knew he was thinking of me in that way, I just knew it to be true, and at this point, I was all in. Magic was real and maybe one day I'd understand it.

I laid my hand on top of his, interlacing our fingers and letting his warmth engulf me. I bit back the gasp as my heart skipped. The moment my skin touched his, I could breathe easier, and the world didn't seem to move as fast. Slowly, I opened my eyes and looked at the dash—120mph and still climbing. He laughed as I shut my eyes again, but the car slowed to a somewhat normal speed.

"It's okay, I'll slow down. If I knew you'd be so afraid, I would've driven your car." His voice flowed over me like silk.

"I'm pretty sure you'd still drive this fast, even in my car." I didn't dare open my eyes. His thumb rubbed the side of my hand. Such a slight gesture, but I had to angle my face away so he couldn't see my smile.

"I promise it's safe to open your eyes." He spoke so gently that I finally obeyed.

Looking over to the gauges, I saw a more manageable 80mph.

"How can you drive so fast through town like that? Haven't you ever gotten a ticket? Or worse?" I looked at him, his golden eyes crinkling.

"I'm a warlock, Josie. No one can even see us right now. I use a shield charm from other cars, so I've never been in an accident or stopped by the cops."

I laughed. "Must be nice. I wish I could say the same thing."

He squeezed my fingers. "You're a warlock too. I can teach you. Normally, we have at least one parent who knows about magic to teach us. You are uniquely different. It's been a long time since I've taught anyone, but I think I could for you. There's a glow off you like nothing I've ever seen before."

"A glow? You mean like my aura?" I asked. My stomach did loops as he pulled my fingers to his lips, kissing them softly.

"Yes, exactly like your aura. Everyone has an aura, but warlocks are different. Ours are brighter and more... solid. Like a shield. But yours is the most vibrant I've ever seen."

"I've been told by several people that my aura is green, but I don't understand what that means."

"It is. It's a bright emerald green, which means you are a healer. People are drawn to you and often come to you when they need you. Maybe it's why I'm drawn to you, but..."

I turned to look at him. "But what?" I wasn't sure why I needed to know, but I did. I felt a stronger pull toward him than I had ever felt toward anyone, and considering I barely knew him, it should have terrified me. Instead, it sent a thrill through my body, waking up every nerve. Heat burst through my skin, and my body buzzed with a strange excitement. Images of what I'd let this man do to me flew through my mind. He steered the car off the road and parked next to the river we'd been traveling beside. My heart was racing. I wiped my palms down on my jeans as he unbuckled his seat belt and leaned over, brushing his nose against mine.

"You're driving me mad, Josie," he growled. "I'm trying so hard not to do the things I want to do with you..."

Sucking in a breath, I ran my hands through his thick hair. "But what?" I asked again. I couldn't stop myself from pulling him into me and grazing my lips along his.

He pulled away, sitting back in his seat. "You don't even know, do you?"

He threw open his door and paced in front of the car, raking his fingers through his hair as he muttered to himself.

I sat in the car, frustrated. What was his problem? One minute, he was inches from my face, and now, he was throwing a fit like a toddler. I threw open my door and stepped out to face him.

"Damned furious wight," he spat in a thick English accent I could hardly understand.

"Excuse me?" I asked, startling him.

"I'm sorry." He looked down, sounding more like himself.

"What was that?" I tried to laugh at his strange words.

"I... I haven't done that in a long time."

"Done what?"

"Slipped back into my native tongue. I'm sorry if I confused you."

I stepped closer and reached my hand up to him. His face pressed hot against my palm. "I just don't understand what's happening."

He leaned into me, wrapping his arms around me. "Josie, you..." His touch sent sparks bouncing through my body. The heat that radiated off us was nearly unbearable. He pulled away quickly and spun around, muttering, "Flap-dragon fustilarian, pigeon egg, ill-breeding sap." I couldn't understand the rest of his words as his accent grew thicker. He paced, kicking the dirt as he went.

"Warren! We need to go. I have to find Rocky," I shouted, hoping a change of subject would calm him. He froze like he'd forgotten I'd even been there, then trudged back to the car. "What the hell is going on? You're freaking me out." I kept the car between us.

"I'm sorry," he breathed. "It's not your fault. You don't know what you're doing."

"What I'm doing?" My heart thrummed in my ears.

"You're using magic." He stepped around the car and stood in front of me. His hand touched mine, sending sparks through my skin. "Dang it, Josie." He cursed under his breath, pulling away.

I turned away, avoiding his gaze. "I'm sorry," I said, barely audible.

"Don't. Don't apologize."

"My magic is forcing you to feel something you don't." I wiped the tears from my cheeks but didn't look at him. I knew what it was to be forced into a relationship, and I'd never want to do that to him, but the sting of thinking he might not want me still burned.

"No, Josie, that is not how magic works. You could never force someone to do something they don't want to do. No magic could ever make me hit a woman, or kiss her." He twirled the end of my braid between his fingers. "Josie, I desire more than just a kiss, but I come from a different era. I hold on to my morals when everyone else is losing theirs."

My heart lightened and I turned to face him despite the tears streaming down my face.

"Oh, my Josefina," he sighed. He pulled me into his arms, my head resting on his chest as he hugged me tightly. He kissed the top of my head gently.

"My ex. He was... charming at first, but after we married..."

His hands stroked my side as I tried and failed to continue past the lump in my throat. "Shhh," he whispered. "Don't think about that right now." He held me for a long moment before I looked up at him.

Refusing to admit it out loud, I felt safe in his arms.

"Better?"

I nodded and stepped out of his embrace. "I think we should go find more information about my... my brother." Standing on my tiptoes, I pressed my lips to his. He growled at the contact but didn't pull away. My body yearned for more, but then a strange tingle came from my fingertips. My lips moved over his mouth, but my mind reached out for the magic I thought I felt. I reined it in, pulling it back toward me. I stepped away, gasping. "Sorry."

"'S'okay," he slurred.

"That's kinda crazy. I-I felt like I had to kiss you. Like I couldn't control it."

"Magic is funny that way. When you're untrained, it's like an untamed beast within you. It can feel your desires and push you toward them against your better judgment."

"So, what exactly am I doing?"

He grinned, saying, "Our souls have a natural connection. They want to be together, but we have our baggage that is stopping us. Your magic is trying to tear down that boundary, forcing us both to admit what we're hiding."

"And what are we hiding?"

He stepped closer, cupping my face with one hand and brushing his thumb over my cheek. "I'm not sure either of us are ready to say yet." He pulled me into a quick kiss before walking away.

I clasped a hand over my mouth to hide the smile growing against my will, my fingers barely able to contain the warmth spreading through me. It had been years since a kiss felt like a promise, and yet his lips spoke volumes—more than words ever could. They didn't just press against mine; they lingered, whispered unspoken vows of something deeper, something real. It wasn't just desire—it was reassurance, a quiet certainty that this was only the beginning.

For a moment, I allowed myself to savor it. His magic brushed against mine, tentative but unyielding, like a thread binding us together. My heart ached with the knowledge that there was more waiting, just out of reach. But I didn't need it all right now. This was enough. For the moment, this was everything.

Reality tugged at the edges of my thoughts, a gentle reminder of the urgency we couldn't ignore. Rocky was still out there, his fate unknown, and the world around us wasn't about to pause for the connection we'd just discovered. I forced myself to lower my hand, schooling my expression into something more composed, though my lips still tingled with the memory of his.

He stepped back, his eyes searching mine as if trying to gauge my reaction, to make sure he hadn't crossed a line. I reached out and lightly touched his arm, grounding him and, in a way, grounding myself. "We'll have time," I murmured softly, the words more for me than him. "But right now, we have to focus on finding Rocky."

He nodded, his jaw tightening as resolve replaced the vulnerability I'd seen just moments ago. "You're right," he said, his voice steady, though his gaze lingered on me a second longer, as if reluctant to break the spell we'd cast.

I took a deep breath, letting the moment settle into my bones. It was enough to carry me through the uncertainty ahead. For now, we had a mission, and while the promise of more lingered in the air between us, it could wait. We had work to do, and Rocky needed us.

He continued to drive, the silence settling between us with comfortable ease. After a while, as my heart slowed, he took my hand again and spoke.

"We need to get your powers in control a little more."

"I think..." I looked down at my hands remembering the strange sensation I'd felt back in his mudroom. "It tingled."

"That sounds right. It's been so long since I've had to explain it. I'm glad you felt it when you did." His grip on the steering wheel tightened as his voice dropped to a whisper. "I wasn't sure if I could take much more."

"Oh, please, did I offend your delicate sensibilities?" I raised an eyebrow at him.

"It's not that. It's just that it's been a very long time since I've..." He cleared his throat and finally glanced over at me. "Since I've wanted someone like I want you, but I want to keep you safe, even if..." He sighed, turning back to the road. "Josie, there's so much more to me than you know, and I don't want to hurt you."

"I..." I licked my lips, looking out the window. "The only person I've been with is my ex. I was with him longer than I was single." I set my hand on the center console, not daring to touch him again. My heart begged for his warmth, but my head told me Rocky was in danger and we needed to focus. "It's not a ridiculous notion."

He smiled and let his body relax. We drove in silence the rest of the way to the police station.

Eleven

Josie

We pulled into the parking lot of the police station sooner than I'd expected, the sun just peeking its head above the horizon. I got out of the car and headed straight for the doors.

"Josie, wait," Warren called, striding over and grabbing my hand. "Are you prepared to hear what he's got to say?"

"What do you mean?" I cocked my head to the side.

"I mean, these kids... From what I've heard, it's not pretty. I just, I don't want you to get your hopes up."

I ripped my hand from his grasp and climbed the stairs to the boxy, red brick building. My anger rose as I flung the double doors open and stormed inside. I must have startled the woman sitting behind the glass window protecting the front desk. Her yelp penetrated the wall, which kept me from going any farther.

She leaned forward, sliding the window open. "May I help you?"

"Sorry, I'm here to see Detective Reed, please." The cool breeze at my back and the widened eyes of the woman told me Warren had finally joined me.

"Is he expecting you?"

"Just tell him it's Josefina. He'll see me."

She tilted her head, looking past me to Warren.

"He's with me," I cut her off before she could even ask.

She sat back in her chair and picked up the phone on her desk. I inhaled sharply as Warren's chest brushed against my back, his hand resting on my hip.

"I'm sorry, Josie—"

I stepped out of his reach. "Don't. I can't give up on him, and I won't. If you already have, then leave."

"Why ask me for help over this detective, then?" he said, his hand falling to his side as his frustration rose.

I pushed past the old memories. "I said it's complicated."

He stepped close, lowering his voice. "I know, but he could've helped you more than me when you thought Rocky was human."

"It's... There was a... We had a big fight back in college. It's fine. Honestly, he doesn't even remember what happened. Besides, I had Caleb."

The woman cracked the window and buzzed us in before Warren could ask more. I took the opportunity and turned away, walking into the station.

The woman at the desk pointed to the stairs at the far end of the building and said, "Second floor. Detective Reed will meet you there."

I rushed down the hall and took the steps two at a time. Part of me hoped Warren wasn't behind me, yet when we reached the top, the tightness in my chest lessened when his arm brushed my side.

"Jo!" Clint shouted as we reached the top of the stairs. "I was expecting my wife to be with you when Mary said that you were here." He strode up to us with a wide grin on his face. His dark blond hair and brilliant blue eyes stood out in any crowd.

The fight we'd had so long ago faded from my mind as he hugged me.

"I take it you must be Warren Harris?" Clint shifted his weight, stretching out his hand in greeting. "I've seen your articles in the magazines my wife has littered all over my house."

Warren nodded and clasped his hand.

"I'm surprised this is the first time we're meeting. I know you own a lot of businesses around town."

"I try my best to stay out of the limelight," Warren said, releasing his hand.

Clinton turned back to me. "So, what brings you to this neck of the woods so early?" You could take the boy out of the country, but not the country outta this boy. Clinton's family were all farmers, he was the rebel.

"I... None of the crappy cops in Deer Run believe me, and I thought you might. Rocky's missing." I wrung my hands together.

"Rocky? The point guard?"

I nodded.

"What makes you think that?" He leaned on the wall behind him and crossed his arms.

"He hasn't been at school since Friday," I managed, my voice cracking under the strain of the sobs threatening to consume me. The words caught in my throat, tumbling out in broken pieces, each one torn apart by the jagged edge of my breath. My vision blurred as tears welled up, distorting the room into a hazy swirl of muted colors. The couch, the walls, the light filtering through the window: None of it felt real anymore.

"He tried to call me over the weekend, but I'd lost my phone." My voice hitched, breaking as a sob escaped. *If I hadn't been so foolish, maybe... maybe I could've answered. Maybe things would've been different.* My chest heaved as guilt clawed at me, leaving my words splintered and uneven.

"His foster parents aren't doing dick about it," I said, louder now, the anger in my tone cutting through the sadness, though my voice still shook. "And the cops at home said he probably just left. They won't do anything because he's seventeen. I..." My voice faltered, trailing off as a fresh wave of grief crashed over me.

I thought of all the kids Nessa had told me about—the ones who never came back. My mind painted a vivid, unrelenting picture of Rocky, broken and abandoned, found in some alley, and it shattered me. The dam holding back my emotions burst, and the tears poured freely. "I just know something is wrong, and it's my fault." The words tumbled out in a frantic rush, as if saying them aloud might somehow absolve me of the crushing guilt.

Tears blurred my view entirely now, reducing the room to nothing but indistinct shapes and shadows. I didn't resist when Warren's arm wrapped around me, pulling me into his chest. The solidity of him was jarring against the storm raging inside me. His warmth seeped into my skin, a stark contrast to the cold weight of despair, but it only made the tears come faster, harder.

I buried my face against him, sobs racking my body, leaving me shaking and breathless. My words were gone now, lost in the torrent of emotions I couldn't hold back. All I could do was cling to the momentary comfort, even as it felt like I was drowning in everything I couldn't fix.

Clinton held up his hands. "Okay, okay, Jo, please stop crying. Let's go to my office."

Warren placed a kiss on my forehead as I wiped the tears from my face and followed Clinton through the maze of desks and officers. He pulled me back to walk beside him and whispered, "How much do you want him to know? Most mundanes can't handle the truth."

"I don't know." As I watched my best friend's husband, I pressed my lips into a firm line, considering if he could, but… "I don't want him to think I'm crazy."

Warren tightened his arm around my waist, then placed a kiss on the top of my head. "You are not crazy."

I shoved him away. "Stop that," I hissed through gritted teeth, keeping my voice low. "I know I'm not crazy, but a man who believes in law and order might think I'm crazy when I bring up vampires and werewolf attacks." I quickened my pace to catch up with Clinton.

He led us inside his small office and gestured to the chairs in front of his desk. "So, tell me more, Jo. Why do you think he hasn't just run off? I know his foster parents haven't been the best. Could he have run away?"

I scoffed.

"Hey, listen. I'm not trying to be a prick. Just doing my job, and I have to ask these questions."

"Fine. I don't think he ran away because he knew scouts were coming to the game on Monday. I saw him Friday night. He and some of his friends had found their way into the gym and were goofing off. I gave him some money. Dumb, I know, but I worry about him. Anyway, Monday when he wasn't in class, I asked one boy he was with Friday about him, and he lied to me about where they went."

"How'd you know it was a lie?"

I raised an eyebrow at him. "How do you know when a suspect is lying? When you're around teens all day every day, you just pick these things up. But it was more than just a lie. He was scared. Like he knew more, but wouldn't tell me. I've tried calling Rocky's cell, but it goes straight to voicemail."

Clinton looked from me to Warren and back. "What's the kid's name?"

"Keith Hartford." I fiddled with the tissue I'd taken off Clinton's desk to wipe my eyes.

"Alright, give me a minute." He stood and walked out of his office, leaving me alone with Warren.

My knee shook. I stood and walked to the wall, leaning on it and wishing I could punch it, but putting a hole in a police station wall was a bad idea. I hated that I cried so easily. Anger and frustration made me cry just as easily as pain and sadness. And now, here I was, sobbing in front of this man I'd only just met.

Warren's big hand rubbed my back in a soothing motion, and I jumped at the contact. Not having heard him move made me wonder if I had been so consumed in my thoughts or...

"Shhh," he whispered. I felt the tingle of magic flow from him and slow my breathing.

"Don't," I barked. Turning around, I shoved him hard in the chest. He didn't even flinch. "Never use magic on me unless I ask." I shoved him again, but I might as well have hit the wall. My resolve faded, and I let him pull me into his chest.

"You're right. I'm sorry," Warren whispered.

I pushed away from him the moment Clinton returned.

Clinton stepped beside us and handed me a tissue. "Jo?" he asked, eyes filled with concern.

"I'm sorry, Clinton. I'm just really worried about him," I said, wiping my face. "There's more." I looked back up at Warren. "We think Rocky... That his father might be my father. My birth father."

Clinton's eyebrows shot up. "How do you know that?"

"Well," Warren said, "I can't be certain without more proof, but I am pretty good at genealogy. I found his lineage, and there was a tag for another child." He brushed his knuckles over my arm. "The girl's name was Josefina Marie."

"So," Clinton dragged out the word. "If that's true, then it makes you family. Right?"

I shrugged. "I guess."

"Well, that helps. Anyone can file a missing report, but when it's family, it's taken more seriously. I'll have you fill one out." He leaned out of his office door, grabbing a nearby officer to get the proper paperwork before coming back in.

He sat on the edge of his desk, handing me another tissue. I took it, wiping my face clean again.

"What did you find out? With Keith?" I asked.

"I called the school and had them put Keith on the line." He pinched his nose between his thumb and forefinger. "Stupid kids," he whispered under his breath before looking up at me. "He knows more than he told me. Even through the phone, I could almost smell his lies. Now, I don't know what that means exactly, so don't go thinking it's a case. He just knows something. Rocky still could have run away."

"Nessa told me about the case you're working. I think this has something to do with that."

"Vanessa." He sighed, almost to himself. "She shouldn't have told you about that." Standing, he circled his desk. "And what makes you think that? The kids who have gone missing are all street kids from Indy. What connection could Rocky possibly have to them?"

My heart was racing. Clinton had to know. It was too dangerous for him to be investigating this without knowing the truth. I looked over at Warren. "Tell him," I whispered.

Warren flicked his wrist, and seemingly by itself, the door shut and the blinds closed. My best friend's husband sank into his chair, nearly missing the seat, slack-jawed, glancing between the door, Warren, and me.

I spoke quickly. "This might be hard to believe, but magic is real." *Yep, we were going to be locked up by the end of the day.*

It took us an hour to convince him not to call the psych ward to come get us. I had to beg him not to say anything to Nessa, at least not until I could tell her myself. I knew asking him to keep a secret from his wife was wrong, but it wasn't his to share. We told him all we knew about the missing kids and the fact they were all Figli Del Mito. He sat and listened to Warren explain everything, like he was giving him a grocery list.

Clinton shook his head. "If these kids are all some kind of... creatures of legends... isn't there a chance whoever is taking them is one of them figly things?"

"Yes," Warren said.

"Then how am I, a human, supposed to find them?"

You aren't alone in your search," Warren said. "There are more of us around than you know." He looked out of Clinton's office window, then walked to the door, opening it a crack and standing aside to allow in the two uniformed officers. The men who walked in were not men at all. One had the pale skin and pointy ears of the fae, and the other radiated magic. They looked so out of place in the dark blue uniforms I couldn't stifle a laugh. Clinton raised an eyebrow at me.

"They're one of us," I said, trying to smother the smile from my face.

He stood so quickly he nearly toppled from his chair, his hand instinctively going to his holster. I rushed to stand between them.

"Clinton, you know these men. Just because you know the truth now doesn't mean you don't know them." My magic tingled, pulling at the tension in the room and relaxing the three officers a bit.

Warren moved between Clinton and me as he spoke. "They can help you in your search for these kids. They will help guide you through our world and protect you from it as well. Other Figli Del Mito officers around the city can help you with your investigation. You need to trust them. We have lived alongside humans since the dawn of time. There is no need to fear us."

"Why aren't they dealing with this, then?" Clinton asked, not moving his hand.

"Because we still operate under your laws. You are the lead detective on this case. We only just now discovered the true nature of this crime. We need to work together on this."

"Please, Clinton," I added.

Clinton blew out a breath before he nodded. "Now that we know these kids aren't just street kids, I want you two to look at this new angle," he spoke to the two officers in the room. "See what you can find and report back to me this afternoon. I'll make sure the captain reassigns you to me for the time being." He turned to me. "And as for you, if you're finished with the report, then head home. This is too dangerous for you to get involved."

"But I—"

Warren wrapped an arm around me. "I'll make sure she gets home safely."

I stepped forward to argue, but Warren's firm hand grasped my arm, pulling me back.

"Please, Jo, go home. My wife would never forgive me if anything happened to you," Clinton said.

I tore my arm out of Warren's grasp and stormed out of the office. Practically running down the hall, I didn't even notice when I ran straight into an officer.

"Sorry," I murmured, as I continued toward the stairs.

Warren caught up with me halfway down. "Slow down, Josie."

"Why? I gotta get home like a good little girl," I mocked. "You want to borrow his cuffs to make sure I cooperate?"

"That's not... That's not fair, and you know it."

"Why? Because the two men I've dared to trust in the last decade want to lock me away in the tower to protect me from the big bad wolf?" We were drawing attention, but I didn't care. "I'm so sick of men telling me what I can and can't do! I mean, all my life Caleb controlled me. He stole my true self from me, and I'll never get that time back. So don't you dare presume to know what's best for me." My words echoed off the stairwell walls.

"Fine, I won't take you home." He glanced to the top of the stairs where Clinton stood, then nodded at him and gripped my arm, dragging me down the stairs and out the way we'd come. I tugged at his grasp, to no avail, and he released me the moment we were outside.

"What the hell?" I shouted at him.

"Will you calm down?" He pulled me around to face him, the building to his back. "Are they in the windows?"

"Are who in the windows?" I snapped at him.

"The man you ran into. He and his partner. Are they still watching you?"

Looking past him to the second-floor windows, I saw them and gasped. The men—and I use the term loosely—stood staring at us. Their flesh was charcoal black and rough. Cracks rippled through them, revealing a molten liquid running just below the surface. Their eyes glowed a volcanic orange. Warren's arms wrapped around my body, holding me in place.

"Let me go! I have to warn him!" I tried to wiggle out of his arms but couldn't. "They... They're..."

"Demons," Warren supplied.

Demons. I was staring at demons. Acid burned in the pit of my stomach as my body melted into Warren. His powerful arms kept me from falling.

"What are we going to do?" I cried into his chest.

"If you go running back in there, they will stop you, and it will get ugly." He pulled out his cell phone and clicked away. "I'm sending a text to the warlock officer, Tanner. If he doesn't already know they are there, he will. I doubt someone sent them there to hurt Clinton, but Tanner can protect him.

I wanted to push him away, but it felt too nice in his arms.

"So, what now? Are you going to take me home?" I whispered.

"No, but..."

I sighed, stepping away. "But what?"

He brushed his fingertips down my cheek. "You need to rest and eat something. Your energy is draining." He smiled. "Nice job, by the way, at calming down the room when we told Clinton there were 'monsters' in his department."

I scoffed and turned to his car.

"I mean it. That was impressive."

"If you aren't taking me home, then what?" I walked around to the passenger side and leaned on the car.

His smile grew. "I'll take you to my place. No, not the bar." He waved his hand in the air, swatting away my scowl. "But my home. We can get some food, and you can sleep while I do some more digging."

I rolled my eyes at him but slid into the car anyway. My stomach agreed with his plan, giving a thunderous growl. The soft leather of the seat hugged me, threatening to pull me into sleep despite my protest. I sighed in defeat, letting him speed off back to town.

Twelve

Warren

I drove us to the back lot of the old brick building, where its ironwork balcony cast long shadows in the late afternoon light. Pulling into a spot behind the dumpster, I couldn't help but smirk as I prepared for the next part. I wiggled my nose theatrically and glanced at Josie, waiting for her reaction. Her laugh was genuine and sweet, but it turned into a sharp gasp as the car shifted beneath us. Not forward or backward like she might expect, but straight down. The pavement sank, the parking lot vanishing from sight, replaced by the walls of a descending shaft. Josie's eyes widened as the tunnel ahead came into view.

When we stopped, I eased the car into gear, driving forward through the dimly lit passage until we reached the end. I slowed to a stop, the soft glow of the headlights illuminating the concrete walls ahead. Josie's hand shot out, gripping mine tightly. Her breath was uneven, her voice shaky. "Claustrophobic," she rasped, barely audible.

"Crap, I'm so sorry." I cursed myself for not warning her about the descent. I squeezed her hand gently, my thumb brushing over her knuckles. "Hang on. We're almost there."

The ground beneath us jostled again as the platform lifted. Sunlight streamed in, casting long beams into the tunnel as we emerged. The moment the car stopped, Josie fumbled with her seatbelt and bolted, dropping to her knees on the cool concrete. She gasped for air, her shoulders heaving.

Guilt twisted in my chest as I got out and approached her slowly, kneeling a few feet away. "May I?" I asked softly, holding out my hand. She nodded, unable to speak, and I reached for her. Channeling a calming spell, I sent a wave of warmth and comfort over her. Her breathing steadied as her muscles relaxed, and she finally looked up at me.

"Thank you," she murmured, her voice barely above a whisper. Relief flooded her face, but a new worry replaced it almost immediately. "Oh crap! My cat!"

"What cat?" I asked, caught off guard by the shifting thought.

"Ollie, my cat! He's at my house all alone. He's been locked inside for days. He usually helps me through panic attacks."

"I can bring him here for you," I offered without hesitation.

"Can you?" she asked, her voice tinged with hope and doubt.

"Wizard, remember?" I said with a small smile. "Just think of your house—close your eyes and picture it."

Taking her hands in mine, I waited as she focused. Moments later, a fluffy orange cat materialized in her lap. She exhaled in relief, running her fingers through the cat's fur.

"Why?" she asked suddenly, her voice thick with emotion. "Why are you being so kind to me when I've been such a jerk?"

The vulnerability in her words hit me hard. I flinched but forced a smile. "You're not a jerk, Josie. Why would you think that?"

She hesitated, biting her lip. "Caleb—my ex—he would've called me one if I spoke to him the way I did to you."

My jaw tightened at the thought of anyone treating her like that. "Then he's a giant twat waffle, and screw him," I said, earning a small, reluctant laugh from her.

Her next words were a quiet confession. "Why do you have to look at me like that?"

"Like what?" I asked, genuinely curious.

"Like you see something in me that I don't."

I leaned closer, holding her gaze. "Maybe I do."

"You know what you are?" she practically giggled. "You're a tootsie pop."

"Excuse me?" I pulled back.

"You know? Hard, crunchy exterior; soft, gooey inside."

I smiled. "Yeah, I guess so." For a moment, the world narrowed to just us. Then I stood, offering her a hand. "Come on. Let's get inside."

I led her through the door to the penthouse, keeping my hand firmly wrapped around hers. I could feel her fingers trembling slightly, but there was a steady warmth in her grip, like she was trying to anchor herself in this space, in the strange safety I was offering.

As we stepped into the expansive room, Josie gasped. I watched her closely, her amazement palpable as she took in the blend of industrial steel and brick, the dark, luxurious furniture, and the towering shelves of books that stretched high above us. The room felt alive—there was magic in every corner, magic I'd woven into this place over centuries. Soft music drifted through the air, the subtle melodies enhancing the mood as she stepped farther into the room.

"This is my home, Josie," I said quietly, my voice almost reverent. "You are the only one who knows it exists. It's my sanctuary."

She turned to look at me over her shoulder, a skeptical smile playing on her lips. "Uh-huh, I'm sure I'm the first girl you've brought home."

I stiffened, the question lingering in the air between us. "No, really," I said, taking a step closer, trying to keep my tone steady. "I try very hard to keep my life outside of my businesses private. I've never brought a girl here... nor to any of my beds."

Her eyes locked onto mine, and I could see the weight of her skepticism. I wasn't lying, but she didn't have to believe me. There was no reason she would.

She hesitated, then spoke softly, her voice carrying more vulnerability than I'd ever heard from her. "Why me?"

I took a slow breath, running a hand through my hair. This wasn't something I'd planned on saying, but somehow it felt right. "There's something about you. Josie, I trust you more than anyone from my past. I..." I paused, the words gathering at the edge of my lips. "I believe you can do anything you set your mind to. You're..." My throat tightened, and I forced a smile, though my eyes betrayed the intensity of the feeling I couldn't quite explain. "You're brilliant. And I want to be by your side the day you see it too."

Before I could finish she threw herself into my arms, her body pressed against mine. The sudden rush of movement that took me by surprise, but I caught her, lifting her easily off the floor, feeling the heat of her skin and the weight of her trust.

Her lips found mine, and the world shifted. Everything else—the penthouse, the city outside, the secrets I'd spent centuries building—faded into nothing. It was just her and me.

I carried her toward the kitchen; she weighed nothing at all, with her legs wrapped around me. She didn't resist. In fact, she pulled me closer. I set her on the counter, my hands tugging at her braid, loosening it until her hair spilled around her shoulders.

"Josie," I whispered into her neck as I ran my hands down her spine, sending shivers of anticipation through both of us.

I felt her arch against me, pressing herself closer, but then her stomach growled loudly, breaking the tension. She pulled away, laughing softly, and I couldn't help but smile.

"I need to feed you, then get you to bed," I said, my voice low but teasing.

Her eyes widened comically, and she looked flustered. "I mean sleep," I corrected quickly, trying to cover my slip.

She raised an eyebrow, clearly amused. "Fair enough. What do you have to eat?"

I turned back to the stove, a laugh bubbling out of me at the sudden shift in her energy. "You're about to find out."

I moved around the kitchen with practiced ease, frying bacon and boiling elbow noodles, chopping cheese and peppers. There was something satisfying about creating from scratch, especially with her watching. Her eyes followed my every movement with an intensity that made my pulse quicken.

"What?" I asked, glancing over at her as I stirred the cheese mixture.

"I hate to admit it, but you're sexy in the kitchen," she said, her voice dripping with playful sarcasm.

I chuckled. "You act like you've never seen a man in a kitchen."

"I haven't," she said with a shrug. "That's woman's work." She mocked a manly voice and air-quoted before rolling her eyes.

I didn't miss the way her gaze softened as she watched me. "I've held many mundane jobs over the years. In the '20s, I was a chef. Probably one of my favorite eras." I met her eyes with a grin. "I don't believe in gender roles. Well, aside from chivalry. That's not a role, it's just respect." I took a step toward her, brushing a strand of hair from her face. "And that includes protecting those I care about."

My lips brushed hers in a soft kiss before I pulled back slightly. She looked at me, her expression serious now. "I'm sorry," she breathed.

I raised an eyebrow. "Don't ever apologize to me."

She laughed softly, but there was a hint of nervousness in her voice when she spoke again. "I don't know what this is yet, but I'm comfortable around you. And your touch..." Her hands trailed up my spine, sending a jolt of electricity through me. "It does something to me I've never experienced before, and I... I want more, but it scares me."

I took a step back, my heart beating faster. This wasn't just chemistry; this was something else. "It scares me too, Josie," I admitted, my voice low. "The last time I let myself love someone, it nearly broke me. I don't know what this is, but... I'm willing to figure it out with you if you are?"

She bit her lip and nodded. I could see the hesitation in her eyes, but there was something else too—something that told me we might just make it through this, together.

I leaned in again, my lips finding hers, and for a moment, nothing else mattered.

She pulled back, and I could feel her heartbeat on my chest. "You'll burn the food if you keep it up," she said, her voice teasing, though I could hear the breathlessness beneath it.

I laughed, reluctant to leave her embrace, but I turned back to the stove, finishing the meal as she sat on the counter, watching me.

I was glad she was there.

Twenty minutes later, I set two bowls down on the bar and when she was finally done eating, I swept her up again, heading down the hall, making sure she was taken care of in every way.

"You need sleep, Josie," I said softly. "And I'll make sure you get it."

She relaxed into me as I carried her to the bed, my chest tight with the weight of everything that had happened—and everything yet to come.

"Sweet dreams," I whispered, brushing a kiss across her forehead.

And for once in a long while, I allowed myself to hope.

I tucked her under the comforter before walking back toward my office. I tried to remember the name of the boy Josie had talked to. Keith? Keith Hartford.

The city's skyline greeted me as I sat down in my black banker's chair and slid up to my desk. Clicking on my laptop brought it back to life. Magic had its unique signature, like a fingerprint, so I placed my fingertips on the screen as a tiny sliver of magic flowed from me to my computer, unlocking it with the unique signature of my magic. Passwords were of little use to a warlock, but magic could keep anyone out.

Pulling up my search engine, I typed his name and school in and hit enter. I clicked on the first social media account I found. This was the kid alright. He stood proudly with the rest of his teammates. His phone number was right there for anyone and everyone to find.

"Kids," I scoffed.

Picking up my phone, I dialed his number, and surprisingly, he answered on the first ring.

"Rocky?" The kid sounded panicked.

"No, but I'm looking for him." I let a little of my magic slip through the phone and relax the kid.

"Who? Who is this?" he stuttered.

"I'm a... friend of Miss Collins's, and we're looking for Rocky. She told me she talked to you and that you lied to her."

"I didn't lie," he snapped.

"Held information back then. And you did the same with Detective Reed."

"How'd you know he called me?" I could smell the kid's fear. There was much more that he could tell me, but in his current state, he never would. I poured even more magic into the phone and almost immediately, his nerves settled, and he spoke clearly.

"I told you I'm helping Miss Collins and now we need you to tell us the truth." I drummed my fingers on my desk, waiting for his response.

"You won't believe me."

"Try me, kid."

He panted into the phone. "You're really trying to help Rocky?"

"Yes, now just tell me." I was growing impatient.

"Fine. He wanted to go to this shop downtown. It was really weird, but he said he'd buy us pizza after. So he drove his truck, and I rode with him. Some of the other guys followed us in their car."

"What store?" I interrupted, fearing I knew the answer.

"Some antique shop. Ob... obs... Something mage?"

"Obsidian Mage?"

"Yeah, that's it."

"What happened?"

There was a long pause on the other end. "Rocky was trying to trade the guy for some weird-looking knife, but he just laughed at us. He told Rocky he'd never have enough for it. I didn't see the big deal, but Rock was pissed. He stormed out of the shop and around the corner, down an alley. He punched the freaking brick wall like it was nothing. I'd never seen him act like that before. But then..."

"What?" I sent even more magic to him to keep him talking.

"Someone, no, something attacked him. I don't know what it was, but it was fast. It slammed him against the wall and bricks went flying. I thought for sure Rock was dead, but he wasn't. He tried to fight off this thing. It was so weird. Rock is tough, but still. He shoved his attacker, and the force threw it back harder than I would have expected. He tried to get back to us, but it came up behind him and grabbed him. Rocky told us to run. We were climbing into the car and I looked back. This thing ha-had fangs. It was biting Rocky. Then it just disappeared. We sped all the way home."

I leaned into my desk, pinching the bridge of my nose. Vampires were involved. Great, just what we needed to deal with.

"See why I couldn't tell Miss C. or the cop? They'd all think I was crazy." The kid's panic was rising again.

I straightened in my chair and spoke with as much magic as I could. "It's okay. You never went into the city, and you didn't see what happened to Rocky. When I hang up, you won't even remember talking with anyone about him. Do you understand me?"

"I understand," he answered robotically.

"Good." Clicking off the receiver, I slumped back into my chair. A large portion of vampires, like Sam, had learned to control their hunger and act like a mundane, but there were still clans that wanted to bring back the old ways. Feeding on mundanes without concern about who saw them was one thing, but to feed on a Figli Del Mito was next-level stupid.

Abandoning my search for the moment, I stood and yawned, only now realizing that I hadn't slept in over twenty-four hours myself. And I'd just sent a lot of magic through the phone lines to get the kid to talk. I staggered out of my office and back toward my room.

I pulled a spare pillow and blanket out of my closet and kicked off my shoes. The couch by the window was large enough for me to stretch out on. So, I laid my head on the pillow and covered myself with the blanket. I watched Josie sleeping in my bed for a long time before I gave in to sleep myself.

Thirteen

Josie

The sun was setting when I woke up later that evening. Panic rose in my chest for a moment before I remembered the red and brown comforter trapping me in the massive bed belonged to Warren. When I sat up, I noticed he was curled up on the couch, sound asleep. I reached out, the silky sheets smooth against my palms, and pulled a pillow to my face, breathing deeply.

His burnt earthly smell lingered there like a summer campfire. I breathed it in again before the thought finally clicked in my head: This was his bed, not a guest bed, but his. A smile crept across my face, knowing he'd given up his comfort for mine.

I slid out from under the covers and tiptoed over to where he slept. Awake, he was a giant of a man: He was well over six feet tall with broad shoulders. But laying here wrapped in sleep, he looked small.

Kneeling in front of him, I brushed his dark hair from his eyes. My fingers grazed over his brow. Sparks bit into my flesh at the brief contact, and I was no longer sitting in his room.

Darkness and a sickly sweet smell surrounded me. My head whipped around to find something I recognized. Warren was asleep here, too. His head rested on the edge of an old lady's enormous bed. The woman looked so frail when she moved to stroke his hair.

He jolted awake at her touch, panic in his eyes.

"What?" He turned to face the woman.

She gave him a weak smile. "I haven't left yet."

"Don't say that. I'm not ready for that." His voice broke. "Charlotte, please don't. Let me save you." He gently touched her face as she wiped the tears from his eyes and stared at him for a long moment before speaking.

"Look at you, Warren, you have the same face I fell in love with so long ago. And look at me, I have lived longer than any of my childhood friends. Longer than any human should have lived. It is time, my love."

"No, Charlotte, I cannot live without you." He was sobbing now.

"Yes, you can. You lived before me and you will live after me. Someday, you will find your match, but I am not her. I have loved you and our life together, but it is now time to let me go."

I blinked and was back in his room, watching him sleep. The tears in his dream now coated his cheeks. I pulled away from him as guilt at the intrusion settled over me. He exuded an air of confidence to everyone around him, but maybe he was more vulnerable than he let on.

"Josie," he whispered in his sleep.

I leaned closer and kissed the tears from his face. He blinked awake and looked at me with sad eyes. His hand slid out from under the cover and cupped my face.

"Josie," he sighed. "What's wrong?" His thumb brushed the tears I didn't know I'd shed from my face.

"I-I don't know how but..." I turned into his hand, avoiding his eyes as I asked, "Who's Charlotte?"

He pulled his hand away, sitting up quickly. His eyes watered at the mention of her name.

"Someone from my past. That is all." He stood and walked to his bathroom.

I had invaded his dreams and stolen a piece of his memory. Ignoring the sting of his icy demeanor, I followed him.

"Excuse me?" I snapped at him. "I didn't mean to see that. You, however, purposefully went into my memo—" I stopped dead. He stood with his back to me, completely naked. My gaze remained on where a phoenix tattoo—much larger than mine—splayed across his back. The black and gray bird stretched from the base of his neck and curved down his hip. Flames engulfed the creature that filled his back. His golden eyes flicked over his shoulder.

I turned my back and uttered, "Sorry, I didn't..." Heat flushed to my face and I buried my head in my hands.

"What were you saying?" he asked. I peered through my fingers to look at him, and thankfully, he'd grabbed a towel and wrapped it around his middle.

"I-I just wanted to say that I didn't mean to do whatever I did. I'm sorry," I said, lowering my hands.

"Don't. It's not your fault." His voice was low, heavy with an ache that made my chest tighten. "I'm sorry, Josie. I shouldn't have walked away."

He took a step closer, and the air between us shifted, thickening with something I couldn't quite name. His gaze softened, but behind it, I saw shadows of a grief so deep it felt like it might swallow him whole.

"Charlotte was my partner a very long time ago," he continued, his tone reverent, as though speaking her name brought her back for a fleeting moment. "She was human, and no matter how much I begged, she refused to let me heal her anymore. She said it would make her something she wasn't meant to be. So I stood by, helpless, watching her wither away and die, knowing there was nothing I could do to stop it."

His words hit like a wave, raw and unguarded, and my heart twisted at the weight he carried. His shoulders slumped slightly, his jaw tightening as if reliving that pain all over again. I wanted to say something, anything, to ease the burden, but the words wouldn't come.

He drew in a slow breath, as though gathering himself, and then his gaze lifted to meet mine. Something changed in his expression, a spark of something warm and alive flickering in the depths of his grief.

"I didn't think I'd ever have that again," he admitted, stepping closer still, his voice softer now, almost a whisper. "Not until..." His eyes locked onto mine, and the intensity of his gaze sent a flush of heat rushing to my face. I swallowed hard, my breath catching in my throat. "Until I saw you."

My chest tightened, the weight of his words pressing against me. Realization dawned, sharp and sudden. "But... I'm not human. Am I?" My voice was barely above a whisper, trembling with uncertainty. "Will... will I age like a human, or like a—"

"Warlock?" he finished for me, the hint of a grin tugging at his lips.

Before I could respond, his hand reached up, his fingers brushing against my hair as he tucked a loose strand behind my ear. His touch was feather light, yet it sent a shiver cascading down my spine. My breath hitched as his hand lingered, trailing down to my neck with a tenderness that belied the strength in his touch.

"Josie," he murmured, his voice rich and husky, "you don't know how long I've wanted to do this."

Heat blossomed across my skin as his other hand slid to the small of my back, his fingers curling possessively as he pulled me against him. His chest, bare and warm, pressed against me, and I felt the steady rhythm of his heartbeat beneath my palms as I instinctively reached out to steady myself.

I tilted my head without thinking, an unspoken invitation that he accepted without hesitation. His lips, soft yet insistent, found the curve of my jaw, trailing down to the sensitive hollow of my neck. A gasp escaped me, unbidden, and the sound seemed to spur him on. His kisses grew hungrier, more deliberate, each one igniting a fire that spread through me.

Butterflies erupted in my stomach, their frantic fluttering mirrored by the erratic beat of my heart. My fingers grazed his bare back, and I felt the tension in his muscles as he arched into my touch, pressing his body harder against mine. The heat between us was electric, pulling me under, consuming everything else until the world outside of this moment faded away.

"Josie," he whispered against my skin, his voice a low growl that sent a thrill racing through me. His hand slid higher, tangling in my hair as he angled my head, his lips returning to mine with a fervor that left no room for doubt. He wasn't just kissing me; he was claiming me, pouring years of longing and unspoken emotion into every touch, every movement.

And I let him. I gave myself over to the moment, to the intensity of his grief melting into desire, to the unspoken promise in his touch.

Here, in his arms, I wasn't afraid. I wasn't uncertain. I was his, and for the first time, I realized that was exactly where I wanted to be.

"Wanna join me in the shower?" he whispered into my ear.

I swallowed hard. I would hate myself for this, but I pushed out of his grasp.

"I..." I what? Didn't want to? Couldn't? Neither of those were true. My body clearly wanted and needed him, but I had only just put the pieces of my heart back together and I feared putting it in a position to get hurt again. Foolishly, I turned to look at him. I had to focus on his eyes to keep mine from wandering. "It's just..."

He stepped toward me, cupping my face in his hands. His lips lingered above my eyebrow. "It's okay, Josie. We have time." He kissed me softly before pulling away and moving toward the shower.

I practically ran out of the bathroom, but his voice froze me in the doorway.

"You're her, you know. The match Charlotte spoke of."

Leaning into the frame to keep from falling, I had to suppress the smile his words brought to my face. Not wanting him to see the weakness in my legs, I waited for the opening and closing of the shower door before I staggered back to his bed.

Warren

I FLIPPED THE WATER FROM HOT TO COLD AND LET IT WASH over me. The electricity of her body still buzzed within me. Every inch of me craved her as I sank against the tiled wall.

"What was I thinking?" I chastised myself. She was still hurting from all the pain her husband had caused her, and now she was breaking over her newly discovered brother. And here I was, acting like a horny teenage boy.

Every part of me wanted her in every way I could. It had been so long since I'd let anyone in, but this woman made me want that, and all I wanted was to hold her and hear her tell me I was enough.

Shaking the thought from my mind, I straightened up and turned off the water. *Get a hold of yourself.* She deserved better than how I was acting. I toweled off and pulled on a pair of jeans before walking to the door.

I leaned against the open doorframe, gazing into my bedroom. She sat on the edge of my bed with her back to me. She seemed lost in profound contemplation, tilting her head from one side to the other and ticking off things with her fingers as she mumbled under her breath.

I couldn't help but smile as my knuckles rapped on the door frame, pulling her from her thoughts.

"I didn't mean to interrupt, but I wanted to—" All thoughts fled from my mind as she stood, eyes filled with tears, and walked toward me. Her small hands wrapped around me, snaking up to the nape of my neck, nails combing through my wet hair, and she laid her head on my chest. I let my hands rest on the small of her back as I breathed her in. She smelled of petrichor.

Her lips never reached out for me, but that was alright. I held her gently, waiting for her to make the next move. Tears dampened my skin as I stroked her hair.

"What's wrong, Josie? Why are you crying?"

"I... Nothing is wrong. Well, that's not true. There is so much wrong, but right now, in this very instant, nothing is wrong. I'm sorry."

"Stop apologizing." I brushed her hair from her face and pressed my lips to her forehead.

"I've... I feel like I'm losing my mind and acting like a crazy woman, and you've been nothing but kind to me." She pulled away and looked me in the eye. "I have had no one treat me like you have, and I'm not used to it. If that would have been my ex there in the bathroom... Well, let's just say I'd never get away with saying no to him."

I pulled her back to me. Just the thought of another man forcing her to do anything against her will sent fire through my veins. The cambion better hope he never meets me. "That is part of why I'm falling for you, Josie. You're your own person and won't take any of my crap. You make me want to be better." I felt her smile against my skin.

"I'm sorry. You were about to say something before I interrupted." She pulled away, tucking her hair behind her ear.

"I was going to show you something. What're your thoughts on firearms?"

Her face snapped back to me with a wide grin. "Don't tell me you collect those, too?"

I laughed out loud and nodded.

She smiled. "My uncle is a collector, too. He taught me everything he knew. I have my CCL as well." She looked around. "Crap! Where's my purse?"

I cocked my head at her. "In the car still. Why?"

"It's a concealed carry purse. It's the only reason I carry a purse."

"Ah, well, it's safe for the moment. You want to see my collection?" I asked her.

She nodded vigorously. I turned her around and led her to the back wall of my room and waited. She cocked her head and stepped forward. As she reached out and touched the wall, I followed her and we were pulled through to the other side.

We stood in a room as large as my bedroom. Tall wooden cases filled with rifles lined the outer walls. I had just about every gun ever made. From flintlocks to M1 Garands and Mausers to the more modern M4 Carbine. I'd dedicated one wall to handguns. I had a slight obsession with the Wild West, so several Colts sat in wooden cases. They were worth too much to carry around, just nice to have. But the Glocks, Rugers, and Smith & Wesson's were my every day carries.

"You're a warlock. Why do you need a gun?" she asked me, not turning around.

"I have seen much of history and lived under the rule of many tyrants. I witnessed the formation of America. They put the power in the hands of the people. I've seen so much, but nothing has changed the course of history like that. I collect guns to remind myself that if a government ever gets too big, it is the people's responsibility to rein them back in." She turned back to me. "Plus, they are really fun to shoot." I grinned.

She looked at the door on the opposite wall. "What's over there?"

I raised my hands at my collection. "You don't think I'd own these and have to go somewhere to shoot them, do you? It's my range."

Her eyes went wide. "Can I?" I nodded. She strode up to the M1 Garand, pulling it from the rack. Her slender hand opened the cabinet below, finding a clip, and walked to the door.

"That's a—" I started, but she raised her hand at me. She walked through the door and set the stuff on the table before walking back in. She grabbed a handgun and mag, depositing them on the table before returning once more for some earmuffs and eye protection.

She looked at me. "You coming?"

I smiled and followed her.

The room had solid concrete walls stretching far in the distance. I had two long ranges and two shorter lanes set up with targets and tables.

She set the rifle on the gun rest as she tapped the clip on the table and smiled. She pulled the bolt all the way back and rested the back of her palm on the lever, keeping it open. Pushing the clip into the gun, she let the bolt slam into place. She sat down at the bench next to the table, putting on her glasses and ear muffs. Her wide grin turned back to me.

My heart pounded in my chest as I closed the distance between us, stepping up to her with purpose. Gently, I straddled the bench behind her, my movements deliberate yet hesitant as if testing the fragile boundary between us. I wrapped my arms around her waist and leaned in, my lips brushing softly against the corner of hers—a fleeting kiss, tender and full of unspoken promise.

I pulled away, whispering, "That was so sexy."

"I know." She kissed me back. "Can I shoot now?" I pulled on my protection and nodded. She emptied the clip, hitting the target each time. She slid out from under the table, looking at her work. "Not bad for not being at the range in years."

I stepped up beside her. "Now, can you hit the target with that?" I looked at her choice of handguns. I'd never been around a woman who was so comfortable around guns, and I had to restrain myself.

"This is what's in my purse. I'm kinda surprised to find it in your vault. It's not a popular brand." She picked up the Bersa BP9CC 9mm and mag, walking up to the shorter handgun range.

She slid the mag into the gun and pulled the slide back, chambering a round. Her forefinger rested just above the finger guard until she was ready. She timed every breath with the press of the trigger. Every shot hit in a tight clump near the center. When the slide locked open, she released the mag, placed the gun and mag on the table and turned around to me.

"Wow," I breathed out, wishing we weren't on a mission to save her brother.

She tackled me into a big hug but pulled away quickly. "Thank you! I can't tell you how much I needed that! I feel a bit better!"

"Anytime! My range is yours." I swept her into a kiss. My mouth lingered longer than I expected. She leaned into it instead of pulling away. I was the one to end the kiss. "It's getting late and I want to take you somewhere. I called and talked to Keith." I waited for her to react, to yell or push away, but she stood there looking at me. "He told me they went to an antique shop I know."

"What was he doing there?" she asked.

"It's not a normal antique store. Everything in it has magical properties. But after they left, someone took Rocky."

"Why didn't you tell me sooner?" Now she pushed away, heading for the door.

My arm wrapped around her waist, stopping her. "Because there's more. I wanted to know if you'd be able to handle yourself in a fight before we left. I'll give you special ammo before we leave, and I want your gun and a spare mag on your body, not just in your purse. Hell, keep the one in your purse and put that one on your person. I have several inside the waistband holsters."

She backed away. "You're scaring me, Warren."

"Good, you should be a little scared." I didn't mean to frighten her, but she needed to have a little fear of what was about to happen. "The one that took him is a vampire and not a nice one like Sam. Some factions want to return to the old ways of using humans like cattle. I don't know what they'd want with a warlock kid, but if they're the ones that took him, I want you to be prepared."

I watched her as she visibly swallowed hard. She turned, picking up the handgun and taking the full mag I was handing her. She slid it in, releasing the slide. "Alright, let's go."

I finished dressing as she put the holster and gun in the small of her back. We walked hand in hand in silence through my penthouse and into my garage. I helped her into the car, closing the door behind her, before sliding into the driver's seat. She didn't even speak as I drove through the tunnel and into the night.

Fourteen

Josie

All the way to the antique shop, I sat, hands in my lap, thumbs fiddling with each other. He parked his car on the street in front of the shop but didn't get out and took a deep breath before he spoke.

"I couldn't convince you to stay in the car, could I?" He didn't look at me.

"Warren?"

"It's just... This man you know is not the same as the owner of the shop knows. I don't... I can't let you see that man."

"Warren," I said softly, gripping his hand. "It's okay. We all have a past. I know the man you are and won't judge the man you were."

He pulled my hand to his lips and kissed my fingers. "Thank you, Josie." He dropped my hand and got out of the car before opening the door for me. The dark wood entrance covered with oddities sent a chill down my spine, but when Warren placed his hand on my lower back, I calmed instantly.

"Don't worry, I won't leave your side," he whispered in my ear.

A lump caught in my throat as he led me in. The winding path snaked through an otherworldly collection of antiques, each item stranger and more unsettling than the last. It was as though the room had been curated by someone with a penchant for the macabre: a collector of nightmares. Cabinets teetered under the weight of ancient trinkets, and shelves groaned with the burden of books whose spines were cracked and faded, their titles long erased by time. The dim lighting cast long, wavering shadows that made the artifacts seem to shift and move, creating an eerie illusion of life.

The space was so cluttered that I had no choice but to walk behind Warren. My hand instinctively gripped the belt of his pants, holding tight as though the thin strip of leather could anchor me in this suffocating maze. My gaze darted from one bizarre object to another—a tarnished music box that seemed to hum faintly, a taxidermy fox with glass eyes too bright to be natural, and a porcelain doll whose cracked face seemed to watch me as we passed.

Then we came upon the clowns. A cluster of them, grinning with mechanical malice, their painted faces frozen in twisted glee. One of them, its speaker barely functional, let out a garbled, jagged cackle. My grip tightened on Warren's belt.

"Does it have to be clowns?" I muttered, my voice trembling.

He glanced back, a crooked grin playing on his lips. "Creepy, aren't they? They've been here longer than I have. Let's just hope they don't decide they like you too much."

"Not funny," I snapped, my steps faltering as a chill ran down my spine. The clowns seemed almost alive, their hollow eyes glinting in the flickering light.

My feet stopped altogether, and I yanked on Warren's belt, pulling him back until his chest bumped into my face. My grandfather's words rang in my ears, warnings from years ago about how objects could harbor evil. I'd never believed him—until now. Darkness radiated from the artifacts, a tangible force that seemed to reach for me, wrapping around my throat and chest like invisible hands. My breath hitched.

"Josie?" Warren turned, concern etched across his face. He pulled me into his arms without hesitation, his warmth chasing away some of the oppressive cold. His hands stroked my back in soothing circles, grounding me.

"Warren, this place holds evil," I whispered, my voice trembling as I clung to him. "I can... feel it."

He pressed his lips to my temple, his touch steady and reassuring. "Josie, I'm sorry. I didn't think it would affect you like this. I promise I'll make this quick, and we'll get out of here. But it's important we talk to the owner about Rocky."

I buried my face in his chest, nodding reluctantly, though the thought of staying here any longer made my skin crawl. "Okay. Just... hurry."

"I will." His voice was firm, yet gentle, as he held me a moment longer before stepping back. "Stay close. I've got you."

I tightened my grip on his belt as we continued through the labyrinth of horrors. Every step forward felt heavier, the artifacts seeming to pulse with malice, but Warren's presence gave me the strength to keep moving. If Rocky's safety depended on this, I could endure it. But I couldn't shake the feeling that the evil in this place was watching, waiting for its moment.

Warren pulled out of my arms. "I need you to trust me, okay? I told you, most people are afraid of me and I play on those fears when I need to, but I swear to you I will never hurt you. Do you understand?" He cupped my chin in his hand.

"Yes," was all I could say. He pulled my face to his, gently kissing me before turning to walk on. He reached his hand out behind him and I took it gratefully.

My eyes stayed fixed on his back, and I let my mind wander, remembering the massive firebird that lay under his tight shirt. It was all I could do to keep from focusing on the surrounding evil.

The shelves finally opened up to a small clearing in front of a counter. The owner stood with his back to us. His frame was nearly as wide as it was tall. He wore a black t-shirt and jeans. He had disheveled and graying, thinning hair. Even from here, I could tell showers weren't his thing.

"Be there in a sec," his gruff voice called out.

Warren dropped my hand and stepped closer to the counter. Magic poured out of him, freezing me in place. This was not the same magic he'd used around me before, but as dark as the surrounding antiques. My feet begged me to move, but my heart told me to stay. "You will be with me now." He spoke with a ferocity that sent chills through my body.

The store owner turned so quickly he knocked over a pile of things at his side.

"Ma-ma-Mage, sir," the man stuttered. "How can I help you?" He quaked in the presence of this new Warren before me, who stood tall and cold.

"A boy was in here over the weekend asking about a knife? I'd like to know about him." Warren looked at the glass cases in front of him like the man no longer mattered.

"The b-boy?"

"Yes, a boy. Josie, do you have a picture?" He called to me over his shoulder. My shaky hands reached for my phone and handed it to him. Warren showed the man Rocky's picture, and he nodded.

"Yes, he wanted the Dragonite Stone Dagger. But I told him it was worth more than he could make in a lifetime."

"What happened after that? Did you see where he went?"

"N-no, sir. He was angry when he left, but he left." The man tried to straighten, but his shaky legs wouldn't let him. "He... he was just a boy. Why do you care?"

The power in Warren's magic pulsed and the man's feet rose off the floor. His massive body hovered in midair like a feather.

"Oh, Enoch, you've never been one to sense your own kind. Maybe that's why you are here dealing out death. He was a warlock. He was in danger and you wouldn't help him, and now a vampire has taken him. Many of our children have gone missing. If I find out you are involved, I will be back." Warren released his hold on the man and watched as he slumped to the floor. "Oh, and I'll be taking this." With a flick of his wrist, he held the dagger in his hand.

He watched Enoch, now sobbing on the floor, with disgust. When I peered over the counter, I nearly gagged. A darkened spot spread down the leg of his jeans.

"Clean yourself up, warlock." Warren spat the word like the man was unworthy of the title.

He reached for my hand before turning to leave. His palm was clammy and shaking in mine as he practically dragged me out of the store and shoved me into his car.

He paused outside his door before sliding in and turning the engine on. He laid the dagger in his lap, pushed against the headrest, and breathed deeply before speeding away from the shop.

Struggling, I yanked my seat belt on before I spoke. "Warren?" What could I say? He seemed just as shaken as I was. I watched him drive, praying he'd respond, but his jaw clenched tighter. When he didn't, I reached over tentatively, laying my hand on his knee. He jerked the wheel, causing me to sit upright in my seat. "Talk to me," I muttered.

The car slowed, and he veered it off the road, parking it in a nearby lot. He rested his head on the steering wheel for a long moment before he spoke.

"I'm sorry." His voice was so weak I had to strain to hear him.

My hand stroked his back until he sat up.

"Josie, I never wanted you to see that side of me and I never want to be that man again, but in our world, I have to be."

Brushing my fingers over his quivering lips, I saw just how broken he was. The powerful warlock who could strike fear in the heart of others with his presence was broken.

"What happened to you?" I whispered, half to myself.

He pulled his face away from me and sighed. "Does the name Vlad the Impaler mean anything to you?"

I nodded, even though he couldn't see me. "You mean Vlad Dracula? As in Dracula?"

"Yes. Back in those days, it was customary for vampires to have a warlock to help them hide from the humans." He sat back in his seat but didn't look at me. I swallowed hard, figuring out where this was going.

"You... You helped Dracula?"

He nodded. "I went by the name Mage back then, and I was as brutal as Dracula himself. I was a young warlock and wanted fame and fortune. Vlad promised it to me. He lied. He dangled his wealth under my nose, but kept me hidden. I'm the only one who truly knows what happened to him... because I'm the one who cut his head off."

Touching him in this state might not have been a good idea, but I reached out, anyway. The spark of my magic was small as my hands found his arm, but he relaxed the moment we connected. He turned his wet face to me.

"I went into hiding for nearly a century. I hated what I had become. But then I met Shakespeare. He showed me that life is both beauty and pain." Tears streaked down his face, and I brushed them away. It had been over five hundred years and still it broke him. I let the ribbons of my magic reach within him. The weight of every death he carried around settled in my chest. His body was so heavy with the pain of his past it broke my heart.

"Warren," I sighed. Unbuckling, I turned in my seat to face him. My hand dragged down to his chest. "You are so much more than this pain. Yes, life is full of darkness, but you can't live in the dark."

"You are my light." He spoke gently before pulling me onto his lap. His lips were salty and soft. His passion boiled below the surface, but he tamed it into a simple kiss.

I pulled away, leaning my forehead to his. "Why do I feel so strongly about you?" I asked myself, but he answered me.

"I feel the same for you." His knuckles dragged across my cheek. "Do you know what twin flames are?"

I shook my head, not daring to breathe.

"It's like one soul split into two. The moment I saw you on the security camera outside my club, your soul called to mine." He kissed my lips.

"I..." I thought back to that night. Although I hadn't wanted to be there, I felt safe once I walked through the doors. "I think I understand. Caleb had been manipulative and downright abusive for some time, but I didn't have the strength to leave him. It's so hard for me to trust, but with you, it was instant. At first, fear consumed me, but now..." His breath tickled my skin as my lips hovered so close to his.

"Charlotte was right—you are my match in every way, Josie." His lips pressed into mine with more vigor than before. My body ached for him. His warm tongue parted my lips, entering me with the fierceness I craved.

He slid the chair back, and I sat down on his knees. Pulling away, I yelped at the pressure on my leg. Reaching between my thighs, I grabbed the dagger I'd forgotten lay there. "What is this thing, anyway?"

"According to legend, people take the Dragonite Stone from the skull of a dead dragon. It gives its user the strength and courage of the dragon it came from."

"Dragons are real?" I unsheathed the dagger. The hilt fit my hand perfectly. The stone was a gorgeous swirl of blood red and green, and the blade was as dark as obsidian. My hand went to touch it, but Warren grasped my wrist before I could.

"Let's put that away." He took the blade and sheathed it, placing it on the dash. He cupped my butt in his hands before he continued. "Yes, dragons are real. Or at least they used to be. Humans hunted them into extinction. So Enoch was correct in saying this dagger is priceless. Plus, it is possibly the sharpest blade known and will never dull. It'll cut off your finger if you slipped." He pulled my fingers to his lips, kissing each one. "And we wouldn't want that."

His kisses sent a shiver through my body, and heat rushed to my core. Laying on his chest, my mind was heavy with thoughts.

"Now what? What about Rocky?"

"Crap, I'm an idiot for driving away. Let's go back to the alley and see if there's a clue there." He stroked my hair.

"You're not an idiot. You wanted to get away from that man. I think I need a shower just for being near him." I kissed him softly. "Let's get back there and hopefully we can find something.

He smiled, kissing me one last time before releasing me, and I slid back into my seat, buckling up before he drove back to the antique shop.

Fifteen

Josie

He parked in the alley at the opposite end of the antique shop and walked around the car to open my door. It might seem old-fashioned, but when he reached in to help me out, my stomach did somersaults and my face flushed. Finding a man who still believed in treating a woman like a queen was rare these days, and I was determined not to stop him.

I wrapped my arm around his and interlocked our fingers as we walked to the spot where someone had taken my brother. If it weren't for Warren's feet moving, mine would have stayed rooted. My heart raced the closer we got.

A sudden chill swept over me despite the warm night. My breath caught in my throat the moment I saw the broken bricks along the wall. Stepping out of Warren's grasp but letting my hand linger a moment before dropping it, I walked to the wall. The indention of the bricks was at least three feet in diameter and six feet off the ground. Tears burned in my eyes at the thought of my brother being slammed so hard into this wall to cause this damage. If they did this to him in public, what would they do to him in private?

Slowly, I reached for the wall.

"Josie, that might not be a good—"

The pain that ripped through my body the moment my hand touched the bricks drowned Warren's words out. My back ached with the force of being thrown into the wall. Invisible hands around my throat cut off my air supply. My vision blurred the longer my lungs ached for breath. In my head, I was screaming, but the panic I expected to feel never came. I actually laughed at my assailant. A courage I'd never felt boiled through my skin.

"Clearly, you don't know who I am." The words came out of my mouth, but it was Rocky's voice that spoke them. The creature that stood before me was nothing like the only vampire I'd ever met. He... No. It was nearly seven feet tall, hairless, with a light blue tinge to its skin. Red stains dripped down its chin and neck. Where there should have been eyes, there were dark pits of nothingness.

Its deep voice scratched out, "I don't care who you are, only what you are, young warlock."

Still, I felt no fear. A deep chuckle rumbled up from my gut.

"I am not just a young warlock, you fool. I am Rockefeller Wolsteincroft."

The vampire's eyes flashed in fear, but it did not back away. The tingle of magic flowed as I raised Rocky's hands. In a flash of light, the vampire flew back hard. I fell to the ground, stood to Rocky's friends, and ran.

The vampire's grip on my wrist and the needle thrust into my neck stole away my momentary freedom. I tried to pull at my magic, but it was an empty well.

"Run," I yelled to Rocky's friends as the vampire pulled me back to it. The creature wrapped its arms around me. I pulled at its arms, but nothing happened.

I strained to see the marking on its wrist. The black and white tattoo was rough, like a child's drawing of a profile of a cat with dots.

"Knowing who you are only intrigues me more." Its voice echoed in my ear.

I held onto the image of the cat as the pain seared through me. The vampire had sunk its fangs deep into my neck. It burned like molten lava through my veins. I felt the ground disappear as the creature jumped skyward.

The pain eased as the vision faded. My feet swayed as I watched Warren, who stood beside me. His face was white as a ghost. My voice failed me. I didn't even understand what I'd seen, let alone how to tell him. I opened my mouth to speak, but my body gave out.

Warren wrapped his arms around me in time to catch me before I fell. I tucked my arms to my chest as he moved at an inhuman speed to the car. He laid me in the seat and buckled me up before getting in and speeding off.

He didn't speak, but stroked my hand. I could hear his heart thumping in his chest. He felt as scared as I did. I pulled at his hand until it sat interlaced with mine in my lap.

I watched the buildings fly by out the window. My fingers brushed away the single tear that fell from my eye.

The line out front of his club came into view. He pulled around back and into his private garage. He turned the car off and dropped my hand. I blinked, and he was at my side, opening the door and scooping me out of the seat.

I didn't even flinch when his bedroom materialized around us. He gently laid me on the bed and sat next to me before he spoke.

"What happened?" he asked, his voice thick and growly with an edge of panic.

"I saw..." Emotions tangled with Rocky's, making it harder to sort them out than expected. "I saw what happened. Felt it all... It was like I was Rocky." Rubbing the spot where the vampire had bitten, a weak attempt at humor followed. "Aren't vampire bites supposed to be sexy?"

"No, I'm sorry, but vampire bites suck." His smile didn't reach his eyes.

"Thanks," I chuckled. "He wasn't afraid. I was only watching, and I was terrified." Bile rose in my throat, threatening to come up. "But he... he mocked the vampire. He laughed in his face. I could feel his strength. He was so brave. The vampire was actually more afraid of him than Rocky was afraid of it."

"He's strong, Josie. We will find him." Warren tried to reassure me.

"The vampire had a tattoo. It was like a pictorial drawing of a jaguar." My voice spoke, but I couldn't focus my eyes.

"Some older clans brand their vampires. I'll talk to Sam about it, but first we need to take care of you."

"I think Rocky is more than a warlock. The way the vampire reacted to his name..."

Warren cocked his head at me. "His name?"

I nodded. "Rockefeller Wolsteincroft."

Warren's eyes widened. "He's one of the lost Wolsteincroft's?" He stood, staring blankly at me. "But his name in the registry, his family's name in the registry, it was Sanchez."

I shrugged. "That's what I've known him as, too. Who are the lost Wolsteincroft's?"

His gaze softened. "That's a longer story. One I will tell you after a shower and food. I don't know if you know this, but somehow..." He stroked my neck where the vampire had bitten Rocky. "There's blood all over you."

I shot out of the bed and ran for the bathroom. He was right. Blood soaked through my shirt. In my panic, I ripped it off even with him standing behind me. There were no puncture marks, just remnants.

In the mirror, I saw him turn. "I'll let you shower and go get some food." The door clicked closed behind him, and I finished stripping my clothes and walked to the shower.

Warren

MY MIND RACED AS I WALKED DOWN TO THE BAR. IF ROCKY was a Wolsteincroft, then so was Josie. I knew she was special, but I thought it was my pull toward her. Now I had even more reason to protect her. Ignoring every call from patrons, I quickly found Sam. I walked behind the bar without glancing up.

"Hey, Warren?" Sam's voice questioned.

"Hey." I still didn't look at him.

"Why do you smell like blood and vampires?"

I finally glanced up. "What? Never mind that for the moment." I shook my thoughts off. "Can you have someone bring me up some food? Lots of protein?"

"Sure. You okay?"

"Yeah... enough for two, please." Sam nodded at me. "Thanks."

I walked back toward my office before remembering I needed to talk to him. I glanced over my shoulder.

"After your shift, will you come upstairs? We need to talk to you."

"We?"

"Please?"

"Yeah." Sam straightened and went back to work.

The crowd parted for me as I walked back up to my office. I stepped up to the bookshelf and pulled the one book I needed from its spot before touching the center book and walking back into my room.

I laid the book on the edge of the bed and strode over to the bathroom door, pressing my ear to it. The shower was still running. I paused at her silhouette through the frosted glass. My heart hurt at the beauty of her shape. How I longed to join her, but my fist closed around the door handle and I pulled it shut.

I heard the chef enter my office, and I waited for her to leave the food on my desk before retrieving it. When I returned, Josie was stepping out of the bathroom.

The sight of her in a pair of my mesh shorts and hoodie felt like I'd walked into a wall. She was toweling off her hair when her eyes found mine.

"Sorry. I didn't have clean clothes. I hope you don't mind I went into your closet?"

For the first time in my existence, I couldn't speak. Hell, I couldn't even breathe. My feet were frozen. I stood there gaping at her. I must have seemed like a fool.

She laid the towel on the edge of the bed and walked over to me. Her bare feet and wet hair were the most gorgeous thing I'd ever seen.

"You okay?" She laughed as she took the plate from me.

I blinked. "Y-yeah," I stuttered like a total fool.

She shook her head and walked to the bed, sitting down. Her hand patted the spot next to her.

"You gonna join me or make me eat alone?" she asked, and I forced my feet to move.

I lay my food on the bed before cupping her face in my hands. "Josie, you are the most beautiful creature I've ever seen." I brushed my thumb over her lips as she laughed.

"Even in these oversized clothes?"

"Especially in those oversized clothes." I pulled her face to mine, kissing her softly. Her stomach grumbled, and I pulled away. "Magic makes you hungry, and I don't even understand the magic you did back there."

"Are you going to tell me about the Lost Wolsteincroft's?"

"Yes, but you need food. I'll tell you the story while you eat."

"Fine." She was sexy even when she rolled her eyes at me.

I reached for the book at the end of the bed and pulled it open. The ancient book was the oldest one I owned. The picture I'd opened it to was of leather-clad warriors holding spears and shields.

"The Wolsteincroft's were an ancient line of warlocks that walked this earth long before I did. The name itself means Wolf Stone. Wolves have always been a symbol of power and freedom. People still fear wolves to this day. But this family... people still fear them today, even though it's been several centuries since anyone has heard from them."

I took a bite of my hamburger.

"What made them so special? Why are they so feared?"

I gulped down my food, fearing telling her the truth. "You know that other creatures besides humans exist. People said that the Wolsteincroft's were a different beast than even a warlock. I never ran across them in my time in Europe, but the stories were that they could turn into a wolf." I flipped through the pages of the book and stopped at one that depicted the transformation.

She took the book and ran her fingers over the image. "You mean like a werewolf?"

"Not entirely. Were's have very little magical abilities, and what they do have is very specific to their kind. The Wolsteincroft's were both shifters and warlocks. Were's shift is painful, but Wolsteincroft's could shift easily with no restrictions and wield magic like no other. As you know, magic costs energy, but for them it's not as high a cost. Does the Battle of Hastings mean anything to you?"

Her eyes went wide, and she froze mid-bite.

"Josie?" She stared off into nothing. "Josie?" I shouted and shook her shoulders.

Finally, she blinked and dropped the book. "I was... I was there..."

I nearly choked. "What?"

"Just now, it was like the alley. Like I was seeing through their eyes. They were there but as wolves. They fought against their king. But why?"

I stared at her a long moment before I continued. She was seeing things no warlock I'd ever known could see. How had she been in Rocky's memories and how had she come back covered in his blood? And now? I shook those questions out of my head, resigned to deal with them later.

"They wanted their freedom. He had kept them as his personal warlocks. They disappeared after that battle. Occasionally, they'd crop up, but never long enough to get caught. They were brutal in their destruction every time they surfaced. Hell, even Vlad feared them."

Josie sat staring at her food. Her hand shook at her side. I reached for her, grazing her arm.

"Josie?"

Sudden understanding flashed across her face.

"If Rocky is one of these Wolsteincrofts, then so am I, right?" Her voice shook as she asked it.

"In part, yes. I couldn't even guess if you could shift into a wolf or not."

"But you said they were all violent brutes."

"Josie, you are not the same. I can feel your kindness within you." I placed our plates on the side table before crawling further on the bed and pulling her to my chest. "You are beautiful, kind, and loving. And so is Rocky. From what I've heard, if he weren't, he would have killed his foster father long ago. But he is as kindhearted as you are."

She snuggled into me. "Thank you, Warren."

I could have her lay in my arms forever. Her scent enveloped me. I lay back on the pillows, bringing her with me. My hands stroked her hair until her breathing slowed.

A knock rapped at the wall, bringing me out of the moment, and I slid out from under the sleeping Josie, laying her gently on the pillow.

Walking to the hidden door in the wall, I waved my hand, opening it to Sam. I motioned him in and walked back to the edge of the bed. She looked so peaceful laying there, but the sun would rise soon and Sam needed to get home.

I brushed my fingers over her face, waking her gently.

"Sam's here. Can you tell him what you saw?" I asked her.

She nodded and sat up, looking a little more than fearful.

Sixteen

Josie

Warren's gentle touch stirred me awake, and I blinked, disoriented by the dim light and the unfamiliar surroundings. My breath caught when my gaze landed on the figure across from us— a vampire. My body tensed instinctively, heart pounding as my mind screamed danger.

The vampire didn't make a move, though. He just stood there, watching his feet, his shoulders hunched as if trying to make himself smaller. Slowly, recognition crept in. This wasn't just any vampire; it was Warren's bartender—Sam.

I swallowed hard, still uncertain. The vampires in stories were always bold and charming, creatures of calculated allure who could command a room with a single look. But this one... Sam seemed almost uncomfortable in his own skin. His confidence behind the bar, slinging drinks and flashing an easy smile, was nowhere to be seen. In its place was a man who looked out of place and uncertain, his posture and downcast eyes betraying an unexpected vulnerability.

My instincts warred within me. Everything about my upbringing screamed to stay guarded, to stay quiet, but the tension in Sam's body and the flicker of unease on his face softened the edge of my fear. He wasn't threatening me. If anything, he looked like he was the one who didn't know what to say.

I glanced at Warren, whose steady presence anchored me, before forcing myself to take a deep breath. The words came out quieter than I'd intended. "Why are you here?"

Sam's gaze flicked up for a brief second, just long enough for me to see the shadow of fear in his eyes. Then he looked away again, as if he wasn't sure he was allowed to meet my gaze.

"To help," he murmured, his voice low but earnest. "Warren asked me to."

I hesitated, unsure whether to believe him. But as I watched him shift uncomfortably, his hands fidgeting at his sides, I felt some of my fear ebb away. Not completely—there was still a wariness that kept me on edge—but enough to talk, enough to hear him out.

I straightened slightly, keeping my tone cautious. "Help with what, exactly?"

Sam's shoulders stiffened, but he met my eyes this time, his expression determined despite the flicker of hesitation still lingering in his features. "With Rocky. I know you don't trust me, and that's fine, but I'll do whatever it takes to make sure he's safe."

His words hung in the air, and though I wasn't ready to trust him fully, something in his quiet resolve kept me from pulling away.

I relaxed a bit as Warren sat on the edge of the bed beside me. He waved his hand, and a chair materialized out of thin air. He gestured for Sam to take a seat. Warren's heavy hand rested on my knee as he spoke.

"I am sorry to ask you to relive what happened, but we need to know who took Rocky and this will help. Can you tell Sam what you saw?" His voice was so gentle I wanted to lean into him, but I resisted and sat up straighter.

"It was strange. I saw what Rocky saw... I felt what he felt, but I couldn't control anything. Like I was a passenger in his mind." When I first saw the vampire before I knew that's what he was, I was afraid of him, but here in this room, sitting in a chair, he looked small. I knew that was a lie; he was at least six and a half feet tall with wide shoulders, but he slouched in the chair, making him less intimidating. His teeth looked like normal human teeth, but I wondered if he had fangs that had retreated into his gums and those red eyes that freaked me out were more of a deep mahogany.

"I'm sorry if I frighten you," Sam spoke, breaking me out of my thoughts. "I know you saw the real me your first time here. I'm sorry."

I slid out from under the covers and walked over to him, the soft padding of my bare feet the only sound in the room. His shoulders were hunched, his head bowed, as though the weight of his guilt was pressing him into the chair. I knelt in front of him, placing my hands gently on his knees, and tilted my head to meet his downcast gaze. "You don't frighten me," I said softly, my voice steady despite the swirling emotions inside me. "You did that night, but now I know the truth."

His eyes flicked to mine, searching for doubt, for fear, but when he found none, the tension drained from his body. He let out a long, shuddering breath and leaned back in the chair, his posture no longer so rigid. I stood, walked back to the bed, and sat down beside Warren. Without hesitation, I reached for his hand and held it in mine, my fingers lacing through his.

"The vampire in the alley scared me," I admitted, my voice trembling just enough to betray the memory's lingering grip on me. "It could never pass for human... I don't even think with glamour." A shiver ran down my spine as the image of its twisted, monstrous face flashed in my mind. The way its eyes had gleamed with hunger, its jagged teeth bared like a predator—those were details I could never forget. I recounted them now, my words slow and deliberate, sharing everything I could remember in the hope it might help them, including every detail of the tattoo.

As I spoke, my voice wavered, and I bit back the tears threatening to form in my eyes. The weight of the memory pressed on me, but then I felt Warren's warmth beside me. I turned my head, resting it against his shoulder, seeking the steady strength he seemed to carry so effortlessly. His arm, strong and reassuring, came around me, pulling me closer.

"You're safe now," Warren murmured, his voice a low rumble that vibrated through me.

His words were calm, soothing the edges of my fear. I leaned into him, letting his presence ground me. In that moment, the world outside faded, and all I could feel was his steady heartbeat against my cheek and the protective warmth of his embrace. He didn't say much more, but the way his hand gently squeezed mine said everything I needed to hear.

Sam stood, rubbing at his temples for a moment before leaning against the back of the chair. "I don't know what clan it is exactly. Newer clans no longer brand their members. What you described has to be one of the ancient clans. There aren't many left, and they have kept themselves well hidden. It will take some digging, but I will see what I can find." He glanced past me and to Warren. "I will need some time off from the bar to find it."

"Do what you can. Let me worry about the bar. Thank you."

Sam bowed slightly and headed for the door. Another wave of Warren's wrist and the wall parted to let Sam out. I wrapped my arms around Warren's waist and squeezed. He kissed the top of my head and squeezed back.

"I need to shower. All I can smell is that rank alley. You should rest," he said. I whimpered as he tried to pull out of my arms. "You can always join me, you know?"

"I know... Maybe I need sleep," I reluctantly said

Warren gently but firmly guided me back down onto the bed, tucking the blanket around me as if it could shield me from the turmoil inside my head. His touch lingered for a moment before he pulled away, his voice low and soothing. "Rest, Josie. I'll be back in a minute." He headed toward the bathroom, his footsteps soft against the floor. The door clicked shut behind him, leaving me alone with my thoughts.

My heart raced as I stared at the ceiling, but my mind was elsewhere—trapped in the bathroom with him. The sound of the shower turning on made my pulse quicken. I'd only caught a glimpse of that body earlier, but it was enough to leave an impression that refused to fade. Every curve of muscle, every line of strength, was etched into my memory, a temptation I couldn't seem to shake.

The room felt warmer, his scent lingering in the air like an invisible tether drawing me closer to the thought of him. My body ached with exhaustion, but my mind was anything but restful. The need to sleep battled fiercely against the pull of my wandering thoughts. Every rational part of me screamed to let it go, to focus on the rest I desperately needed, but my traitorous heart and the butterflies in my stomach had other ideas.

I sat up, my eyes locking on the bathroom door as the water continued to run behind it. The thought of him standing there, vulnerable and bare, sent my thoughts spiraling. My fingers twisted in the blanket, an outlet for the tension building in my chest.

No. I need to sleep.

I forced my eyes shut and flopped back onto the pillow, determined to drown out the images my imagination conjured. *Sleep*, I told myself firmly. But even as I repeated the command in my head, I wasn't sure which side of this inner war would win.

I couldn't stop my feet from moving out of the bed and toward the door. Every nerve vibrated with the thoughts that ran through my body. I didn't need sleep; I needed him.

My heart stopped at the sound of the shower door opening and closing. I leaned into the door, hand on the handle, and listened. A war battled within me as I stood there in the quiet. My mother had raised me in a Christian home with traditional Christian values, and for the longest time, I had followed every religious law put before me. But after Caleb—the abuse and neglect—how could a loving God sit there and watch me suffer in silence? If he brought down the walls of Jericho with a simple man, why would he allow the pain I felt at the hands of another man? But Caleb wasn't any other man. He was a demon... or at least part demon.

For so long, I was angry and felt betrayed by the God I'd given my childhood to. Yet something in the back of my mind told me He was still watching over me. I took a deep breath and walked back to the edge of the bed and leaned against it. My body ached at the need it felt, but I couldn't drop the sour pit in my stomach at the memory of my first drunken night at college and waking up in Caleb's bed—naked—not remembering what happened. The guilt and shame still lingered, and I didn't want to rush into a physical relationship with another man. Caleb had been the only one I'd ever been with, and I was certain with Warren's age he'd had many partners.

The creak of the door brought me out of my own thoughts, and I jumped to my feet.

"Warren," I said, wiping the tears I didn't know I'd shed from my face.

"I thought you were asleep?" he asked, pulling a shirt over his head.

"I'm tired, but I couldn't shut my mind off."

He crossed the room in three quick strides. "From what?" he asked.

"You." I slumped back down to the bed. "I tried to join you but I... I couldn't.." My face flushed at the admission.

"Josie, the last thing I want is to pressure you. I'm here no matter what and won't leave your side."

I shrugged. "I know it's just... I don't know, it seems foolish. I mean, I'm forty years old and not a virgin, but still... something about it just feels wrong. Like God's watching me or something."

"Well, I've known a lot of famous people from history, but Jesus wasn't one of them. I'm not that old." He laughed and sat next to me. "From everything I've studied, God sees everything, and if your instincts tell you not to do something, then don't. I'll respect it."

"But I'm sure you've had many more partners than me."

"Probably. But never causally. Every single one of them meant something to me. And compared to you, they are dim memories." He wrapped his arm around me. "Josie, you are my everything. I will want you in fifty years from now, the same way I want you today. When you are ready, we will be ready."

"My mom always told me to wait for marriage. I was drunk the first time and then after that, Caleb always guilted me into it. Even after we were married, it still didn't feel right."

"Well, warlocks don't have marriage in the traditional sense, but we have a bond that forms even deeper than any human marriage."

"How's that?"

"We have a ceremony of sorts just like a marriage, but we tie our magic together"

"Oh, really?" I asked, feeling a bit more intrigued.

"Yes. It's not as big and fancy as a traditional wedding, but more intimate with just a few friends." He pulled me into his arms before crawling onto the bed with me. "Now, we really should sleep.

Seventeen

Warren

The obnoxious vibration of my phone from across the room was the only thing that could make me leave her side. Josie lay there so peacefully I couldn't bear to wake her, so I slid my arm out from under her neck as gently as I could. I ached for the first time in a very long time, but smiled at the way she fit so perfectly against my body.

Forcing myself to walk across the room, I picked up the phone that was buzzing again, and flopping onto the couch took great effort.

"Hello?"

"It's me, Warren. I have news." Sam's voice on the other end woke me to full attention.

"Sam? What time is it?"

"It's a little past noon. Have you been asleep since I left?"

"Mostly," I said. "What did you learn?"

"I had to be sure before I told you." His voice shook as he spoke. "I took the time to do a little research. The symbol Josie saw was an old one from the Aztecs. It is part of the Ocēlōt—jaguar warriors—clan. They were once a mighty force to be reckoned with. After the fall of the Aztec empire, the vampire clan went underground. No one has heard from them since." He paused for a long moment before he continued. "It's her... There were rumors after that she fled to central America, but I... I didn't want to know. Now I'm sure of it. It's her clan."

"Sam, I'm sorry to drag you into all this. Get some rest." I rubbed the sleep from my eyes.

"There's more," His voice broke as he spoke. "There's been strange activity by the old factory down on Ninth Street. It could be them."

"What kind of activity? If they've been hiding for so long, why would they leave a trail now?"

"I-I'm sorry, I don't know why. There's been a lot of violence in the area. I headed down there before I went home. There's a clan there for sure. I could smell it, and I didn't even get close."

"Crap," I whispered. Jemisha was the craziest of vampire queens, and if she was here, she was certainly involved in the kidnappings and murders. But I couldn't ask more from my old friend. "Stay home, Sam. Hell, go to Europe at sunset. Just don't go anywhere near her," I begged.

"But Warren... You know I'm the only choice."

"I can't ask that of you. I know what she did to you last time. It took you centuries to get past that. I won't let you."

"You know no mundane cop will get within a hundred yards of that place. She'll welcome me with open arms and maybe share what the hell she's up to." Silence hung in the air for a moment. "You know I'm right."

I breathed out. "Seriously, Sam, don't do anything until we talk to the station. I won't send you in there alone."

"Okay," he said.

"Promise me, Sam. No heroics?"

"I swear, Warren. I'll stay home, drink, and rest until I hear from you." He hung up without another word.

Sam had been more than a bartender to me. He was like a brother, and I'd be sending him into the devil's lair. I let out a heavy breath. Josie rustled the blanket, rolling over to face me. Her eyelids barely cracked open.

"Warren?" Her hand ran down the pillow and bed where I had been a few minutes before. "Come back to bed."

Her colorful locks fell down her face. Standing, I smiled at her petite frame curled up in my massive bed. I knelt on the bed beside her, brushing her hair from her face. She rolled over onto her back and grabbed me by the hips. She pulled with little effort and made an *umf* sound when I didn't move.

I couldn't help but laugh at the pout face she made. She crossed her arms and refused to look at me. The temptation was right there, practically begging me, but I wouldn't cross that line until she was really ready. I knew with all my soul there'd never be another for me but Josie, and I wouldn't break my word to her. Not now, not ever.

So, I sat on the edge of the bed with my back to her and spoke.

"Sam called," I said in a rush, and looked over my shoulder to see her reaction.

Her eyes went wide, but she made no move in the bed.

"He's learned a few things." My eyes traveled lower, and the need to kiss her increased. "We need to get up and head back to the station to talk to Clinton." I stood, but her hand grasped mine, holding me in place.

"Josie, we need to go."

She sighed and pouted up at me.

"Josie, I... I don't know how to say this, but... would you trust me if I said we will have all the time in the world after?"

All the words I never thought I'd say again came bubbling up to the surface.

She sat up and glared at me in the eyes as if peering through my soul. "Warren." Tears glistened in her eyes. "I-I've never understood what love is supposed to be like, so I might be wrong, but..." Her words caught in her throat.

"Josie, I-I think—No, I know I love you."

She beamed at me. "I love you, too."

"You remember what we talked about last night? About a warlock tying ceremony?" I asked.

She nodded.

I knelt before her and continued. "Josie, I wish to be linked to you deeper than anyone in my long life. When this is all over, would you do me the honor of tying our magic and lives together?" I held her shaky hands in mine.

Tears flowed freely down her cheeks as she nodded. "Yes."

My fingers wrapped around her wrist, glowed for a moment, and released her. An intricate braid of silver wrapped around her arm, and a matching one bound around mine.

"Every warlock will know that you are mine and I am yours."

"So, does this mean we're engaged?" she asked.

"Essentially." I shrugged, standing up.

She jumped to her feet, wrapping her arms around my neck, kissing me. She let go, dropping back to the floor, and headed to the bathroom. "Now, let's go find my brother."

Josie

WARREN MAGICKED ME A PAIR OF JEANS FROM MY HOUSE, but the hoodie I wore still smelled like him and I refused to give it back. I was getting used to his driving, so the blur of buildings out the window no longer made me queasy. His fingers gently interlaced with mine the moment we pulled away from the club. If it weren't for the worry in the pit of my stomach, I'd be happy.

My body had relaxed into the chair when my phone rang. Leaning over, I pulled it from my back pocket and looked at the screen.

"Crap. It's my mom," I whispered.

"Do you need to answer it?" Warren asked me.

"If I don't, she will only keep calling." I clicked the green phone. "Hello, Mom."

"Where are you? Your car isn't in your drive or at the school?" She didn't even bother with small talk. I had too much running through my mind and wasn't sure where to begin. "Well?" she barked.

"I'm fine, Mother."

"I called the school, and they said you took some time off. What is going on, Josefina?"

"I could ask you the same thing," I muttered.

"Excuse me?" I couldn't tell from her tone if she'd heard me.

"Nothing."

"No, it's not nothing, young lady. You answer your mother right now." She always knew how to push my buttons and send heat rising within me. She knew what I was, and she'd lied to me. My intuition was correct, but I never liked confrontation. I'd rather push past the small things and move on, but this wasn't small.

"I'm waiting..." Her shrill voice snapped at me.

"Pull the car over, please, Warren," I said as calmly as I could.

"Warren? Who the hell is that? Josefina, are you being held against your will?"

"For heaven's sake, Mother!" I snapped.

"Don't you swear at your mother."

The car rolled to a stop at a small park, and I threw the door open and stomped out before he had even shifted to park.

"Josie." I heard his cool voice call to me, but I ignored it.

"Mother, this isn't the time or the place to be having this conversation. Know we will have a long talk when this is over."

"Over? When what's over? What's going on?"

"I don't have time," I barked.

"Make time."

My mind raced to Rocky being held against his will, being poked and prodded or whatever torture he was enduring, and my rage boiled over. "No, Mother. You no longer get to tell me what to do! I'm a grown woman who's done being controlled. You know, I know you do, and you lied to me. It's your turn to talk to me!" Thunderclaps echoed overhead as I paced the playground.

"I-I don't know what you mean." Her voice shook now.

"You know exactly what I mean. My father wasn't some lowlife who spent my childhood in prison. I want to hear it from you!" I was screaming now.

"I-I-I'm sorry, Jo. You're right. But how?" I could hear the tears in her voice.

"Warren, he's a warlock. And Rocky, he's my brother, and someone has kidnapped him. I need to hear you say it, Mother!" I was fighting the tears myself now.

"I'm so sorry. I didn't know about Rocky. Honestly! But yes, your father... He was a warlock."

"How? How did you meet him? What happened?" I slumped down into the swing.

"He was so charming. I fell in love with him almost instantly. We spent several months together before I learned what he was. I-I panicked and ran away. Only after that did I learn I was pregnant. I never told him, but he knew. The inheritance your grandmother set up for you, it was all from him." She went silent.

"Why? You could have told me," I breathed.

"Would you have believed me? Would anyone?"

"If you told me when I was younger, I would have. And all these years with Caleb..."

"Caleb? What does he have to do with anything?"

She really didn't know.

"He's..." I couldn't say the word demon to my mother. "He's something else out of myths. His abilities kept mine from emerging." My heart broke upon saying it out loud.

"Your... abilities?" she whispered.

"Yes, Mother. I'm a warlock, too, and if you hadn't hidden it from me, I wouldn't be in this mess I'm in now."

"Mess? Are you all right, Jo?" Worry replaced the guilt in her words.

"I'm fine. Warren is helping me find Rocky. There're a lot of kids missing or worse right now, and I have to find him before something happens to him."

"Jo, I'm so sorry I lied to you. I thought I was keeping you safe."

"It's fine. I gotta go, Mother."

"I love you," she said in a rush.

"Love you," I said quickly before hanging up.

Slowly, I stood up and headed back to the car. Warren sat on the hood, cross-armed, watching me. He opened his arms as I approached. I curled into his embrace without a word. I refused to cry. Not for her lies.

"You okay?" he finally asked.

"She left him when she found out what he was. My house, my car, my money: It's all his. He sent her money over the years. He knew about me, yet he never came looking for me." I let a single tear fall for my father.

"I'm sorry, Josie. It's hard for warlocks when their mates abandon them. I know it sounds crazy, but we are far more fragile than we seem. It's not an excuse for him abandoning you or your mother's lying."

Tears fall from his eyes. "Charlotte? I'm so sorry, Warren." I brushed the tears away.

"It was a long time ago. And now I have you." He pulled me into a soft kiss before releasing me. "Don't be too hard on either of them. Our world has been very secretive for millennia. Let's get to the station." He took me by the hand and opened the car door for me.

He grasped my hand once back inside and brought my fingers to his lips. "We will find him, Josie. I love you."

I wiped the tear from my eye and smiled. "I love you too." We drove the rest of the way to the station in silence.

Eighteen

Warren

We walked into the police station hand in hand this time. The lady at the front desk called for Clinton when we asked and buzzed us in. There was a strange hum over the bullpen as we walked toward the detective's office. The eyes watching us burned on my back.

Clinton stood and greeted us as we stepped into his office. The blanket strewn across his couch and the dark circles under his eyes told me he had slept there. Josie dropped my hand to wrap Clinton in a hug.

I gently cleared my throat. He pulled away and straightened before he spoke.

"You two look better than you did the other day."

"Thanks, Clint." Josie blushed.

"I take it you have new information? You learn anything?" Clinton looked at me as he asked.

"Yes, I have information. Are the other two here? I'd rather tell the story once."

Clinton nodded and picked up his phone. A moment later, a knock on the door signaled their arrival. They closed the door behind them and we sat.

The fae officer spoke. "Miss Josefina, we never properly introduced ourselves." I am Lance Bilchak, and this is my partner, Tanner Johnson. He's not bad for a warlock."

Josie took their hands, shaking them. "Pleasure to meet you."

"I spoke to our friendly teen, Keith. They went to a pawnshop that I know, so we went and checked it out. They took Rocky from the alley." I gripped Josie's hand. "Josie... saw what happened. It was a member of an ancient vampire clan. My bartender is a vampire, and I had him look into it. He tracked them down to the old factory down on Ninth Street."

"Why would you take her there? I thought you were going to keep her safe?" Clinton stood, rage burning in his eyes.

"I kept her safe. If it weren't for her, we wouldn't have known who took him." I tried to keep my voice calm.

"Fine, but who's this bartender? Why send him?"

"He's a vampire." My irritation matched his now.

Clinton turned his attention to the officers on the couch. "I'm guessing we have vampires on the force too? Why not send them?"

"Because they smell like cops." I nodded to the men. "No offence." They nodded back. "I needed to send someone I could trust and someone who wouldn't get caught. Sam will be fine," I told myself as much as the others.

Clinton stared at me.

Josie's voice cut through the thick tension like a blade. "Alright, enough of this pissing match. Call it a tie—you're both equally rugged and intimidating, okay?" Her tone was sharp, but the gentle touch of her hand on my arm tempered the anger burning in my chest. I let out a slow breath, forcing myself to ease the grip I hadn't realized I'd tightened.

"She's right," I admitted, breaking my glare and glancing at the others. "This isn't helping. I'm sorry. We need to work together if we're going to get through this."

Clinton cleared his throat, cautiously stepping into the truce. "What if we send someone with your guy, Sam? Not inside, but close enough to give backup if things go south. An earpiece or something so he's not out there alone. We can have a few officers stationed nearby for support."

I mulled over the suggestion, my mind weighing the risks and logistics. After a moment, I nodded. "It's a good idea, but we need someone who can keep a low profile. Tanner's a warlock—he can cloak himself better than a fae could around vampires. I'd suggest sending him."

"Sounds good" He glanced over at Josie before coming back to me. "But from now on you keep her out of this," Clinton barked.

Josie glared at me in warning. My eyes watched her as I spoke. "I can't do that. She is her own woman and I wouldn't dare to tell her what to do."

Her eyes softened, and she mouthed, "Thank you."

Clinton took a deep breath before responding. "If you get hurt, you know my wife will kill me?"

"I don't plan on getting hurt. I need to find my brother and nothing you say can stop me, so you might as well let me help." Josie's smile dared him to challenge her. God, I loved this woman. I beamed at her defiance.

Clinton pinched the bridge of his nose and exhaled hard.

"So, what's it going to be? You gonna let me help or what?" she asked him.

He sighed under his hand. "Fine. You've never been so persistent, Jo. I'm not sure if that's a good thing or not."

"I've been on a short chain for too long. I'm only now becoming who I should have been all along." She held my hand tighter.

"Okay, so this vampire of yours, when is he going to find a way in?" The detective watched me.

"Sam is going to get into the clan tonight." I bit the inside of my lip as I told him.

"What makes you so sure you aren't sending Sam to his death? It takes months to train an undercover cop. You can't throw him in there and expect him to swim," Clinton told me.

I laughed. "Sam is not your typical vampire. He's nearly as old as I am. Typically, vampires belong to a clan of some kind. They can go a little mad if they don't. But Sam's different. He's been a lone vampire for a long time and many clans have tried to recruit him, but he's refused them all."

"So you think he could walk through the front door of this place?"

"Probably. If I'm correct in assuming who the queen is, she'll welcome him with open arms."

"But Sam's awkward, Warren?" Josie spoke.

I tried not to let my concern show on my face. "Yes, he's shy. He's a lone vampire because of what happened in his first clan. But I have faith he can pull it off. He can be scary when he wants to be."

Clinton stood, cracking his knuckles. "You know I'm breaking about twenty federal laws by letting all these civilians do a cop's job?"

"Vampires don't work within human laws, so why should you?" I asked.

"Because if I get caught, it will be my job." He pointed out the window. "They don't know about this scary underworld, and to my captain it would look as if I were doing an illegal search."

"Well, it's a good thing they abandoned the factory years ago. You can search it without a warrant," I told him.

"Fine, but what about the officers? If I send SWAT in there, they'd get slaughtered."

"About that, sir," Officer Tanner spoke up. "We have our own radio codes. Word's already out among the Figli Del Mito officers. With your permission, sir, we can set officers around the area and watch out for our undercover civilian."

Clinton's eyes went wide as he stared at his officers. He slumped back down in his chair, head in his hands. "You gotta be kidding me," he said half to himself. "What else don't I know about my world?"

We sat in silence for a long moment, waiting for the sergeant's decision.

Finally, he lifted his head. "Very well, set up a team of your guys around the area and report in every two hours. If we find any hard evidence that the kids are there, we go in."

Josie jumped to her feet, ran around the desk, and hugged him. "Thank you, Clint!"

He released her quickly. "You're welcome." He eyed me. "Now, please take her home and keep her safe."

I stood, nodding. She let me guide her out of his office and through the building. The queasiness in my gut only grew as we walked. Out of the corner of my eye, I saw the demons from the last time we were here. Their hollow eyes watched us walk toward the stairs.

Their footsteps followed us downstairs and out the front door. Rage and fear boiled up within me, and I knew they wouldn't let us leave without a fight. Josie's life was all that mattered.

I pulled my keys from my pocket and called the magic deep within me.

Ninteen

Josie

A knot formed in the pit of my stomach as we walked out of the police station. Warren had wrapped me tight against him and his arm trembled, but that was impossible. He was so strong nothing could scare him.

He released me once we got closer to his car, then pulled my face to his, kissing me hard. "Josie, please get in the car." He placed the keys in my hand and turned his back to me.

"Warren," I whispered, too frightened to speak any louder.

"Please, Josie, it's the only way I can keep you safe." He didn't turn to look at me, but his magic pushed me back.

I took a step back but refused to leave him. A shimmering bubble formed around me as I watched and tried to push through the magic, but couldn't. He had trapped me inside of the shield.

The two volcanic demons approached as I pounded my fists against the protective barrier he'd erected. "Please, Warren!" I begged. Dropping to my knees, I pulled at the magic within me and pushed with all my might, but nothing penetrated his shield. Tears fell down my face. I couldn't watch him take them on alone, but I was useless behind his barricade.

The creatures stood in front of him now. My heart beat hard against my ribs.

"We know what she is. If you give her to us, we won't kill you." Its raspy voice sent chills down my spine.

Warren tightened his fists. "I don't think so." His voice dripped with rage.

"Wrong choice, Mage."

"If you know that name, quake with fear." Sparks emanated from his hands.

"We fear no warlock. We are golem. You may destroy this form, but our master will reform us." They spoke together as one voice.

"And who is this master of yours?"

"You will find out soon enough."

Warren blocked me from view, but I leaned over to see the creatures. Their blackened skin glowed red hot and molten lava dripped down the monsters' bodies.

"You will not take her." Warren's voice rang out in a crisp tone.

"That's where you're wrong." One of the golem lifted his hand and blasted a volcanic eruption at Warren.

He raised his arms and formed a shield at the last second. Volcanic rock fell to the ground with a thud. "Nice try," he said.

"Stop playing with them, Warren!" Tears burned my eyes as Warren danced around the creatures like they were puppets.

"Listen to your mutt. Just give her to us."

Rage poured off of him so thick the air turned sour. He raised his hands and blasted the air toward the golem, pushing it back. The second creature stepped around Warren and headed toward me.

Standing to my feet, I slammed my back against the shield. The monster's hands touched my shield, pouring lava over the bubble. The heat penetrated the magic, sending sweat dripping down my face. I shook with the fear of death by a volcano. A buzz of electricity popped in my ears and the lava dripped into my sanctuary.

"Warren!" I screeched through my tears. He turned to me, shooting my attacker with water. The creature's skin hardened the moment the cold liquid hit him. Warren pushed his hands forward, and the golem went flying. He slammed hard against a wall, shattering into a thousand pieces.

The lava flowed closer to my feet, but Warren's shield kept me trapped. He ran toward me, but the monster near him yanked him back. The second creature slammed him into the asphalt. It walked straight for me, leaving Warren unconscious on the ground.

It stepped up to what remained of the bubble and reached into the hole. I summoned my magic to stop the creature, but it did nothing. My shield shattered, and the golem grabbed me around the middle.

Its molten-hot hand seared into my flesh like a branding iron, sending waves of blistering agony through my arm. Warren's name tore from my throat in a raw, desperate scream, but he remained frozen, a statue in my peripheral vision. White-hot pain lanced through my body, making the world swim in a haze of tears and darkness. Through my fractured vision, ethereal silhouettes materialized from the shadows like smoke given form,

The creature's roar thundered through my bones like a sonic blast, rattling my teeth and vibrating in my chest cavity. Before I could draw another breath, it splintered in a catastrophic burst that sent shockwaves rippling through the air. My eyelids slammed shut against the searing white flash, but phantom colors still danced behind them, a kaleidoscope of agony that pulsed in time with my racing heartbeat.

"Josie." Warren's voice broke through the ringing. "Hold on."

We were moving, but all I could tell was my head was in Warren's lap. I closed my fingers around his as I slipped into unconsciousness.

WARREN'S MUFFLED VOICE WOKE ME. I FORCED MY EYES open to surrounding darkness. How long had I been asleep? I tried to sit up, but the pain sent me back down to the bed. Looking around, I found we were back in Warren's penthouse.

I pushed the blankets aside, the cool air brushing against my skin as I sat up. My hands trembled as I lifted my shirt, revealing the damage beneath. Angry red welts snaked across my stomach, their jagged lines raw and swollen like fiery trails etched into my skin. My breath hitched at the sight, fear and confusion twisting in my gut.

Gingerly, I pressed a fingertip to the edge of one welt, testing the pain. A sharp sting shot through me, and I yelped, pulling my hand back instinctively.

Footsteps echoed down the hall. Warren wrenched the door open and stood just inside the doorway, eyes wide. "Josie!" he gasped. He practically ran to the side of the bed. "I thought—I was so worried! If it wasn't for Tanner and Lance, we'd both be dead."

Slowly, I sat up. One officer I'd met in Clint's office, Tanner, stood in the doorway watching us.

"Tanner helped heal you, but you should lie still. Healing takes time." Warren sat beside me.

"What... what happened?" I asked.

"Tanner and Lance showed up just in time to save the day. I woke up to see you fall to the ground. I feared you were gone. Tanner drove us here, and we have been alternating healing you." He brushed the hair from my face.

"And you? I saw how hard he hit you. Are you okay?"

"My head's still ringing a bit, but I'll be all right." He lifted my shirt, looking at the burns. "I think you need a little more healing. You up for it while you're awake? You were squirming a lot while you were asleep."

I swallowed hard. "Does it hurt?"

He sighed. "Well, it doesn't feel good. We are speeding up the body's natural process of healing, making what should happen in days happen in hours, so it is uncomfortable. But you're tough." He kissed my cheek.

I nodded, and he waved for Tanner to come closer. "It's Tanner's turn, but I'll be here with you." He crawled farther onto the bed, shimmying in between the headboard and me, letting me lie back against his chest. I gripped his hands as Tanner knelt beside us.

"This shouldn't take long. Just one more healing and I think we can let your body take over," he told me.

Taking deep breaths, I braced for the pain. Tanner laid his hands gently over my burns. His fingers alone sent sharp needles to my core. I couldn't even imagine the agony his magic would bring. My skin tingled and burned as he pushed his magic to me. I pushed against Warren, sucking in my breath.

"Shhhhh." Warren's thumb caressed my hand. "I gotcha," he whispered in my ear.

My fingers dug into him as my skin boiled from the inside out. I gripped him tighter. Tears trickled down my cheeks. Closing my eyes, I focused on my breathing. In and out. In and out.

Icy chills replaced the burning.

"That should be enough for now. I think Warren can do it one more time later if you need it. You were very brave. Hell, Warren did worse when I healed the cut on his head." Tanner laughed.

"Thanks," I breathed out, not opening my eyes.

"Thank you, Tanner. Tell Lance thank you for us, too. You guys saved our lives," Warren spoke.

"It was our pleasure, Mage." There was a soft click of the door as Tanner left the room.

Opening my eyes, I glanced down at my stomach. The welts had retreated into smooth pink skin. Warren's fingers brushed over the raw flesh, and I sighed at his touch.

"I thought you were dead. My world stopped spinning." His arm wrapped around my chest, holding me tight against him. "I never want to feel like that again."

"I never want to feel that fear, either. When that creature slammed you to the ground, my heart stopped." I turned in his grasp and pressed my lips to his jaw.

He kissed the top of my head. "After you rest, more training needs to happen before we do anything else. I can't lose you."

I nuzzled against his neck. "Okay. We will stay here until I have better control of my magic. I want to protect you as much as myself. If I would have known how to use my magic, I think I could have helped against those two."

"I know you could have, Josie." He pulled my face up to his, kissing me deeply, then backed away slightly. "How are you feeling?"

Sitting up on my knees, I pulled the shirt over my head and tossed it to the floor. Leaning in, I whispered, "You tell me."

He pulled me down into a fierce kiss.

Twenty

Josie

My body ached all over when I woke the next day. Warren lay on his stomach, taking up more than half the bed, only wearing boxers. His muscles flinched as my fingers traced down his spine. It was so tempting to just dip my hand lower beneath his shorts, instead I gently rubbed his back.

"You keep that up and I'll go right back to sleep," his muffled voice told me.

My heart froze for a long moment. The thought of being lazy and lying next to this man as long as I wanted spread a sense of calmness over me that I had never experienced.

A smile spread over my face as I asked, "And what's wrong with that?" I leaned in, kissing the back of his neck. He rolled over and grinned at me. "We're grown adults, so why can't we stay in bed all day?" I asked.

His fingers trailed down my neck, over the t-shirt I'd stolen from him, and rested over the still-pink flesh of my stomach.

"Lying next to you is too tempting for me. Besides, you need to train." He gave me a sad smile.

I dug my nails into the nape of his neck and pulled him into a kiss. He was right. If I stayed here much longer, there was no telling what I might do to this man.

"How about a compromise? Let me lay here in your arms for a moment, then train?" I leaned down, trailing kisses down his jaw. I didn't wait for a response before laying my head on his chest.

"You drive me mad, woman." He kissed my forehead and pulled me closer.

The steady rhythm of his heartbeat lulled me to a place between dreams and sleep. There I saw all the possible endings. From the death of Rocky and the other kids to the ending of our world. But here in Warren's arms, I knew everything would be alright.

He leaned in to kiss my cheek. "How about some food, then training?"

I sighed, "Sounds good."

He laid back down on the pillow and lifted his hand. Twirling his fingers around, he closed his eyes.

"I thought you were going to make food?" I asked.

"Shhhh."

I laid back onto the bed, studying him. A moment later, the bedroom door opened on its own. Two trays of food came floating in the room, then rested gently on the bed before us. A stack of pancakes waited on one plate and bacon and eggs on the other. A glass of orange juice sat in the tray's corner.

I sat up, nearly toppling the food to the bed. "What the?"

Warren sat up beside me, pulling the food toward him. "I told you I could cook using magic, but normally don't. Today I didn't want to leave your side." He grinned at me.

"Well, okay then." I pulled the food to me and took a bite of bacon. The salty maple flavor exploded over my tongue as I moaned, "It's delicious."

"Hey now, I'm the only one who gets to make you moan like that." He leaned over, kissing my neck.

"You did," I said between bites. "How does this taste so amazing?" I asked quickly, taking another slice of bacon.

"It's no different from if I went to the kitchen and made it myself... except quicker. There's much for you to learn, Josie, so eat up and let's start."

We ate breakfast in a comfortable silence, the clinking of silverware filling the gaps where words didn't need to be. When the plates were cleared away, I leaned into Warren, seeking the warmth of his presence and the comfort of his steady breathing. I burrowed closer, ready to settle back into the cocoon of his embrace.

Before I could get too comfortable, he slipped out from under the covers, his movements smooth and deliberate. My moment of peace was short-lived as he turned back, a mischievous glint in his eyes, and gently but firmly pulled me toward the edge of the bed, forcing me to sit up.

"Come on," he said with a grin, his hands steadying me. "You're not spending the whole day in bed. Time to get moving. Ready to learn your strengths?" he asked.

I eyed him, then down at myself before I spoke. "You're gonna teach me to wield magic while we are both half dressed?"

He rolled his eyes and led me to the bathroom. We showered, and I forced my hands to myself. As much as I enjoyed the feel of his body against mine, I had to learn more about this new world if I were to be a part of it.

We stepped out, dried ourselves, and I grabbed my now favorite hoodie and threw it on while he grabbed a pair of sweats.

He led me back through his gun room where he'd stored the dragonette stone dagger and then to his gun range and grinned down at me. With a flick of his wrist, everything changed. The shooting lanes and all the equipment vanished. The light gray walls brightened to a light turquoise, and hardwood planks replaced the hard concrete floor.

With another flicked of his wrist, he now stood in his signature tight suit. And man, was it sexy. I gasped when I looked down at myself. I, too, was no longer in his clothes but my own. The outfit I had worn to the club the night we met was now wrapped around my body—shoes included.

Jumping back, I asked, "What? How?"

"I'm a warlock, remember?" He laughed.

"I know that, but this is my dress?" I stroked the fabric over my hips.

"Magic can do about anything. You can do anything, Josie." He stepped closer, rubbing my arm. "You are stronger than you believe. I think you could out magic me once you learn to harness it."

I smiled, but not quite a happy smile. Fear and excitement intermingled within me. I loved the idea of being able to out magic Warren, yet somehow it terrified me.

"I... I don't think I could ever be better than you." I stepped back.

"Maybe not right away, but you have the magic within you to be great." Out of the corners of my eyes, I saw him watching me. I couldn't look at him when he was giving me such credit. "It's a lot to take in, Josie. We will keep it basic for now."

"Can I have something more comfortable before we start?" The dress he chose clung to my every curve and the shoes were every bit of three-inch heels.

He sighed, "Oh, but you look delicious in that dress."

I shot him my best glare. He laughed and flicked his wrist. My jeans and his hoodie replaced the dress.

"Thanks."

"You're welcome. Now," With another twirl of his hand, an oversized love seat sat on the floor behind us. "Sit, and we will explore your magic a bit."

I sat next to him on the couch and pulled my legs up against my chest.

"Do you know where magic comes from?" he asked. I shook my head before he continued. "Warlocks are more in tune with their bodies and the world around them. We can manipulate the very matter of things. That water I pushed at those monsters— I pulled the moisture from the surrounding air and multiplied it. We can't create something out of nothing. If we were in the vacuum of space, we'd be as magical as a human.

"So far, you have only used your magic by gut instincts alone. You've been reacting to things around you. We need to get you to think about it before you use it. I want you to close your eyes and just feel for your magic. Tell me what you see, hear, or smell."

Hesitantly, I closed my eyes and reached for it like I had before. The tingle hit me before anything else did. "Have you ever been around a Van De Graaf generator? It feels kinda like that. Like I'm standing next to one of those and all my hair is standing on end. It kinda tickles." Breathing deep, I could smell the magic. "It smells... It smells like petrichor.

Like I'm standing in the middle of the forest during a rainstorm. I can... I can actually hear the raindrops." I felt the smile grow on my face, and I didn't want to open my eyes.

His fingers traced the edge of my lips. I pulled myself away from my magic to see him smiling at me.

"What?" I asked.

"Your smile is infectious. You seemed so happy."

"I was... I am. My magic feels like home. I have always loved the rain, and now I know why. What does yours feel like?"

"Mine? Feels like the heat of a campfire on a cool summer night. Everyone's magic reminds them of something different. Some think about the weather. Some think of smells or tastes. It's a unique feeling for each warlock."

"Can all warlocks do the same things or does the way one's magic feel let them do different things?"

"You're quick. Everyone has the same potential, but some are better at certain things than others. Since you can sense the rain, I believe you're a water warlock. I'm fire and blood. I can still wield the other elements, but fire is my strongest. Some warlocks have rare abilities. Blood magic is something I can do, although I don't enjoy it."

"What does that mean? Blood magic?" I asked.

"I can use someone's blood to connect to them. I can track them, feel what they feel, or even manipulate them. I don't use it often as it feels unnatural." Warren stood, offering me his hand. He pulled me to the center of the massive room.

"Now, think about the rain you could smell." He instructed me.

I closed my eyes and pulled myself back into my magic.

His voice broke through the silence. "Call that rain toward you, toward us. Let it flow through you."

When I tried to call it, nothing happened. I tried again and still nothing. I let out a small growl through my clenched jaw. My eyes snapped open and glared at Warren as he laughed.

"Easy now. You're thinking too much. Let it happen." He stepped closer. "Try again."

I closed my eyes and found myself back in the rainstorm in my mind. Then he was there with me, pulling me into his arms. Warren's mouth found mine and kissed me hard in the rain. I let him twirl me around. Laughing, we pulled apart.

I opened my eyes and felt the raindrops on my skin. It was a soft, warm rain that made me think of spring.

"See, you have to feel it, not think about it." He laughed as he pulled me closer. I rested my head on his chest as we stood in the rain.

"What if I wanted to make this soft rain into a storm?" I asked, not lifting my head.

His thumb stroked my back under my shirt. "Recall something that makes you angry."

My mind went straight to the monsters that took my brother. I jumped as a lightning bolt struck the corner of the room. The booming thunder clap echoing through the space made me cover my ears.

His chest rumbled with laughter. "I'll try not to make you angry."

I jabbed him in the ribs. The rain dissipated as I pulled out of my magic. "What else can I do? You could change this entire room with a flick of the wrist. How did you do that?"

"I will explain that, but we will hold off on trying it. Let's go sit back down."

I followed him back to the couch and slumped down beside him. Despite our recent meal, my stomach rumbled.

He flicked his wrist and fresh baked bread landed in his lap. "I told you before that magic has a price. You need to build up your strength or it could kill you. I recommend a high protein and carb diet for warlocks. You will also probably want to sleep more while getting used to the magic use. As far as how to conjurer things, though, that's one of the easier magics we do. I'll explain how I got your dress. It's simple, really. I thought of you the first time I saw you. I pulled that dress to me like you pulled the rain to you. So maybe after we eat some more and rest, you can bring some more of your clothes here so you don't have to steal mine. All you have to do is picture where they are in time and space and will them to be here."

Leaning my back against him, I closed my eyes and my walk-in closet came into my mind's eye. The stack of jeans sat next to a pile of t-shirts. I pulled them off the shelf as if I stood in front of them. Their weight fell into my lap, forcing my eyes open. Warren grinned down at me.

"Josie," I heard him shout and jump from the couch. My vision grew hazy as he lifted my limp body into his arms.

Twenty-One

Sam

The night air sent a chill down my spine. No, it wasn't really the air... I'm a vampire, so I didn't notice the cold. It was where my feet were taking me that gave me the uneasy feeling. I hadn't stepped foot into a clan in centuries, and I wasn't happy about heading toward this one. I'd do anything for Warren, though.

Ignoring the screeches from the bars, I kept walking. The streetlights vanished the further from civilization I walked. I passed the ruins of a building and walked farther into the abyss of night. Beggars and street women were all that remained this deep in the slums. A man in a ragged coat shook a can as I neared. Kneeling down, I handed him some change. His eyes pleaded with me.

"Tanner?" I whispered in the darkness. Warren had said Tanner was a warlock officer that would meet me here and keep an eye on things from the outside.

He nodded, handing me a tiny earpiece and muttering his thanks for the change.

I pushed the concealed mic and receiver in my ear and walked on.

"Just in case... Tell Warren thanks," I whispered into the mic. I walked straight to the old factory's doors. Before I could reach for the handle, a tall, dark figure stood before me.

"And just where do you think you are going?" His deep voice echoed in the night's silence.

Looking him in the eye, I said, "I... Tell Jemisha it's Sam." As I spoke, I stepped back.

Out of the corner of my eyes, I saw him look me up and down before talking into his wrist. I kicked at the rocks at my feet as I waited. The venom in my veins raced, making my heart beat so loud I was sure this vampire could hear it. If I didn't calm down soon, I'd tip them off to the fact I wasn't here to join her clan.

"You've got this," Tanner's voice echoed in my ear.

Turning my back to the door, I mumbled, "I can't."

"Yes, you can. If you get into trouble, say... pineapple, and we will break down the doors." The way he said "pineapple" caught me off guard, his tone soft yet laced with an unexpected humor that made my tense shoulders relax. It was such a random, silly word to throw into the moment, and his delivery was so casual that it felt absurdly out of place.

I nodded before remembering they couldn't see me. I was about to respond before the door opened and another vampire stepped out into the night.

"You Sam?" he asked.

"Y-yeah." I hugged my arms tight around my chest.

The vampire scoffed. "From the stories she's told, you're supposed to be some bad ass. You look like a loud fart would knock you over." The two vampires laughed.

"Yeah." I was used to the jokes at my demeanor. I might be tall and stronger than the average human, but my baggie clothes and mild-mannered attitude didn't fit what most vampires thought I should be.

"Whatever. She was happy to discover you've finally accepted her invite. Come on." He jerked his head toward the door and kept it open for me as I walked through.

The stench of copper and fear assaulted all my senses the moment I stepped inside. The factory floor was clear of all machines and nearly all rubble. Nothing in plain view from the street. Not even a single vampire stood between us and the back wall.

We walked past the crumbling remains of the brick columns to a set of concrete stairs leading down into the earth before he spoke again.

"So, what made you change your mind about joining us?" he asked.

"I'd rather talk to Jemisha, if you don't mind." I tried to mimic Warren's cold and calculating tone.

"Fair enough. She's happy you're here. Got plans and she thinks you'll be a help."

I didn't even know how to respond, just kept walking

The descent into the underground corridor felt endless, the narrow stairwell pressing in around us like the weight of the secrets it concealed. Each step echoed ominously, the sound swallowed by the oppressive silence. At the bottom, the air was cooler, damp with a faint metallic tang that clung to the back of my throat.

As we stepped into the hallway, darkness closed in like a living thing. The faint flicker of torches on the stone walls cast long, dancing shadows, distorting the space into something otherworldly. My instincts kicked into overdrive, and I let my gaze sweep over every detail—the uneven floor, the subtle dips in the ceiling, the faint scuff marks on the walls. Every feature became a potential marker, an anchor point in case I needed to spirit—something only vampires or air mages could do—out of here.

Spiriting required knowing exactly where you were going, and this labyrinthine corridor felt like a place meant to swallow the unprepared. I mentally traced every turn we took, the layout slowly building in my mind like a map. The uneven cadence of our footsteps on the stone added to the unease; even the sound of our breaths seemed to bounce back at us, warped by the tunnel.

At last, we reached a door—a hulking slab of reinforced wood, its iron bands tarnished with age. The man ahead of me stopped, his knuckles rapping against the surface in a sharp, deliberate rhythm.

I tensed, eyes darting to the edges of the doorframe. The faintest line of light seeped from underneath, and my senses sharpened.

"Enter." Her icy voice rang out from behind the door. The vampire opened the door, letting me pass through before closing it behind me. I was alone with my most hated emissary.

The sudden brilliance of the massive candle chandelier hanging from the center of the ceiling forced me to shield my eyes. As my vision adjusted, the room came into focus— a lavish and unsettling mix of luxury and menace. Dark purple walls, almost black, wrapped around the space, their surface interrupted by a gleaming wall of weapons, each meticulously displayed as though ready for war. Across from the weapons stood a towering four-poster bed draped in deep red silks, where a tiny vampire lay sprawled on the crimson bedspread, her delicate form at odds with the bloodied human lying motionless at her side.

Jemisha stood; her short but curvy frame sauntered right up to me. My body stiffened as she brushed a finger over my cheek. Over her shoulder I caught the fainted glint of glamour against the wall beside her bed and knew instantly she was hiding something and then I saw it: a faint outline, barely visible, blending seamlessly into the purple. A hidden door, its presence betraying Jemisha's paranoia and cunning. Only someone who truly understood her—and her penchant for secrets—would have noticed it.

My fangs throbbed at the scent of fresh blood. I bit back the urge to feed as I stared at Jemisha. She brushed back her long blonde hair and kissed the human with bloody lips. "You may go," she told him, and I stepped aside to let him pass.

"Oh, how I've missed you, my Samuel." She stood on her tiptoes, pressing her bloody lips to mine. Her tinny aroma sent pangs of desire through me. It was stupid of me not to have fed before coming here. I stepped back.

"I heard you've been looking for me?" I gave her a slight bow.

"Why did you take your time? And why now?"

I ran through the reasons Warren and I had talked about. "I have spent far too long alone and need to be with my people again," I breathed out.

"And what about that Warlock of yours?"

"He is not mine," I said with all the coldness I could muster. "He was something to use until I got bored. I am over waiting on lowly humans. I wish to feast again like we once did."

"After all this time? You wish to give up on your anti-human diet?"

I took a deep breath. "I find I am hungry. Nothing will satisfy the desire that burns within me." Staring into her eyes stirred up old feelings, making my fangs throb even more.

She grinned before stepping around me, cracking the door open. "Prove it."

One guard stepped in, dragging a sickly looking human inside and handing her off to his queen before stepping back out. The emaciated woman might've collapsed if Jemisha wasn't holding her up.

"If you wish to join us, this is the price of admission. I was going to give her to the dogs, but this will be fun to watch." She dropped the girl, who sank to her knees sobbing. I stared into Jemisha's eyes for a long moment, wishing I could do anything but what she wanted, but I knew it would mean certain death.

I bent down low, leaning closer to the woman. Her eyes pleaded with me. "My way will be painless, I promise. I am sorry."

The woman shook beneath me. My fangs pulsed in time with the blood rushing through her veins. I pressed my lips to her neck, calming her heart.

"I'm waiting." Jemisha's voice interrupted my spell.

The woman jolted, but I continued to kiss her neck, sending as much magic into her as I dared. Finally, I opened my mouth and sank my fangs deep into her flesh, drawing the last of her blood into my body. Human blood had become tainted, but this poor woman was so high my head buzzed as her body stilled.

Clenching my jaw tight, I laid her gently on the ground before standing to face Jemisha.

"Well done, my lover." She stepped over the body and wrapped her arms around my neck, pulling me into her lips. My stomach churned as she licked me clean of blood before releasing me. "You may stay." She opened the door, dismissing me.

"Ah man, you got to finish off the whore? I was hoping to watch the dogs have her." The vampire who had brought me to Jemisha now walked me to my room.

"Wasn't much left." I tried to sound nonchalant. He walked me down the hall and nodded to the door at the end.

"You can have that room. If you play your cards right, I think Jemisha will share with you."

"Yeah." I shrugged. "Thanks."

Shutting the door behind me, I didn't even bother to look around before heading to the tiny bathroom. The blood I had stolen came up in heavy heaves. My muscles burned with the retching.

"Sam, just breathe. You did what you had to, and at least she didn't die a violent death." Tanner's voice echoed in my ear.

I retched more.

"I can't." My body collapsed to the floor as I took gulping breaths. I had to get it together. If someone heard me, I'd be dead.

"Yes, you can." Tanner's voice softened. "Sam, you can do this. I've got your back. Do you hear me?"

"Yeah," I whispered.

"Good. Now dust yourself off. This won't get easier, but I won't leave this mic."

My chest loosened at the thought he'd be on the other end, no matter what. "Thanks." I straightened myself up, wiping the blood from my mouth, and walked back to the bedroom.

"Whatever you hear from here on out, remember that I am on your side. Always." I am the Blood Beast, after all. Maybe it is time I reminded them of that. Kicking off my shoes, I laid down on the bed, resting my eyes. This was going to get ugly, and I had to prepare myself for the worst of it.

Twenty-Two

Josie

The phone rang before sunrise, pulling Warren from the bed. I groaned and buried my face in the pillow, but his tense voice as he answered the call pried my eyes open. Something was wrong—I could feel it in the way his shoulders stiffened. By the time he hung up, his expression was grim, and my heart sank.

"Lance wants us at Clinton's office," he said, pulling on a shirt. "Sam made it in, but... he had to do some questionable things to get there."

The words hung in the air like a storm cloud, heavy and foreboding. I sat up, suddenly wide awake, my mind racing with questions. What could Sam have done? And more importantly, was it worth the cost?

Clinton's office felt stifling, the air heavy with tension as Lance finished explaining what Sam had done. Tanner had stayed behind in order to keep an eye on things at the warehouse while Lance came to update everyone. My stomach churned, a sick knot forming as the words settled in.

"He drained her?" I blurted, my voice sharp with disbelief. "How is that supposed to make us trust him?"

"It wasn't just about us trusting him," Lance said, his tone measured. "It was about getting the queen to trust him."

Clinton leaned forward in his chair, his jaw tight. "And that makes it okay? This is the kind of crap that blows everything up, Lance."

I nodded, crossing my arms as anger bubbled beneath my skin. "He's supposed to be on our side, not terrorizing innocent people to earn points with the queen."

Warren, however, didn't flinch. He leaned against the wall, arms folded, his expression calm but unreadable. "It was a calculated risk, and it worked. Sam got in. If he hadn't done it, we'd still be out here in the dark with no idea what's going on inside."

"You're defending this?" Clinton snapped, his glare aimed at Warren now.

"I'm saying it's done," Warren replied evenly, his voice like steel. "We needed him in, and he got in. Sam's not perfect, but he's doing what he has to do. You all wanted a way into the queen's inner circle, and now we have one. Maybe focus on that instead of wringing your hands over what's already happened."

I stood there glaring at Lance and Warren both. Despite necessity, I wasn't about to let this stand. Sam couldn't be trusted, and I wouldn't trust him. "We need to find another option," I said

"You need to understand—" Lance started.

"Understand? Understand what? Understand that he killed a woman? Understand that he ended a life? For what?" My voice rose with every question until my speech turned to enraged shouts.

"Look, I get it's not ideal, I know, but undercover cops often skirt the laws—"

"Skirt the law... Sam shattered it!"

Lance took a step back from me.

Warren raised his hands and stepped closer. "Josie, you need to calm down." His voice raised to match mine.

"Calm down? You want me to calm down? How the fudge am I supposed to be okay with this?" I watched Clinton, who had stood from his chair and was now backed up against the wall.

"Josie, look at your arms." Warren took another step closer.

Fur crawled up my arms, and I stumbled backwards into the wall. My eyes searched for answers on Warren's face.

He grinned. "I guess this answers the questions of your lineage."

More fur sprouted. My throat constricted and a thousand pound weight settled over my chest. Air refused to come as I slumped to the floor, gasping.

Pain rippled through my body, sharp and relentless, like my bones were trying to break free of my skin. My hands clawed at the floor, nails already lengthening into something monstrous. My breath came in ragged gasps as panic clawed its way up my throat.

"I can't—I can't stop it!" I cried, my voice barely human.

"Josie." Warren's voice cut through the chaos, low and steady. He knelt beside me, his hand warm and grounding against my arm. "Breathe. Focus on my voice. You're okay. I'm right here."

His calm tone was a lifeline, pulling me back from the edge of hysteria. "It hurts," I whimpered, tears streaming down my face.

"I know it does," he murmured, his hand moving to cradle my face. His thumb brushed my cheek, wiping away the tears. "But you're stronger than this. You've got control, Josie. Just breathe with me."

I locked on his eyes, grounding myself in their steady determination, and for a moment, the storm inside me slowed.

"Look at me, Josie," he said, reaching out a hand toward me. "May I?" I nodded and took his hand in mine. The instant our fingers connected, his magic washed over me and settled my mind. The fear that had strangled me a moment ago fled my body, and I leaned my head into his chest. His powerful arms wrapped around me. "I got you, Josie." His hands stroked my spine.

Only when my breathing slowed did he release me. My arms had returned to their normal skin, and I could think clearly. I glanced up at Warren and whispered, "Thank you." He leaned over and kissed my forehead before he turned around to face the others.

Clinton still stood up against the wall, but the others had relaxed slightly.

I groaned. "I'm some kinda ancient warlock? I don't know. Some kinda shifter warlock or something..." I tried to dismiss the questions I still had about myself.

"The Wolsteincrofts?" Lance asked. His eyes went wide as he leaned on the chair in front of him.

I nodded. He sat on the edge of the chair with the weight of the news. "Then Rocky..." I nodded again, and his jaw dropped.

"Yes, Rocky is a Wolsteincroft too."

Lance lifted his gaze, but not to me. "We have to get him out of there. Now." He pleaded with Warren.

Warren agreed. "I know. We will, but we need to figure out what she needs these kids for." He wrapped an arm around my waist. "I'm sorry, but this isn't about just Rocky. We need to stop her, and the only way to do that is to understand her plans. We need to let Sam do what he does best."

"And what's that?" I asked.

Warren's body shivered as he stood, helping me to my feet. I backed away and sat in Clinton's chair, watching him. Warren's eyes never left mine.

He took a deep breath before he spoke. "You know how I'm known as Mage to some, and how that name puts fear into those who cross me? Well, Sam didn't always go by the name Sam. His history is even darker than mine. People called him the... the Blood Beast." He nodded. "About the same time I was aiding Vlad, he was making a name for himself in Italy. He wasn't killing humans like Vlad was, but his own kind. He became known as the Blood Beast for his relentless murder of rogue vampires. Back then, being a lone vampire was simply not done, and he got good at hunting them down. After a while, he'd learned his queen was using him to kill those who opposed her. He turned on his clan, using his skills to weed out the evil from within. He killed most of them and caused the rest to flee. After that, he became a lone vampire. He's stayed mostly hidden for centuries. Until I found him, really. I helped him, but now I've sent him into the dragon's lair."

My heart ached for Sam and Warren both. His face held the weight of his actions. I stood and wrapped my arms around his middle, hugging him tight. I was not ready to forgive their nonchalant attitude over the death of this woman, but I also couldn't stand around watching him hurt.

"Jemisha was his queen. She is now the queen of the clan we are hunting," Warren said.

I pushed away from him. "And Sam's in there alone? What if he's found out? Or worse, what if he goes all Blood Beast again?"

"He won't."

"How do you know? What if he kills everyone, including the kids we are trying to save? If he tried to kill her once, why would she even trust him?"

"That was a long time ago." Warren reached out for my hand, but I refused. "He has changed. He was a young vampire then, but over the centuries, he has grown and has control over his lust…"

"He had to kill a woman to get in with the clan; can you honestly tell me she won't make him do worse things?" My anger was building. My hands were shaking. "Keys!" I demanded, thrusting out a hand. Warren directed a questioning gaze at me. "Give me your keys now! If I stay here a second longer, I don't know what'll happen, so give me your keys." I waited.

Warren didn't move, so I closed my eyes and pictured the keys in his pocket and snatched them out.

When their weight fell into my hand, I stormed out of the office, practically running to the stairs, not caring that the entire precinct was watching me. Taking the steps two at a time, I reached the bottom before I heard him.

"Josie, wait!" Warren was right behind me. I rushed out the doors and ran for his car. He was waiting for me when I got there, forcing me to stop in my tracks. "Warlock, remember? You stole my keys in a police station. Please, let me take you home. You're upset." He reached for me. "We could go to my range?"

Darting around him, I said, "No."

"Sam will be alright and he will get the information we need to save Rocky. Josie, I love you and want to protect you." He tried to reach for me again, but I smacked his hand away.

"How? How can you love me? How can I love you? I've only known you for what? A week? Maybe two weeks? That is not enough time to fall in love. I don't care what you say. This..." I pointed between us. "This isn't love, it's magic. I know you said magic doesn't work like that, but how would I know? You're using your magic on me, making me feel these things, and I'm done! I will find my brother on my own!" The look of hurt on his face nearly broke me. I pushed past him and around to the driver's side, then slid into the car and took off without waiting to adjust the seat.

As I sped out of the parking lot, my grip tightened on the steering wheel. I drove without a destination in mind. I had to get away. My heart wanted to go back and apologize, but logic told me I was right. I mean, how many people actually fell in love this quickly? What I felt had to be magic. Right?

My vision blurred, forcing me to pull over. I parked and got out of the car, slamming the door behind me. I gasped for breath as I paced the little alley I had parked in. My world was spinning out of control and I couldn't stop it. I took heaving breaths, but nothing eased the pain in my chest.

"Oh, my Josefina. I thought you had controlled these silly panic attacks." His familiar voice froze the blood in my veins. My gun was just a few feet away, locked safely in the car, but I couldn't move even if I wanted to. "My love, why don't you turn around and look at me? It'll make things easier." My feet moved at his command. "There, that's better."

Caleb's dark eyes stared back at me, drinking me in. My body became frozen, but not from fear... He had control over it.

"If I would have fully understood what you were all those years ago, I would have killed you then. But as it is, my mistress has need of you. Come." His voice rolled over me, forcing my feet forward.

I summoned all the strength I could and reached for my magic. It exploded out of me in a burst of light, breaking his hold on me. I turned and ran.

"Oh Josefina..." I heard him speak behind me. "Get her," he commanded someone.

The snarls that followed me sent chills down my spine. I dropped Warren's keys and ran faster. But it was no use. The vampire at my back slammed me into the wall, pinning me in place. It was the same one that took Rocky. I squirmed in its grip. Its mouth drew closer and closer to me. The stench of old blood seeped from it. I kicked at it, but it didn't flinch.

"Bring her," Caleb spoke. The vampire gripped my neck, lifted me off the ground, and walked back down the alley. I clawed at its hand fruitlessly. It stepped up to its master and dropped me in a heap at his feet. I gasped for air. "Now, will you be a good girl, or do I need to let him feed a bit?"

I shook my head. "I won't run." My voice was hoarse.

"Good." He knelt in front of me. "Leave," he spoke to the vampire, and with a pop, it vanished.

He gripped my chin and raised my face to his. He pressed his lips roughly into mine before he stood. "Now stand and walk."

I stood on weak legs and followed him. Remembering what Warren had said about blood magic, I dug my nails into my palms, drawing blood, letting it fall to the ground. We walked past Warren's car. I fell into it, streaking my blood over the door before standing up and following my ex into the car parked at the end of the alley.

I sank into the leather seats and prayed Warren didn't give up on me for the words I'd spoken so harshly to him. How I wished I'd never said them. I felt the tears well up, but Caleb watched me. I took a deep breath and reached for my magic. A brick wall stood between me and my magic. I clawed at the wall with my mind, but it was unmovable.

"It won't work. Your magic is mine now." Caleb smiled as the tears fell from my face.

Twenty-Three

Warren

My heart shattered as she sped out of the parking lot, leaving nothing but the roar of the engine and a hollow ache in her wake. Never in my long life had I felt a tie to another soul like I did with Josie. And in a single heartbeat, she'd destroyed me.

I stood there numb, my hands trembling at my sides, staring at the fading taillights as if willing her to turn back. Time stretched, each second an eternity. It wasn't until Clinton's hand landed firmly on my arm that the weight of her words truly hit me.

The impact drove me to my knees. I clutched at my chest as if I could physically hold myself together. The world spun around me, the edges blurring into an unrelenting haze, and the thunderous pounding of my heart filled my ears. Somewhere in the haze, Lance's face swam into view as he knelt in front of me, his sharp gaze laced with concern.

"What happened?" he asked softly, his voice grounding me just enough to form a response.

"She... she left," I managed to say, my voice cracking under the strain.

"Why?" His question hung in the air, and I struggled to find the words.

"She blames magic for what she feels... for what we are," I whispered, my throat tightening.

Lance's expression darkened, his brows knitting together. "But it's more than that, isn't it? She's your match."

"Match? What does that mean?" Clinton asked, his tone edged with confusion.

Before I could muster the strength to answer, Lance did it for me. "A match is much like the human concept of a soulmate, but deeper. It's a bond between two souls so profound that it becomes unbreakable. They will always be connected—always able to feel each other."

The words cut deeper than I wanted to admit. I sank onto the asphalt, my hands shaking as I cradled my head. My breathing grew ragged, and my stomach churned like it was twisting in on itself. *Get it together.* The thought flared like a desperate command. *I'm ancient. She's just a girl.* Acting like a fool wouldn't change anything. I had to pick myself up, focus, move forward.

But I froze, the weight of the lie pressing against my chest, burning in my throat like fire. Who was I kidding? She wasn't *just a girl.* She was everything. The connection between us wasn't something I could sever, no matter how much I told myself otherwise. Josie was my match, and now, with every second she was gone, it felt like the very essence of me was unraveling.

The distant sound of a phone ringing didn't even register until Clinton's panicked voice cut through the fog in my mind.

"Slow down, Nessa. What do you mean, she's in trouble? How do you know?" His tone was sharp, his pacing frantic as he gripped his phone like it might shatter in his hands.

I shook off the lingering sorrow and straightened, watching him with growing concern. Lance stood beside me, arms crossed, his stoic expression betraying a flicker of unease.

"You what?" Clinton's voice pitched higher. "Hang on, let me put you on speaker." He jabbed the button and thrust the phone toward us. "Say that again."

"Josie's in trouble," Nessa's voice rang out, firm and unyielding.

"What do you mean?" I finally spoke, stepping closer.

"Who's that?" she snapped.

"It's Warren Harris," Clinton answered quickly.

"The Warren Harris?" Her disbelief was palpable even through the phone. "What's he doing there?"

"Long story. One I'm not sure you'd believe—" Clinton started, his tone evasive.

"She's a witch, isn't she?" Nessa interrupted, her words landing like a slap.

Clinton froze, his jaw tightening. Lance and I exchanged a glance, both of us silently grateful she wasn't physically present to drill us with those piercing accusations.

"Why would you say that?" Clinton asked cautiously, his tone edging toward defensive.

"Because it makes sense." Her voice was matter-of-fact, as if she were explaining something as obvious as the sky being blue. "And so are you, aren't you, Warren?"

Her directness was disarming, leaving a heavy silence in its wake. Clinton opened his mouth, likely to deny it, but she steamrolled over him.

"Oh, come on. I've known for years Jo wasn't a normal human—neither am I. I'm an empath, clairsentient, and claircognizant. Basically, I just *know* she's in trouble, and I can feel her fear. Something is very wrong."

Clinton stared at the phone like it was a venomous snake, weighing whether to drop it or endure the bite. His silence stretched, thick and uncertain.

"Don't make that face, Clint," Nessa scolded, her tone sharp with impatience. "I've told you this a million times, and you laughed it off. Magic is real. Get over it."

Her words hung in the air, challenging him to deny her yet again. Clinton's mouth worked for a moment, his usual confidence shaken, before he finally snapped his jaw shut. Whatever he'd been about to say, he swallowed it, and I couldn't help but admire Nessa's audacity. She wasn't here, but she had us all on edge like she was.

Clinton shifted his attention back up to me.

I shrugged. "I reminded you that there is a lot more to your world than what you had initially seen. "Nessa, do you know where she is?"

"No, I can't see her, just feel her. What's happening?" I could hear the tears in her voice.

"Someone took her student, Rocky..." I glanced at Clinton, not sure how much to share. He nodded, so I continued. "It was a vampire clan, and we've been looking for him. We had a fight, and she ran off."

"Vampires? Huh, so she's living the books she used to love. Not as romantic as the stories, though. You..." she hesitated. "You love her, don't you?"

I gulped down at the stares the others were giving me. "Yes." Clinton seemed as if he would burst into flames, but Lance smiled. "But she doesn't love me back, so it doesn't matter."

"You're an idiot. Don't be the jerk in the romance novel who thinks the girl doesn't love him and so he pushes her away and acts like a dick, only to learn later she does have feelings for him. Josie does love you; she's just scared. And right now she needs you, so stop acting like a moron."

She loves me. I let her words settle over me a moment before I moved. If Josie truly belonged to me, I would tear this city apart to find her. I pulled my phone out of my pocket and scrolled through apps, finding what I needed.

"I have a tracker on all my cars. It's stopped... here." I showed the others the map on my phone. "We should start there."

"Find her," Nessa spoke. "I love you, Clint. Be safe and let me know what you find." She hung up before he could respond.

Twenty-Four

Warren

The ride to my car was silent and intense. The only sounds were from my phone calling out directions. I could feel the hurt radiating off Clinton, but I didn't have the emotional bandwidth to deal with it at the moment.

I stepped out onto the sidewalk without waiting for the car to come to a complete stop. The coppery tinge of her blood lingered in the air, leading me to my car parked in a dark alleyway. I followed her trail of blood drops to the curb, where they vanished. She was gone, and it was my fault. I stood there staring at the spot where she disappeared.

"Where is she?" Clinton screamed and shoved me into the street.

Instincts took over. My hands ignited in fireballs. I turned to face the detective. His face went from stone to melting ice the moment he saw me. He took a step back, hands in the air.

"Never threaten me. I am not in the mood to deal with your petty crap. Josie is my match and just know that I will raze hell to protect her." I vibrated with rage at the ones who'd taken her and needed an outlet quick before I took it out on this human. "Move. I need to see if I can track her!"

"I'm sorry. Jo's like my little sister." Clinton's eyes dropped as he moved out of my path, letting me pass.

I flicked my hands, extinguishing the flames. Lance stood in the alley looking as fearful as Clinton. I didn't care. I only wanted to find my match. Walking past them, I found my keys laying in the middle of the alley. I picked them up and walked back to the car. Blood was smeared over the window.

I swiped my finger over the tacky crimson liquid and brought it up to my nose and sniffed. Her fear washed over me in an instant. I had to brace myself against the car to keep from falling. She was terrified. The copper tang bit at my tongue as I licked the blood from my finger.

She stopped here, pacing in the alley. He was here... Caleb... He took her...

"Caleb." I spat the blood from my mouth.

"What?" Clinton regained his composure.

"Caleb took her," I said again.

"How? How can you tell?" Clinton asked.

"Magic," Lance answered. "Blood magic is rare. Warren is one of the few warlocks with the ability."

"Can you tell where he took her? Or why?" Clinton stepped closer to the car.

I shook my head. "Caleb's a half demon. He's blocking his intentions from me and has shielded his car." I hung my head. A sharp, searing ache gripped my chest, radiating outward as if my very soul were being ripped apart. My breath came in ragged, uneven gasps, the air heavy with the metallic tang of blood and the faint, acrid scent of burning magic. Unable to contain the storm surging inside me, my fist lashed out, slamming into the car window.

The glass shattered instantly, exploding outward in a chaotic spray of jagged shards. Tiny fragments sparkled in the dim alley light as they fell, catching the faint glow of a nearby streetlamp. Warm blood trickled down my knuckles, mixing with the crimson streaks already staining the window from her. The sharp sting of the cuts was barely noticeable beneath the all-consuming fire raging in my chest.

The mixture of our blood shimmered unnaturally as it hit the shards on the ground, a sudden pulse of raw energy coursing through it. A low hum built in the air, growing louder with every passing second until it was deafening. Sparks erupted from the dashboard of the car, crackling violently like miniature bolts of lightning.

Then, without warning, an explosion of light detonated from inside the vehicle. It was blinding, a white-hot burst that engulfed the alley in an instant, forcing me to shield my eyes. The force of it threw me backward, and I stumbled, landing hard on the rough asphalt. Heat prickled against my skin, and the echo of the explosion reverberated in my ears like the roar of a tidal wave.

When the brilliance faded, the alley was gone. The world spun violently before settling into something entirely different. I was no longer outside. The cool scent of leather and polished wood enveloped me as I blinked, disoriented. My hand, still slick with blood, rested against the smooth upholstery.

I was sitting in the back of a sleek limo, its plush interior glowing faintly from soft, ambient lighting. The smooth leather beneath me was cool, but I barely registered it. My senses were in overdrive, and everything felt wrong. The air smelled faintly of ozone and something floral, mingling with the metallic tang of my own blood. I couldn't place where I was—everything beyond the confines of the car was a blank void—but one thing was clear: I wasn't alone.

Across from me sat a man with sharp, angular features, his smirk cutting through the tension like a blade. His eyes gleamed with something dark and knowing, a predator's gleam, as he leaned back casually, utterly at ease in the chaos he had no doubt orchestrated. His presence was suffocating, his confidence radiating off him like heat from a furnace.

But there was something else—something faint yet unmistakable. Josie. I could feel her, as though her presence had been stitched into the very fabric of the space around me. It wasn't just her magic, though, that pulsed faintly, erratically, on the edges of my awareness. It was her essence, her very being, tethered to mine like a lifeline in the storm. She was here, somewhere close, and the thought both calmed and terrified me.

"Well," the man drawled, his voice smooth as velvet, yet sharp as a knife. "I see you still can't resist my charm."

The mocking chuckle that followed made my skin crawl. He leaned forward slightly, his piercing gaze locking onto mine as if daring me to make a move.

"Where is she?" I demanded, my voice a growl. My fists clenched, the sting of my earlier injuries forgotten as fury coursed through me. But he wasn't looking at me.. not really. He didn't react to my words or my fists. *I must be connected with Josie, seeing what she sees.*

His smirk widened, his confidence unwavering. "My mistress will be pleased to have both Wolstencrofts caged," he said with dark amusement. "It'll make for a stronger warrior for her."

A cold, twisting fear rooted itself in my chest, but before I could process his words further, her voice pierced through the fog.

"I won't be her warrior," Josie said, her tone steady despite the faint tremor beneath it.

The man, who I now realized must be Caleb, laughed—a cruel, guttural sound that sent a chill racing down my spine. "Not you," he sneered, his disdain dripping from every syllable. "You're far too weak to be a soldier. No, she's creating a new breed of warriors."

Her magic flared faintly in my awareness, her defiance resonating like a distant thunderclap. The bond between us surged, grounding me even as I struggled to comprehend the surreal scene unfolding before me.

The limo blurred, the space folding in on itself as I was yanked back into the cold, unforgiving alley. Reality snapped into place, harsh and unyielding, the smell of oil and asphalt hitting me like a slap.

"I know where he's taking her," I murmured, my voice a harsh rasp as I struggled to steady my breathing. Josie's presence still lingered, a faint beacon guiding me forward. I couldn't see her, but I could feel her. And I wasn't going to stop until I found her.

Twenty-Five

Josie

The leather seat beneath me felt like ice, stiff and unforgiving, but it was nothing compared to the chill running through my veins. My heart pounded so loudly I was sure Caleb could hear it, each beat a deafening reminder of how trapped I was. The soft hum of the limo's engine did little to mask the weight of his presence beside me. He lounged like a predator, his every movement calculated and deliberate, and though he hadn't lain a hand on me yet, the memory of his cruelty coiled tightly in my chest. My palms were slick with sweat, and I clenched them into fists to keep them from shaking. Every second stretched endlessly as I racked my brain for a way out, but the darkness outside the tinted windows only mirrored the hopeless void I felt inside. The faint pulse of my magic flared erratically, a desperate, frightened thing I couldn't control, and I bit down on my lip to keep from crying out. I couldn't let him see my fear, even though it threatened to consume me whole.

Warren's magic surrounded me for a moment, but a moment was all I needed to know he would save me. Even after the words I'd said to him. My throat constricted at the thought of losing him. I couldn't separate the magic from my feelings, but it didn't matter. I knew with every fiber of my being that it would practically kill me to lose him. But in that single instant, our minds made a connection, and I knew I would never have to face that fear.

He was coming for me.

"We're here," my demon of an ex said.

The car slowed to a stop, and someone opened the door from the outside. I glared at Caleb, not daring to move. With a flick of his finger, a force shoved me down to my back on the seat. I tried to sit up and scream, but I couldn't move and couldn't make any sound. My eyes burned and tears fell automatically. I couldn't move, at least not on my accord. It was as if a shield surrounded me, guiding me in the one direction I didn't want to go.

His magic pulled me out of the car. An old run down factory stood in front of me and a shiver ran down my spine. I could only assume somewhere inside was the ancient vampire bartender we had sent in to spy for us. Two broad vampires stood on either side of a peeling blue door. Momentarily free from Caleb's control, I stepped back—a lame attempt to escape—and hit something solid.

Caleb's thin fingers wrapped around my waist, sliding under my shirt. "Don't worry, my dear. They won't bite..." He chuckled into my ear.

His hands urged my feet forward like a puppeteer orchestrating his marionette across the stage. Every step I took was not my doing, but his. My arm's hung loosely at my sides. The night air was warm against my skin, yet the surrounding atmosphere sent chills down my spine.

The vampire opened the door without looking at us. I stood frozen in place, digging deep, and fought his control with everything I could. Still, I could not run. My feet planted in front of the threshold refused to move.

Caleb pressed into my back, wrapping his arms tight around me. "Awe come on, babe. You know how much fun I can be. You stop struggling and I'll make you enjoy this," he purred, nuzzling against my neck.

My stomach curdled at his words. I remembered being tied to the bed against my will. I remembered being put in my place when out with our friends. A wife is to be seen, not heard. I remembered all the terrible nights I'd tried to say no, but he'd "convinced" me, anyway. My skin itched at the thought. His fingertips moved lower, sliding inside my pants. I took the step through the door on my own.

He followed quickly behind me, tucking his hand into the back pocket of my jeans. I cringed inwardly, but hardened my nerves and leaned into him. If I was going to survive this, I needed to fake cooperation. He pulled me closer. I could smell the spicy tang of him. Despite all the bad, there were some good moments. I would hold on to those memories to keep pretending. I had to hold on long enough for Warren to find a way to save me.

Together, we ventured further inside. The factory floor stretched out before us, barren and lifeless, stripped of machinery and any signs of activity—except for the faint scurrying of rats in the shadows. Dust coated every inch of the place, causing my nose to tickle, but I couldn't rub it with Caleb at my side. The emptiness felt oppressive, the silence broken only by the soft echo of our footsteps. I couldn't make sense of it; there was nothing here, no indication of where we were heading or why.

He led us to a set of stairs that plunged into the earth. I gulped hard before descending. Basements meant no simple escape, and I only saw the one set of stairs: One way in or out. The air grew colder and stale as we reached the bottom. The coppery bite was thick the farther we walked.

"First, we will meet the mistress, and if she allows it, you can stay with me in my quarters. Much better than the cages." He leaned in, kissing my neck.

The halls were all painted a dark shade of red and were much cleaner than upstairs. But still, the lingering stench of death hung over me. I was in a vampire's lair. Back when I was in school, I had longed for a sexy vampire to come swoop me off my feet and we'd live happily ever after. This was not that at all: there was nothing romantic about these vampires.

Down the hall, two more stiff vampires guarded another door. They stepped aside as we approached. Caleb knocked, then pulled me tighter against him, giving my butt a squeeze through my pants. I swallowed the vomit crawling up my throat. "Don't worry. Stick close to me and keep quiet. I know you know how to be a good girl." He squeezed harder. I stared at the door, not even wanting to breathe.

"Enter," came a female voice from inside.

The door creaked open, and we stepped inside. My breath caught as my eyes landed on the first face I saw—Sam's. He sat on a massive four-poster bed against the far wall, completely naked. For a brief moment, pain flickered across his features before he replaced it with a scowl, his expression radiating annoyance, as if we'd interrupted something. Heat flushed my cheeks, and I quickly averted my gaze, my heart racing.

I scanned the room, desperate for a distraction, searching for the woman who might have been with him. The room was enormous, almost cavernous, with walls painted such a deep shade of purple they were nearly black. The color seemed to absorb the dim light, casting long shadows that crept along the floor like living things.

Before I could take in anything else, the woman who spoke was in front of us. She was tiny even compared to me, but her curvy features put me to shame. I'd say she was gorgeous... until she smiled. Sharp fangs projected down past her red lips.

"Oh, my pet, you have returned. And you brought me a new morsel? Is this...?" she sang.

"It is. Jo, this is our queen, Jemisha. Jemisha, this is Josefina Wolsteincroft." Caleb pushed me forward half a step, forcing me to bow to the vampire.

She circled me. I stood like a statue while she scrutinized me. She smacked the pocket that Caleb's hand was in and he quickly removed it. She moved back around to face me.

"She is attractive. I understand why you wanted her. If she cooperates, you can have her."

"Thank you, my queen." Caleb turned to leave.

"Not so fast. I said if she cooperates. First, take her to the lab."

I felt Caleb stiffen at her words. "Yes, my queen." He gripped me by the upper arm and dragged me out of the room.

He didn't loosen his grip until we were down the hallway, and even then he wasn't gentle. We walked and walked. I doubted we were still under the factory. Left turn. Right turn. Straight ahead. They had created their own elaborate catacombs under the city. And I found myself trapped in them.

After what felt like an hour, Caleb finally slowed his pace. A bright light shone ahead of us, pouring from an open doorway. He guided me inside without a care for the bruise now forming on my arm from his hand. He released me, and I dropped to the floor.

"Once they are done with you, I will retrieve you. If there's anything left of you, I will carve out what you owe me for leaving me." His voice dripped with malaise. He slammed the door behind him without another word.

I sat there, refusing to cry, no matter how much I wanted to. *Warren's coming for me. I have to be strong.* I stood and took in my surroundings. It was a small room with one door. Nothing special. Nothing I'd call a lab. I waited.

My legs ached when someone finally walked through the other door. The woman was tall and skinny. Threads of brown hair peeked out from under her surgical cap. She wore green scrubs and a white coat. She was looking at a clipboard in the doorway. If I weren't in a vampire's lair, I'd say she was a doctor. When she finally raised her eyes, I saw her red gaze staring at me.

"You Jo?" she asked.

"Yes, ma'am." Something about her demeanor made me want to be proper.

"Good. This way, please."

I followed her through the door and down the hall. Everything gleamed white. She led me through another door to a small room. At first glance, the chair in the middle of the room resembled a dentist chair, with restraints...

I stopped cold.

With a hiss, the woman shoved me into the chair and two assistants I hadn't noticed strapped me in. Thick leather held my head, wrists, and ankles in place. I tried to struggle, but it was hopeless. The binds that held me down were too tight.

The woman hovered above me with a needle thick enough to make a horse cringe. The green liquid in the syringe resembled curdled milk.

"Hold still. It'll be easier." She plunged the needle into my chest.

Twenty-Six

Sam

I paced in Jemisha's room as acid boiled in my gut. They took my best friend's girl, and I could only watch helplessly as they did God knew what to her. Reaching into my pocket, I pulled out the small earpiece Tanner had given me and whispered into the mic. "Tanner? Warren? Anyone?" Then I placed it in my ear, waiting for a response.

"I'm here, Sam." His voice came almost immediately, and I breathed a sigh of relief.

"Tanner." I sat on the edge of the bed. "They have Jo. Some cambion brought her in. I assume that was her ex?"

"I think so. Warren's a mess," Tanner said.

"I have to get her out of here."

"You have to figure out what they're doing. Where's the queen, anyway?"

"She left after Jo. She said they were taking her to some lab and she wanted to watch. I tried to go with her, but she wouldn't let me." I rubbed at my temples. "It's my fault."

"How?"

"I should have killed Jemisha centuries ago." Saying those words out loud made me sick. I'd loved her once and some part of me still wanted to save her, even knowing what kind of woman she was.

"If it wasn't her, it would be someone else. At least with it being her, we had an in with you. We can stop her together." His magic surrounded me like a blanket, wrapping me in his presence.

I jumped up at the sensation. "What was that?" I asked.

"I-I don't know?" His voice shook.

"You felt it too?"

"It was like you were right here for a moment."

"But that only can happen with ma—"

The door swung open and Jemisha strode inside.

"Who are you talking to, my love?" She wrapped her arms around my neck, pulling me down.

I hardened my gaze as I spoke. "I was debating on taking a hot shower. After all the lovemaking we've done, I feel filthy." I forced my lips to hers before pulling out of her grasp and walking toward the bathroom.

"I could join you," she proposed.

"That would defeat the purpose of the shower and we'd never get clean," I called, not daring to glance at her before shutting the door to the bathroom.

Leaning against the door, I clutched at my chest.

"I don't think she noticed," Tanner said in my ear. "But you better get rid of the earpiece, just in case."

I nodded my agreements and reached for it.

"I'll still be here for you, Sam."

His words comforted me as I pulled my only line of communication out of my ear and crushed it between my fingers. The excuse of a shower did sound comforting, so I flicked on the water and waited for it to warm up. When the steam billowed out from behind the doors, I stripped out of my pants and stepped into the cascade.

I let the tiny pieces of broken plastic and wires drop to the floor and watched as they circled the drain. I was officially on my own.

My body sank to the floor as the water rushed over my back. I'd been on my own for so long that I should have been used to it, but I was struggling with the weight of solitude now. It wasn't just that I was alone, but that I had a mission and no backup.

Warren was cut off from me, his steady presence severed—a lifeline I hadn't realized I'd come to depend on. The emptiness where our connection had been was a gaping void, a cold reminder that I was utterly alone. Worse, I'd just destroyed the only link to Tanner, the last fragile thread that might have anchored me to some semblance of hope.

I hugged my knees to my chest, my body trembling as I tried to hold myself together. My breath came in shallow gasps, the air feeling too thick, too suffocating. The Blood Beast stirred within me, a dark, relentless force clawing at my sanity. Warren had been the only one who could keep it at bay, his magic a soothing balm that held back the storm. Without him, the beast surged closer to the surface, whispering promises of power and vengeance that made my stomach churn with equal parts fear and temptation.

Tears blurred my vision as I rocked slightly, gripping my knees tighter. I was on the edge, teetering dangerously close to giving in to the beast's seductive pull. Its hunger gnawed at me, a primal force that promised release from the pain, the emptiness, the crushing weight of failure. But I couldn't—I wouldn't let it win. Not yet.

I buried my face in my knees, forcing the tears back, willing myself to focus. I had to fight it, had to find some way to keep going. For Tanner. For Warren. For myself. Even if I didn't know how.

No. I spoke to him. *I won't let you take over again.*

'I'm here for you, Sam.' Tanner's voice echoed in my head. 'I won't let you fall into blood lust either.'

'T-Tanner?' I thought to him.

'Sam?' His voice sounded as shocked as my own.

'How? How can I hear you?' I checked my ear to make sure I had destroyed the earpiece. 'Is it your magic doing it?' I asked.

'No. I was thinking—'

'What?' I stood, letting the water run down my back. 'What were you thinking?'

'About what would happen if I lost you,' he whispered.

My heart pumped faster.

'Then I heard your fears of what you used to be as if you spoke them to me,' he continued. 'I wanted to remind you that you weren't alone and then I heard you.'

'Telepathy communication only happens if you have that magic or with your match. I'm not a warlock,' I reminded him.

'I know you're not a warlock and that vampires don't believe in one true mate, but...' When I didn't respond, he continued. 'When you smashed the earpiece, it was as if you had smashed my heart. I... My chest aches and all I can think about is you. I've been sitting in this van a block away since you went in and the thought of leaving tears at me. But now... It's taking all my strength to not rush in after you.'

My heart called out to his, the pull undeniable and constant—a steady ache that I couldn't shake no matter how much I tried. It wasn't just attraction or infatuation. It was something deeper. Something primal. And yet, as much as I felt it, as much as I couldn't deny that I cared deeply for Tanner too, the concept of him being my soulmate felt impossible.

I hardly knew him. Our only in person interaction was him outside the warehouse pretending to be homeless to give me the mic I'd just smashed. The only other interactions we'd had were through the speaker and mic for the past few days. How could such a thin connection create the foundation of something as monumental as a soulmate bond? It didn't make sense, and my mind wrestled with the absurdity of it, even as my heart argued otherwise.

Vampires outlived every other creature in this world, an unending existence that defied the natural order. Could someone like me, someone who'd walked through centuries, truly be tied to just one other being for all eternity? What if it was a mistake? What if the connection was one-sided, a cruel trick of fate? Tanner barely knew me, and I barely knew him.

The rational part of me struggled to reconcile the idea of a soulmate with the cold reality of my nature. I'd loved before, deeply and passionately, but I'd also lost. I knew what it was to bury a piece of myself with someone I cared for. The thought of tethering my heart to someone again terrified me. And yet, the bond I felt to Tanner wasn't something I could easily ignore or rationalize away.

I clenched my fists, frustrated at my own thoughts. This wasn't supposed to happen. Soulmates were for poets and dreamers, not for creatures like me. But no matter how hard I tried to push the idea away, I couldn't shake the feeling that maybe—just maybe—Tanner was the exception to every rule I thought I knew.

'Tanner, I—'

"Samuel," Jemisha's voice sang from the other room. "My love, I'm bored."

I cringed. Bored to Jemisha usually led to foul things I no longer had any desire to do.

'Go. Do what you need to do to come back to me,' Tanner said.

'I can't. Not now...' Guilt built up in my gut.

'But she'll kill you if she knows. So go. I'll be right here in your mind whenever you need me.' He didn't speak again, but I sensed his presence as I stepped out of the shower and into the room where the vampire queen waited for me.

Twenty-Seven

Warren

I was going to owe Clinton and Vanessa new carpeting from the circular track my angst had created in their basement. Someone had taken my match and there was nothing I could do to get her back. Not alone, at least. And yet, we hadn't prepared for war.

So I continued to pace, unsure of what else to do with my pent up energy. I wanted to unleash my magic, but I knew that would only wreak havoc.

A throat cleared, and I jumped upon finding Vanessa standing behind me.

"Sorry," I said, "did you say something?"

"Yes, I asked you several times if you were hungry. I've made dinner." She pointed to the stairs and my eyes followed her gesture. One of her children peeked his head out from the first floor. "The kids would love to have you sit down and eat with them."

I knew she was trying to distract me from my grief, and I sighed, dragging my feet to the stairs, following her up to the dining room. Three small children sat anxiously waiting with their hands on their laps. Clinton sat at the head of the table and Vanessa took her chair at the other end of the table and gestured for me and to sit beside the smallest of the children.

A plate of sliced meatloaf sat at the center of the table, along with mashed potatoes, gravy, corn on the cob, and green beans. I sat and pulled in my chair. "This looks delicious," I told her. "Thank you."

"The kids helped," she said proudly. And all three of her children sat up straight, beaming ear to ear.

I grinned and flicked my wrist. The food rose from the serving dishes, swirling around the air before landing on each of their plates. Their eyes went wide with wonderment and their jaws dropped. For a moment, a tiny piece of my heart lightened at the joy on their faces, but it was fleeting. My Josie would've loved to see their smiles, too.

I kept a grin plastered to my face for the kids' sakes. We hadn't told them yet that Josie was missing, only that I was a friend helping their father with a case, which wasn't entirely a lie, but there was no need for them to worry about their aunt.

I ate in silence, listening to the family talk as though nothing was wrong, going about their everyday life.

The kids had been to the park, and they told many stories of playing pretend—of the dragons they'd fought off and the demons they'd slayed. But my own demons still needed to be defeated, riddling my heart.

I forced the food down, not because it was tasteless, but because how could I possibly eat, how could I possibly go on, knowing they had Josie trapped and, for all I knew, tortured for only God knew what purpose.

We had to figure out what the vampires were doing and why. Not sit around the house doing nothing.

Three days. Three days without a word from Sam. The emptiness stretched out endlessly, each second a relentless reminder of how little control I had over the situation. My fingers tapped absently against the table, a restless rhythm that matched the frantic whirl of my thoughts.

The stillness of the house was suffocating. The faint ticking of the clock on the wall grated against my nerves; every tick was a countdown, though to what, I didn't know. The not knowing—that was the worst part. Was Sam hurt? Was he trapped? And what about Josie? Was he not contacting me because she was already gone? My mind conjured a hundred grim scenarios, each more vivid than the last, and I could do nothing to stop them.

I ran a hand through my hair, leaning forward until my elbows rested on the table. My head sank into my hands, and for a moment, I let the weight of it all press down on me. Three days without news, without a sign, without her. My chest tightened, the ache spreading with each breath, and I clenched my jaw to hold it together.

I sat staring at the plate for a long moment before Clinton finally spoke. "Come with me," he said, and I looked up at him. All five of them were watching me wide-eyed.

"What?" I finally said.

"Just put the fork down and come with me, Warren." Clinton's voice was almost brotherly.

I set the fork down, scooted out from the table, and followed him to the front door.

"You need to get out of here," he said, when we were out of earshot of the family.

"Why do you say that?" I asked, slightly defensively.

"Because you were staring at that plate for ten minutes. Vanessa called your name about five times."

"Oh," I said, staring at my feet.

"Jo's been like a little sister since we met in college. I can't imagine what you're going through. If someone ever did anything to hurt Vanessa or one of my kids, I would probably forget that I've been a cop my whole life.

"I know there's not much we can do for her now, but why don't you relieve Tanner? He's been there for a week, and I don't think he's left that van. I think he could use a shower and a good night's sleep. So why don't you watch over the warehouse?"

He handed me a set of keys, and it took me a moment to realize they were my own. I shook my head as I reached for them.

"You're probably right," I admitted. "Thank you. Thank you for everything that you've done." I turned the knob and walked out into the night.

WHEN I REACHED THE VAN. TANNER REFUSED TO LEAVE, SO instead I sat with him and watched over things while he slept.

I saw the truth in Tanner's eyes the moment he told me he thought Sam was his match. It was so rare for warlocks to have a match outside their own race, but Sam had been my friend for generations, and I hoped Tanner was right.

He slept fitfully and woke only a few hours after I had arrived.

"Do you wanna talk about it?" I asked.

"Do you?" He retorted.

"Fair point." I said, and we sat in silence, watching the monitors the police had placed around the building. Vampires walked the perimeter. Some came in, some went out. But no sign of Josie or Sam or anything amiss.

Twenty-Eight
Sam

Josie's face haunted me over the next week. I knew asking to see her would raise suspicion—I had to tread lightly here—but I also knew what she meant to Warren. I owed the man my life. I had to get to Josie.

Jemisha's room was suffocating, its opulence a prison of silk and shadow. The guards stationed outside watched my every move with hawk-like precision, their eyes a constant reminder of the invisible chains binding me. Jemisha kept me here, a tool for her whims, a pawn in her game. But tonight, while she was away, I would break those chains—if only for a moment. I had to know if she was still alive.

I waited, my body tense, until the guards' footsteps echoed down the hall, fading into the distance. This was my chance. I slipped through the door, easing it shut without a sound, and stepped into the dark corridor. The contrast was jarring; the bright glow of Jemisha's gilded room left my vision swimming in the shadows. I paused, blinking rapidly, willing my eyes to adjust.

The air was cooler here, the damp scent of the factory's underbelly creeping in. I ran my hand along the smooth wall, letting its texture guide me. Each step was careful, deliberate.

At the corner, I hesitated, my pulse pounding in my ears. To the right were the stairs leading back toward the factory floor—and the guards. Left was uncharted territory, deeper into the maze of hallways and secrets. I turned left, the sound of my own breathing too loud in the oppressive silence.

The floor beneath my bare feet was cold, each step a sharp reminder of how exposed I was. My fingers skimmed the wall, searching for anything—a doorway, a sign, a clue. The hall stretched on, the faint glow of distant lights casting long, eerie shadows.

I stopped at the sound of muffled voices ahead, pressing myself flat against the wall. My heart thundered as I strained to listen. The words were indistinct, distorted by the distance, but the tone was harsh, commanding. I crept closer, careful not to make a sound, my senses on high alert.

I had to find her. I had to know Jemisha hadn't broken her yet. Every fiber of my being screamed at me to keep moving, to find answers, but the weight of what I might discover threatened to crush me. Still, I pressed on.

My eyes slowly regained their sight. The long corridor held many doors. I tried the first one. Locked. I concentrated my senses on the room. No heartbeat or scent of blood. I kept moving, investigating in each room with my ears and nose. I found nothing in that first hall.

Making a right turn, I continued to explore the compound. I was so focused on the rooms that I didn't sense her until I nearly ran into her. The ever-present stench of death overwhelmed me. I quickly reined in my senses before I gagged.

"Jemisha," I started in surprise.

"My pet. What are you doing out of my room?" She ran her finger down my chest. "I was about to come play."

With a roll of my eyes, I batted her hand away. "I'm bored, I needed to walk." I spoke as nonchalantly as possible, even though the voice in my head was screaming at me to run. But I was the Blood Beast. Jemisha needed me, and I'd make her work for it.

"You're... bored?" She stepped back, placing a hand on her chest. "Well, I apologize, sire, for not entertaining you enough." She gave me a mock bow. "What is it you wish of me, your highness? I could always bring another man into our bed. If I recall correctly, you seem to enjoy men as well?" Her voice was icy.

My thoughts raced to Tanner before I could stop myself. Even though I hadn't known him long, I knew without a doubt that I wanted no one other than him, but I had to push him out of my mind to keep him safe from Jemisha.

"I do," I said, pushing past her before she could sense my emotions, and walked on. "Staying locked up in that room is not an option for me. I am not your pet. Having lived in solitude for a considerable time, I can easily survive on my own again."

Her sigh of defeat made me grin. I hated reverting to the old me, but it came so naturally. I heard her feet turn and her steps hurry to catch up to me. "Very well. I won't keep you locked up anymore. From now on you may be at my side. We will rule this world together. Is that a more entertaining prospect for you?"

In answer, I reached over and wrapped her arm in mine. She stank of blood, but I smiled down at her, anyway. She smiled back and squeezed my arm as we walked.

"Do you know where you're going?" she asked after a long moment.

"I am simply walking with a beautiful lady."

"How about I show you something? I need to check in with the doctors anyway, and since you want to be more involved, you might as well come with me."

Doctors? What in the world does she need with doctors? "Sounds delightful." I kept my face stone. I was finally going to get some answers.

We walked for a long time, turning left, then right. The scope of this place baffled me. She guided me down one last hall and into a small room. The brightness burned my eyes. She walked up to the only other door in the room and knocked three times.

Within moments, it opened, and an average-looking vampire wearing hospital scrubs stood in the doorway, wide-eyed and shivering. "M-my queen," she stuttered, then bowed. "What brings you here today?"

"I have come to check on your progress and show my partner the operation."

The doctor bowed again and held the door open, guiding us inside. Surrounding the desk area in the center were rooms. The girl led us toward a hall on the far side of the desks.

"We were about to start a procedure in the surgical suite. If you'd like to watch in the observation room?" the doctor prompted.

"Delightful," Jemisha answered.

We walked further before the doctor lead us into a small room with chairs in front of a massive window. I tried to keep my heartbeat steady as I turned to look into the surgical room.

Warren's match sat strapped into a chair surrounded by masked vampires. Her eyes were wide, silently pleading with me. I couldn't react. I had to repeat this fact in my head. Jemisha's presence made it impossible for me to send any strength to her through my magic.

I sat next to my enemy and did my best to smile at her. The doctor left and two nurses returned with her. My heart raced as I watched on, helpless. They injected Josie with vile after vile of liquid and drew so much blood it surprised me they hadn't killed her. They huddled in a corner and discussed, studied the computer screen, and started the process all over again.

Glancing over at Jemisha, she was biting her lip, drawing blood. Her eyes soaked in every detail of what they were doing to Jo, and I was sure she was getting off on it. My stomach churned, and I had to look away from her enjoyment.

Jo's color drained and the fight in her diminished the longer we sat there. Bile rose in my throat. They were killing her slowly, and while I was strong enough to kill them all right there and take Jo and run, that would defeat the purpose of me being here. Jemisha was never smart enough to act alone, and I had to get to the bottom of her plans. I had no choice but to watch the torture unfolding in front of me.

Only when Josie passed out did they stop probing her. They cleaned her up and scrubbed the room before they dragged her limp body out of it. My legs burned to follow them, but I stayed planted in my seat.

Finally, the doctor from before came in and sat next to us. "It might not have seemed like it, but it was productive. We are narrowing in on the genes that give her magic like no other warlock. Her brother is stronger, so we might have better luck with him."

"Are they your only subjects?" I asked.

"We have others, but none like them," Jemisha's cold voice said.

"What happens to her now?" I tried to sound indifferent.

The doctor glanced at Jemisha, who nodded. "We will give her some magic to heal and rest, and we will try again tomorrow. This is the fourth testing we have done on her. Each time she gets weaker, but we feel we can push her a little longer before she succumbs completely."

"Very well. Thank you." Jemisha stood.

I gulped. I have to get her out of here and soon! Taking Jemisha's arm, I stood up and left the lab. My blood ran cold at the thought of leaving Josie and the others there alone, but I needed to get them all out.

I steadied my voice before I spoke. "Jemisha, darling, I think I need a night out. To hunt like the old days."

"Oh, that sounds fun. Might I join you?"

"You know I do my hunting alone." My voice hardened.

"Umf. I will miss you. You promise to return before morning?"

I slammed her into the wall, lifting her by her butt to my face. My fingers dug into her skin. I leaned in, kissing her neck. She moaned. My lips found hers and I plunged my tongue into her mouth. As quickly as I had pinned her down, I walked away. I had to get out before I vomited.

Twenty-Nine

Warren

I paced the tiny living room, trying not to trip on the toys. Clinton told me he "couldn't trust that I wouldn't do something stupid" and between him, Lance, and Tanner, they'd all forced me to stay with him and his wife until we decided what to do next. It had been a week. I hardly slept. Hardly ate. Despite Nessa's many attempts to mother me, I just couldn't.

Screams from upstairs interrupted my thoughts, and on instinct, I ran toward the sounds. Vanessa was struggling to get the youngest into his pajamas.

"I don't wanna!" he shrieked. "I'm not tired," he said with a yawn.

She yanked the shirt from his head and tossed it to the floor. "Fine. Sleep naked. I don't care..."

The kid made a face behind her back. I couldn't help but chuckle. She turned and glared at me. I've faced down demons, vampires, and werewolves with minimal fear, but her expression terrified me.

"Think it's funny? Been fighting with him all day and I'm done." She picked up the shirt and stood. "I'd like to see you do better." She shoved the kid's pj's into my hand. I picked them up with two fingers and held it out. The boy glanced at me and I grinned.

I dropped the shirt, yet it still hung in the air. Their youngest boy, Finn, audibly gasped. He stood and walked around it, searching for the trick. I spun my finger, and the shirt followed. It danced around the kid and he giggled. It hovered just above his head. He raised his arms and let the shirt fall over him.

He ran over to his mom, kissing her cheek before running to me and wrapping his arms around my neck.

"You gonna be Aunt Jo's new husband? The last one was bad. But I like you." He untangled himself from me and crawled into bed before I could respond.

I turned and saw Nessa standing in the doorway with a grin on her face. She shook her head at me as I walked past her. I headed back down the stairs to resume my pacing. She followed.

"You have a way with kids. You ever have any?" she asked when we got back downstairs.

"No. We can't have kids with just anyone. I thought—hoped... but..."

"Don't. Don't you dare give up on her now. I've known Jo since we were three years old. There ain't no one stronger than that girl. To deal with her ex and now all this... She's gonna be just fine." Her tone did not match the confidence of her words. Her face had grown gaunter in just the few days I'd been here. I knew she wasn't eating or sleeping either. *She knows more than she was telling me... I think I prefer it that way.*

"It's... they're doing something to the kids that they've stolen." I nodded over toward her husband, who sat at the table hovering over his laptop. "They need her for something but—"

DING DONG. The front door bell made me jump. All three of us exchanged glances.

DING DONG. Clinton rose and went to the door. His hand rested on the hilt of his holstered gun. He opened it a crack, keeping his foot on the door's edge.

"Yes?" he asked.

"It's Sam."

I breathed a sigh of relief. Clinton opened the door fully. My old friend stepped into the living room, looking as worn and ragged as I felt. Without a second thought, I wrapped my arms around him in a tight embrace. "We thought you were dead. How'd you get here?"

"No. She's kept me as her pet, though, so I kinda wish I were. Tanner called me an Uber. Jemisha's only now let me see into her plans a bit. I... I..." He wobbled on his feet.

I guided him to the couch, where he slumped down. He was pale and a little green.

"When was the last time you fed?" I asked.

"I have been avoiding it as much as possible there. You know how they are."

"You can't starve either. Did you at least stop at your place first?"

"Tanner told me where you were. I came straight here. I need to talk to you and get back before sunrise."

"You need to feed. I can call Tanner and have him bring you something."

"He doesn't have the time, by the looks of him." Nessa walked over, watching Sam swaying on his feet. "Hi, Sam. I'm Nessa. I'm Jo's best friend. Thank you for helping them. Now I can help you." I hadn't noticed the knife in her hand until she sliced through her arm. Sam jumped back with a hiss.

"No, I-I can't..."

"You need blood or you'll get sick or die, right? You won't kill me if you don't drain me. And you won't turn me?" She regarded me in question.

I shook my head. "It's more complicated than the teen books say." I turned back to my friend. "Her safety is my priority, so I will not allow you to harm her. I'd do it myself if my blood wouldn't kill you." I reached for Nessa's bleeding arm and pulled her closer. Clinton's hand was back on his sidearm. He stood at the bottom of the stairs.

Sam shifted his gaze from me to Nessa and back. I lifted her arm to his face and nodded. He finally took her wrist in his hands and lowered his mouth to her flesh. "I'm sorry," he whispered.

She shoved her arm against his lips. He bit down and drank. She hardly made a sound, but her face scrunched in pain. There was nothing seductive about a vampire's bite. It was a necessity. His color returned as he drank.

"Sam. That's enough. She hasn't eaten much either." I spoke after a moment. "Sam," I said louder when he didn't stop.

His eyes flicked up to mine. They glowed blood red. I let my magic loose and touched his shoulder. His eyes calmed and slowly he released her arm. He wiped his chin before saying, "Thank you."

I handed her off to her husband. "Make her eat something. Chocolate, the darker, the better, and some orange juice." He nodded and walked her into the dining room.

I sat beside Sam. "Now, what's happening?"

"I don't know everything, not a lot, but they are injecting them with all sorts of stuff and testing their blood. They are trying to find the genes that make the Figli Del Mito what they are. I... she forced me to watch. I'm sorry, Warren, I couldn't stop... It was Josie. They said Rocky's stronger and they are going to keep testing him."

I shook my head. "Josie's not..."

"No! She's fine... well, as okay as she can be. They are healing them after and letting them rest, but still... I'm not sure how much longer she can last."

"We need a plan. We have to get them all out of there, and soon." Clinton rejoined us. "But I'm sorry, Sam, we need you to go back. Let me get you a new earpiece?"

He nodded his head. Clinton walked back to the table and pulled something out of his bag. He handed Sam the new receiver. "Take this. Keep it in your pocket if you're not alone. Let us know when you can talk and we will keep you updated. He set a pad of paper and pen on the coffee table. "Any layouts you can remember will help. When you're done, I'll drop you off in town."

Sam took the pen and wrote everything he had seen while there.

It was nearly dawn when Clinton and Sam stood to head back into town. Sam glanced back at me before they left.

"If-if something happens... Tell Tanner..." Tears welled up in his eyes.

"I will."

Sam nodded and walked out with Clinton.

I laid my head down on the end of the couch and let myself hope, if only for a moment, that everything would be alright.

Thirty

Josie

My body ached. Every movement sent pain shooting down my spine. My breaths were shallow. The simple act of taking a full breath felt like an elephant sitting on my chest. I lay curled on a cot in the corner of my room. I was too tired to even cry. Yet sleep eluded me.

I wouldn't survive many more sessions with the good doctor. I wanted to scream, to claw my way through the door, but I couldn't even heal the puncture wounds that remained on my body. I'd meet my end in this place, and the last words I'd uttered to my match accused him of enchanting me into love.

I'd been wrong. He was far away from me, yet I could still feel him. Our souls had a connection. His worry seeped into me—flashes of anger and rage mixed with moments of deep sorrow. Emotions I knew weren't mine filled me. I was exhausted, both physically and mentally. I wanted it all to end.

I rolled over, groaning, and stared up at the ceiling. They had painted the concrete walls a taupe shade. A solid metal door stood between me and freedom. Not to mention the vampire on the other side. The rest of the room was bare, but at least it was clean. They were big on cleanliness around here.

When my ex had first brought me here, they had stripped me down and given me a thorough scrubbing. My skin was raw and bright red by the time they'd dressed me in scrubs. A chill ran down my back at the thought. They'd regarded me as if I were simply a piece of new equipment, not a human with actual emotions.

Slowly, I rolled back over to my side and tucked my knees to my chest. I begged sleep to come, but every time I closed my eyes, her face hovered above me. The doctor who had seemed so sweet the first time I met her was far from a good person. She put on this air of doing "God's work." Whatever god they worshiped... I didn't dare to explore that thought deeper. Her self-righteous attitude would piss me off in the real world, but here, it terrified me. She would kill without batting an eye because she was doing what she thought was right. I didn't know her end goals, but still... This woman—vampire—would stop at nothing until she found what she was looking for. I'd be dead by then, though. Tears leaked from my eye, running across the bridge of my nose.

'Jo? Jo, can you hear me?' A voice spoke in my head, causing me to jerk up in bed, instantly regretting the quick movement. I doubled over, retching on the floor. I could have sworn... but no, I couldn't have. 'Yes, Miss C., you heard me. It's Rocky. We can project thoughts to each other because of who and what we are.'

'Wait, you know?' I felt foolish, hoping he could actually hear me.

'Yes, I've known since before I came to your school. Father sent me.' Rocky's voice echoed in my head.

'But... your father's...'

'He was your father, too. You can't see him still?'

'See him? He's dead...' My thoughts came out harsher than I meant to.

'I know he is; I saw it happen. I can see the dead and I assumed you could too.' His voice sounded more gloomy than the sweet kid I remembered.

'There's nothing special about me. I didn't even know what I was until after you went missing... Wait, backup, you can see ghosts?' I rubbed at my temples.

'That's how I knew who you were. Father came to me and said you needed me.'

'Uhm.' I scoffed in my head. 'And here I thought I was taking care of you.'

'I chose to be in that house to keep the others safe. No child should ever deal with parents like them.'

'You're a good kid, Rocky.'

His laugh echoed in my head. 'I might be a kid, but I've seen far more than any normal eighteen-year-old has ever seen.'

'Wha-what do you mean?'

'Before their deaths, we traveled the world. I've known what I was since I was a baby. Others have been hunting us most of my life.' His voice shifted and the bitterness of an old man emanated from my little brother.

I sat there, dumbfounded, for a long moment. I didn't know what to think, let alone say. The student I had been so worried about over the past six months was not only my brother, but had encountered far more trauma than any one person should have to endure. My heart ached to hug him, but I had no idea where he even was.

'I don't need your pity, but your help. We need to get a message out because I know what she's planning. Can you connect to Warren?'

The anger in his voice snapped me out of my stupor.

'Warren? How do you know about him?'

'Jo, I'm your brother. I can feel your emotions. And you've basically been screaming for the past hour. He's your match, isn't he?' His voice softened.

'I-I don't know. I'm not sure I understand what that even means. I... I know what I feel and I-I do love him.' The admission lifted a weight off my chest.

'If he is truly your match, you can directly connect with him. You can already feel his emotions, can't you?'

I nodded before realizing he couldn't see me. 'Yeah.'

'When you connect with him, you can see what he sees. It's like an out-of-body experience, but you can give him the information he needs. You can even borrow his magic to give you strength.'

I thought back to the limo ride here. 'Can... can he do that too?'

'Yes.'

'On the way here, I think I felt him. It was a strange tingle. Like a cold chill, but it lasted longer. I felt stronger after.'

'That was probably what happened.'

'But I...' I wrapped my arms around my chest, not willing to admit what I needed to. 'I was horrible to him. Why would he help me?'

'He still loves you, Jo. He helped you then, and he will help us now.'

I focused my energy on my breathing, trying to even it out. *How can I possibly do magic this big? It's been less than a month since I discovered there were more than humans in my world. I can't do this.*

'Yes, you can.' My brother interrupted my thoughts. 'Relax. Think about him. Focus on his features. Did he teach you how to pull things through space to you?'

'Yes.'

'It's kinda like that, but instead of you pulling him to you, you have to pull yourself to him. Use him as an anchor and walk to him.'

'I... I don't think I can.'

'You are stronger and braver than you believe. I trust you, sister.'

'What am I supposed to tell him if I even can connect to him? I don't know what the hell's going on here.'

'No, but I do. They like to talk and they are arrogant. They think I sleep a lot more than I actually do, so I've heard more than they'd like. I'm betting they don't have a clue we can get a message to the outside.'

Rocky spent the next hour—or what felt like an hour—relaying everything he had overheard when they'd thought he was asleep. It was so much information to take in and none of it was pretty. My stomach soured with every word he said. I retched more bile when he finally finished.

I lay back down and let the tears flow. This Jemisha was a small puzzle piece in a much larger picture, but still she was a monster straight out of my nightmares. I wasn't sure if we could defeat her, but we had to try.

'I'm sorry to rest this all on your shoulders, Jo, but you are the only one who can get a message out.'

'What about Sam?' I said, remembering he was here.

'Who's Sam?' Rocky asked.

'He's a vampire friend of Warren's that came here undercover to get information. We could tell him and he could tell the others.'

'Sorry, Jo, I've only seen the doctors. She doesn't allow anyone else inside. If either of us sees him, though, we can tell him. But I need you to connect with Warren. It's our best chance. Please try, Jo.'

'I... I need sleep...' I lied. Yes, I needed sleep, but I doubted it would come. My stomach twisted in knots at the thought of what Warren would say. Would he reject me and leave me here to die? Would he even talk to me?

'Okay. Rest now, but try when you wake up. We need help, Jo. I won't die here and neither will you. You hear me?'

'Yea.' I rolled over and tried to block him out of my head.

'Good night, sister,' Rocky whispered.

A weight settled over me, dragging me under. The doctor's face never appeared. Just total blackness and silence. I slept for the first time in a week.

Thirty-One

Warren

I couldn't sleep. I tossed and turned in the guest bed at Vanessa and Clinton's house. Sitting around doing nothing was never my strong suit.

Josie's sorrow seeped into my soul. I wanted to tear down the walls of the factory and destroy every last vampire in that clan.

The fan spun around and around as I lay on my back, staring at the ceiling. Josie's image would appear every time I closed my eyes, and the torment in her eyes broke me. The thought of her alone and afraid made my blood boil.

'Please,' a tiny whisper fell in my mind. I sat up, looking around. No one else was in the room. I listened for one kid down the hall asking for yet another glass of water. Nothing. The only sounds I heard with my warlock hearing were the in and out of the children's breathing and the snores from Clinton.

'Josie?' I pushed the thought to my match.

No words returned, but I felt her sigh of relief. I lay back down and closed my eyes, drawing her form in my mind. The curve of her hips and the way she placed her hands there when she was mad. I smiled and kissed her below her ear because of the scowl on her face. The scent of her washed over me.

My match's form went from standing in my kitchen with only my shirt covering her to sitting in a chair being stabbed with something. Her face and body were tight. Tears streamed down either side of her face. I gripped the sheets. Without hesitation, I pulled myself to her.

The moment our bodies connected, I felt her pain. Fire ignited within my veins at the new liquid injected into her body. The doctors stood over her with clipboards writing what they saw. Another vial brought ice. I took the brunt of the pain and allowed Josie to breathe easier.

The doctor walked to a phone on the wall and spoke in an eerily excited voice.

"I think she is getting stronger. She isn't fighting as much." She hung up the receiver and walked back to where Josie lay.

'Josie, hold on. We can make it through this. I am coming for you.'

She didn't reply.

'Josie, I love you.' I tried again.

She was still too weak to speak, but I felt her smile.

"And why are you smiling?" the doctor asked her.

She raised her head a fraction of an inch. "Because he is coming... The Mage..."

A flicker of fear crossed the doctor's face before she whispered something to one of the nurses and stormed out of the room. They unstrapped Josie from the chair and hauled her to her feet. I felt her energy drain with every step. I lent her some of mine, helping her back to the cell the doctors called her room.

She collapsed onto the bed and I poured as much magic into her as I could. The fire and ice liquid dripped out of the holes they had stabbed into her as my magic pulsed through her. Slowly, I felt her strength return, allowing her to sit up. She hugged her knees to her chest and wrapping her arms around them.

"Thank you," she whispered into the dark.

'My Josie. I love you. I will watch as every last one of them bakes in the morning sun.'

'I tried to come to you. I couldn't.' Her voice was weak.

'But I heard you. I came for you, my love.'

'Why? Why, after what I said to you, would you come for me?' Her heart was breaking saying the words.

'Because you are my match. Nothing you say or do will ever make me stop loving you. I would raze hell itself for you.'

'But I... I don't...'

'Stop. You deserve love. You deserve love that would stop at nothing to see you happy. I can't promise I am perfect, I know I deserve all the anger you threw at me that day, but I swear to you right here and now that I will find you and I will spend the rest of my existence making up to you. Just please hold on a little longer.'

She nodded her head and hugged her knees tighter.

'I have to go, Josie. I need to wake Clinton and make a plan.'

'Wake Clinton?'

'He insisted I stay with him so I didn't go charging in, but I am coming for you now. Do you hear me?'

'Wait! I need to tell you something. This is so much bigger than Jemisha and the kids. They... They're preparing for war.'

'War? With who?'

'The humans and any faction that sides with them. It's the... the bar... I saw it. Rocky told me Jemisha is working with some supernatural faction that wants to take over the government. She's experimenting on us all in order to create these super soldiers. She already has an army of them, but now that she has us, she wants to take our abilities and create more. After he told me her plans, I-I saw it like I saw what happened to Rocky or what happened when I touched that book, only this time I moved forward in time. It was just like the carvings on your bar. If she figures out how we have the abilities we do and how to extract it, she'll give her soldiers to this faction and they will burn the world. She's close. You have to hurry.' She leaned back against the wall and closed her eyes. Her tears dried and only anger remained on her face.

'I will, my love.'

I pulled my consciousness back to my body. The fan still moved in its never-ending circle above me. I stretched out my aching arms and legs. A gasp from the doorway made me jump out of the bed, and I spun on my heels, ready to fight.

"We thought you were dead! What the hell?" Nessa spoke.

I relaxed slightly. "Sorry, I connected with Josie. I've only seen it once before; it can look freaky."

"Connected?" Clinton asked.

"It's kinda like astral projection. I could see and feel what she felt. My consciousness left my body and joined with hers. So yeah, I probably appeared dead."

"Just glad the kids didn't see it," Nessa said.

"Yeah, sorry about that."

"So? What happened? If you connected with her?" Clinton continued.

I rubbed at my temples. "I think I could use some coffee."

They glared at me.

"Sorry, that took a lot out of me and I haven't slept. Needless to say, we need to make a plan and go in tonight, but I can't do any of that without replenishing my energy and coffee will help. I'll fill you in as it brews."

Nessa nodded and led the way back downstairs to the kitchen. Clinton and I sat at the bar as she made a fresh pot. I told them everything I'd seen and what Josie had told me. I even went into the details of the art on my bar and the seer who'd given it to me.

"The seer told me years ago that I would live to see the events come to pass. I thought she was insane—I never put much stock in seers, but Josie... she saw it too."

"If this queen... Jemisha? If she's creating these genetically enhanced monsters, how are we to stop them?" Nessa asked, handing me a mug of coffee. "And if she's not alone..." She poured herself a mug and sat with us.

"Thanks. I don't know. And I really hate not knowing." I watched the black liquid swirl around in the cup. "We need to do something unprecedented."

"What's that?" Clinton asked.

"We need to unite the Figli Del Mito."

Thirty-Two

Sam

J paced the small room that I'd been calling home. Tanner had contacted me through our bond and relayed the message from Warren about what they'd learned and were planning. My skin crawled at the thought of the woman I had once loved creating such monsters. It boggled my mind to think she wasn't working alone, either. In all my years with her, she'd never once followed another's lead. What had this group offered her? This would not be another war in a long line of human wars... it would annihilate the human race. And then what would the vampires do? I laughed out loud. What was she thinking? If the humans were all dead, how could the vampires survive?

Warren had told me to stay put, but I couldn't. I needed answers. I cracked the door and peered down the hallway. Empty. I stepped out as if I was going nowhere. My hands fiddled with the contents of my pockets as I tried to look casual, but the thrumming of my heart would give me away if I didn't calm down.

Breathe in. Breathe out. I repeated the mantra in my head, even though I didn't need the oxygen to function. The act was grounding—a tether to control the racing of a heart that now pumped venom in lieu of blood. My footsteps echoed in the quiet hall, each sound bouncing back like a reminder of how empty the space was.

But something felt... wrong. The air was thick, oppressive, carrying a weight I couldn't place. It wasn't just my nerves; it was the kind of sensation that prickled at the back of my neck and tightened my chest. I glanced over my shoulder, the shadows stretching longer than they should, but I saw nothing. Still, the unease gnawed at me, a subtle hum in my senses that whispered I wasn't alone.

I shook my head and pushed forward, forcing my focus on the path ahead. Whatever it was, I'd deal with it. I had to.

Jemisha's room stood unguarded, which meant she was elsewhere. Good. Jemisha was always good at keeping secrets, but I had long ago learned her tricks. I took one last look around before unlocking the door with my magic and darting into her room, relocking it behind me.

I let out a long breath. Her room was lavish—as she was in everything—but the hidden door had stood out to me from the very first time I saw it. Her magic concealed it from everyone, but it shimmered in the darkness like a beacon. I strode over to the panel in the wall and pushed it open. A set of stone stairs descended further into the earth. Looking around her bedroom once more, I walked to her bed, knowing she slept with a wooden dagger under the pillow. I grabbed it, tucked it in my pants, and quickly headed back to the stairs. Before I could stop myself, I stepped through the wall door and let it seal closed behind me.

The lower I walked, the mustier the air got, nearly choking me on the dampness. When my foot finally found the bottom, lamps magically lit, and the space opened up into a room lined with desks. I walked from desk to desk, searching through books and notepads that bore centuries' worth of research. The genetic make-up of different magical creatures lay mapped out. My heart sank at the thousands she had murdered in the name of "science."

The table furthest from the stairs held documents of a new breed. A bit of lycanthropy DNA mixed with vampire venom. Another page showed vampire and warlock. Digging through the records, I found only one with traces of all three creatures. I sank down in the chair and stared at the desk. There were hundreds of pages; hundreds of creatures she had created.

"Why, Jemisha? Why?" I whispered to no one.

"Because of you, my love."

I jumped at her words. The papers I held fell to the floor as I kicked over the chair. Jemisha stood not five feet from where I had been sitting. How had I not heard her? She wore a silky red robe. The flaps draped open, revealing the tiny lace covering her body.

"What… what do you mean?" I asked.

"You, my love. This is all your fault." She slowly untied the robe, letting it fall to the floor. My heart stopped. The sheer fabric revealed every bit of her body. I couldn't keep mine from reacting. Her eyes flicked lower and grinned. "You left me broken and lost all those years ago. I've been clawing my way through the ranks of the Corps de l'Ombre ever since, looking for my place in this jacked up world. The Figli Del Mito will rule the world once again and the pathetic humans will grovel at our feet. If you would have stayed with me, maybe I wouldn't be so angry."

I kept my eyes on hers. "How?"

She stepped closer. Her hands trailed up her body. "We have many steps in place to overthrow the humans, but my monsters outshine them all. Once those brats give up their secrets, no one will stand in our way. Everyone has grown too accustomed to living in hiding and it is time we join society. The humans greatly outnumber us, which is why I created my little pets. They can withstand the force of the nation's armies. And once I create more with the Wolfencroft's DNA, we will be unstoppable."

She closed the gap between us. Her hand traveled from my chest to my stomach, pulling a groan from my lips as she stroked me lower. Her fingers grasped the hair at the base of my neck and pulled my face to hers. I kissed her roughly, forcing my tongue into her mouth as my hand wrapped around the hilt of the dagger behind my back.

My other hand grasped her thighs and lifted her tiny frame up. She wrapped her leg around my hips, grinding her core against me. I walked to the table, slamming her down, trailing my lips down her cheek to her neck. My fangs throbbed as I nipped at her. She rocked against me, begging me to take her. I bit down harder until blood erupted from her neck. She gasped and pulled me tighter.

"Please," she begged, her hands fumbling with the clasp of my pants.

"I'm sorry, my love," I whispered as I plunged the wooden dagger up through her ribs and drove it deep into her heart. Her eyes went wide and her breath grew ragged. "You have to be stopped."

I released the hilt, leaving the dagger in place. My bloody hands stroked her hair. "You left me no choice." She smacked at my back with the force of a child. "Settle," I whispered. I stood there, holding her down, until her breathing slowed and stopped altogether. Her body stilled and those once vibrant eyes darkened. I kissed her forehead one last time.

Blood coated my clothes and hands. My chest tightened. They'd know it was hers. I ran to the stairs and up to the door. Peeking into her room before I opened the door all the way, I found it empty. I quickly stripped out of my clothes—taking the earpiece from the pocket—and threw them down the stairs.

I showered in her bathroom before dressing in some clothes that I kept in her room. I strode out of her room like I hadn't murdered their queen. No one passed as I walked to the factory floor. The vampires at the door raised an eyebrow when I stepped into the night.

"Doing some hunting for our queen," I said nonchalantly. They shrugged and let me pass. Step by step, I walked until I was out of sight and hearing distance. Then I ran. I ran as fast as I could, not caring who might see me. I ran, cowardly as it was. I couldn't get Jo out of there alive on my own. I needed help.

'Tanner... Tanner. Sh-she's dead, and if they find me, I am too.'

Thirty-Three

Warren

"**S**he's dead," Sam's voice came through the phone's speaker in hushed whispers.

The words hit me like a jolt of lightning. For a moment, everything stopped. My heart skipped a beat, and my mind rushed to catch up. *What?* I couldn't process it fast enough.

Clinton and Nessa froze, their eyes locked onto me. Clinton's face paled, his lips barely moving as he whispered, "What did he say?"

Nessa's breath caught in her throat. "Sam," she breathed, her voice trembling, "what do you mean, she's dead?" Her eyes flicked nervously from me to Clinton, her panic rising.

I stood there, frozen. For a terrifying instant, it felt like the world was unraveling. I thought of Josie—her warmth, her spirit, everything about her. Not my Josie. He couldn't be talking about Josie. My chest tightened with rising fear.

I was about to speak when Sam's voice came through again, sharper this time, as though he could sense our confusion. "Jemisha's dead," he clarified.

The air between us seemed to still. Nessa's face went pale, her hand falling to her mouth in disbelief. Clinton's posture sagged as if a weight had been lifted off him. He looked at me as though waiting for some kind of confirmation.

I blinked, the world snapping back into focus. "Jemisha?" I repeated, trying to make sense of the flood of emotions crashing through me.

"So, we should be able to overtake them with less of a fight?" Clinton asked.

"I wouldn't be so sure about that," Sam said, gulping in air. "Once they find her, they will seek vengeance. I left her in a secret room, so we might have a few days before they find her unless someone knows about the hidden room, and if that's the case, then we're screwed, so we need to act fast." Sam hesitated before he spoke again. "I'll be there before sunrise. We need to come up with a plan before we move."

I resumed my pacing. My body refused to sit still. I needed my match safe and sound with me. If it were up to me, I'd charge in there right now to find her, but I had to be smart about it.

"So... we wait?" Nessa sat on the armrest of the couch.

"We wait," I echoed.

We all stared at nothing in a long silence. Even my feet stilled. Every scenario played out in my mind: We'd get there too late and Josie would be dead. They changed her somehow in their attempts to create super soldiers. What if she'd become one of them and I had to fight her? Or... no, I refused to finish that train of thought.

I dropped onto the couch, my legs suddenly feeling like lead. My hands, trembling, lifted to cover my face, as if I could somehow hide from the overwhelm. My chest ached with the weight of Josie, trapped and vulnerable, somewhere in that hellhole. The anger, the fear, the helplessness—everything hit me all at once. I tried to breathe, tried to calm the storm in my head, but it was impossible. My body shook as tears leaked from my eyes, burning against my skin. I hadn't meant for it to happen, hadn't meant to lose control, but everything felt so raw. I couldn't fix this. I couldn't be there with her. My heart shattered in my chest as I sat there in the dark, wishing I could be with her, wishing I could take away whatever nightmare she was living.

I started when a hand landed on my shoulder.

"We'll find her. I just know it." Nessa's soft voice calmed me. She sat next to me and wrapped her arm around my back. The tears came faster. My body shook with the force of my fear.

"I can't lose her." I sobbed.

"You just met her. How in the world can you feel so much for a woman you hardly know?" Clinton asked with an air of sadness.

"She's my match. She is my equal in every way possible. I'm not sure any human could ever understand. It's... it's like the first time I saw her my world stopped—and that was through a camera lens. When I touched her, I felt it. My heart synced with hers and they beat as one. I feel everything she feels. I've known every time she's been in danger since that moment, the reasons I can't sleep. She's scared and in pain and there's nothing I can do about it. Without her, I cannot breathe." I knew he couldn't understand, but I was too exhausted to continue. Without her, I'd never fight again.

"I'm... I'm sorry, Warren. We will find her together." Clinton sat on the other side of me, putting his arm around me.

It had been centuries since I'd had a family, and this felt deeper than any family I'd ever known.

We sat there like that for a long moment until a knock at the door broke us from our trance. Clinton and Nessa both stared at me. I stood and walked over to the door, looking through the peephole.

"It's Sam." I stepped back from the door and opened it. The sun was peeking over the horizon. "Get in," I blurted.

Sam's eyes darted around the space. He walked over, opened the door under the stairs, and pulled the coats out of the closet, making room for his tall form. He then sat on the floor, resting his head on the back wall, hiding from the light peeking in through the windows.

I knelt in front of him. "You okay?"

He shook his head. "Not even close…"

"You wanna tell us what happened?"

"Not… not really, but I know you need to know."

Clinton led us down to the basement, his footsteps purposeful and steady as he glanced back at us. His hands were quick, pulling heavy, room-darkening curtains across the basement windows, blocking out the sunlight that threatened to flood the space. The thick fabric billowed slightly as he tugged them into place, darkening the room to an almost suffocating degree. The harsh daylight was replaced with the cool, dim light of the basement, and with it, the oppressive weight of the situation seemed to settle in. The unfinished concrete walls were bare—save for the crayon art—but it would shield Sam from the sun. We had to weave around toys and clothes to find seats. Sam sat with an exhausted huff.

I could feel Sam's discomfort, the slight tension in his shoulders as the light was blocked, but we had no choice. Sam needed to be shielded from the sunlight, and the basement, with its sealed-off windows, was the safest place to hear whatever he had to tell us. The air felt thick with anticipation, and even though the room was dim, I could see the weight in everyone's eyes—the urgency, the fear, the need to act fast before anything else went wrong.

Clinton turned toward us then, pausing for a moment as he adjusted the last curtain, ensuring no light slipped through. "We need to focus," he said, his voice low, tinged with the gravity of what was at stake.

We spent the next few hours listening to Sam recount everything that had happened to him in the past few weeks. Right up to the part where he found Jemisha's secret room, and he stabbed her. His eyes filled with tears as he told of her final breaths.

I rested a hand on his shoulders. "Old friend, I'm sorry. I know you loved her once."

"I did. Despite everything she has done to me, I loved her once, but..." He wiped the tears from his cheeks and glanced up at me. "How will I ever forgive myself?"

"You did what you had to do." I tried to reassure him.

"Here." We both glanced up as Nessa spoke from in front of us. She was holding a pillow and blanket in one hand and a cup of what resembled a bloody Mary in the other.

She handed it to Sam. "I might have liberated a few bags of O negative from the hospital I volunteer at." She shrugged with a smile.

Clinton rolled his eyes and crossed his arms on the other couch. "I didn't hear that," he whispered.

Sam took the cup and drank. He downed the contents in a matter of moments. He wiped the blood from his chin and handed her the cup back. "Why?" he asked. "Why are you so kind to me? You know exactly what I am and what I am capable of, and still, you are kind. I don't understand it."

"I am an empath, remember? I see more than what a person shows the world." She put a hand to his chest. "I feel who they truly are, and what you are is kind and gentle. Despite your need for blood to survive, you don't take more than you need. Even when you were starving and we practically forced you to feed on me, you were still kind. So I return your kindness with kindness." She handed him the pillows. "Besides, I'm a mom. I have learned to be nice even when others are not. We can't do anything until nightfall, so get some rest." She glared at me. "I mean both of you!" she ordered.

"Yes, ma'am," we both agreed. I stood, letting Sam lay on the couch, and watched as Nessa's motherly instincts took over and she tucked in the ancient vampire as if he was one of her children. She even kissed him on the forehead before walking upstairs.

"That is one good woman you have there, Detective," I told Clinton as we followed her up the stairs. Despite telling Nessa I'd rest, there was no way I could sleep. There was too much that needed done before we could go in tonight and save Josie and the rest of the Figli Del Mito being held there.

"Yes, she is," he breathed out. "So is yours, so let's go get her."

I agreed. But how? Even with Jemisha dead, there was still a clan of angry vampires between her and me. Not to mention her army of genetic hybrids. And if they found her body before we got there...

A knock at the door greeted us once we arrived upstairs. Clinton went for the gun at his side, but I walked right up to the door.

"It's Lance and Tanner," I said.

"How?" Clinton didn't relax.

"I'm a warlock. We can sense other warlocks." I shrugged and unlocked the door to let them in.

"We could hear everything. I smelled the vampire the moment we pulled up." Lance spoke without greeting. They had parked their patrol car out front and were still in uniform. I stepped aside to allow them in.

"Is he—Is Sam alright?" Tanner asked, scowling at his partner.

"Yes, Tanner, he's sleeping right now. Let's hash out a plan and you can go see him." I rested my hand on his shoulder and he seemed to relax.

"What are you thinking?" Lance asked. His voice was much colder than Tanner's.

I shook my head. "Even with Jemisha dead, it won't be easy. There's a maze of tunnels down there. Sam could help us find them, but I'm not sure he is prepared to go back in. And still, she has created an army. We need to gather the other Figli Del Mito." I led them back into the dining room and sat at the table. "My bouncer is a werewolf. I know I could talk to him about the packs, but getting them to work with the fae and the vampires will be the tricky part."

"My seelie court is close, and it has huge numbers. And, as you know, the seelie are always up for a fight." Lance smiled. "I can take you with me to appeal to our queen for aid.

Thirty-Four

Warren

*L*ance and I left Tanner to watch over Sam and took the cruiser into town. The houses became more and more decrepit the longer we drove. Entire families poured out of the front doors, readying for their day. Their eyes followed us as we drove past. I shifted in my seat and watched them back. My magic hovered on the edge of my consciousness, ready to unleash its fury at a moment's notice.

We crossed over a river and turned into a crowded parking lot. Lance put the car in park and turned off the engine. I stared at him, wide eyed. I opened and closed my mouth several times, unsure of what to say. He laughed.

"Perfect place to hide the entrance to the seelie realm," he spoke before stepping out of the car.

I followed and watched as the crowd moved toward the entrance of the Indianapolis Zoo. I turned my head to Lance and laughed. "Really?" I asked with a shake of my head.

"Why not? We can communicate with animals and in this town, it's the largest natural environment."

"But…"

"No one has ever questioned me before. Besides, I get in free when I'm in uniform." He smiled and headed toward the gate. I hesitated a moment before following.

"But aren't there risks of someone accidentally stumbling upon it and getting into the realm?" I asked once I'd caught up with him. The seelie were by far the most unknown of the Figli Del Mito. They kept to themselves and the rest of us respected that.

"First off, no one enters the seelie realm without the permission of the queen. And second, few would be at risk of finding the doorway where it's hidden." He stepped up to the gate and gave the girl behind the glass a grin.

"Oh, good morning Officer Lance. You're back already?" she asked.

"Had a rough shift last night. You know how those red pandas make me smile. Thought I'd watch them play a bit before heading home," he said.

"Sure thing! Who's your friend?" Her eyes drank me in.

"Well, you know..." He shrugged.

She giggled and handed him two tickets. "Have fun." She blushed.

"Thanks, hun."

We walked past her and kept moving. This early in the morning, and we still had to push through a crowd. I scoffed as the fae walked around the people like they weren't even there. He walked at a leisurely pace and didn't pause until we crossed a small set of train tracks.

He took a deep breath. "Welcome to Africa." His arms raised in a gesture to the surrounding enclosures. Then he smiled and kept walking. An elephant was playing in the water. "I love Africa. Spent much of my childhood there. Maybe someday I will set these beauties free." He shook his head and walked toward the fence where the elephant and cheetah cages met. There was a gate labeled "employees only," and led to a pathway between the enclosures. He stepped right up to it and pushed it open. I hesitated, looking around, before walking through the gate.

"Where is the entrance? I'm tired of this game," I hissed.

Lance chuckled and kept moving. He opened another gate and stepped right into the Cheetah's savannah.

"Cheetahs? Really? Won't they attack us?

"No," Lance said, ignoring my panic.

"Fine, but won't someone see us?" I asked, still refusing to follow him.

"I glamoured us the moment we stepped through the front gates." He spun around, arms raised, face lifted to the sun. "It is gorgeous here, isn't it?"

"Yes. Beautiful. Let's get on with it," I said in a clipped and sharp tone. The fae and their nonchalant attitude would drive me mad. We needed to save Josie, and he was playing with the big cats.

"Very well." He gave an exaggerated bow, then continued to walk into the center of the enclosure. A few of the big cats stood and watched us pass.

"I thought you glamoured us?" I whispered.

"Of course we are, but not to them. Their eyes are far sharper than those of the humans. Humans see what they want. Animals see everything." He watched them. "They won't hurt us if that is what you are afraid of."

He stepped half a pace to the left, cocked his head, and grinned. I tried to match his position, but couldn't see what he saw. He pulled me in front of him and tilted my head for me.

It was as if I were looking at the edge of a fire. Everything appeared slightly blurred. Light shimmered off the hazy ring in front of me. I stared at the spot for a long moment before I spoke.

"Why here?" I asked without looking away.

"The queen rather enjoys the company of the cats. Occasionally, one will step through and our queen has to bring them back, but not before she runs with them, of course. Their captivating blend of beauty and grace, coupled with their formidable hunting prowess, holds her in awe." He stepped around to my side. "Are you ready?"

I nodded. He gripped my hand and pulled me through. Ice prickled my skin like a thousand needles, then a rush of heat flooded me. I gasped in a breath in a new realm.

The sounds of bird and squirrels playing in the trees hit my ears before my eyes adjusted to the bright light.

When I could finally see again, tall trees and lush grass surrounded me. Flower petals fell like rain from the sky. I turned to my companion. Lance no longer wore his police uniform: A loose fitting green wrap covered his waist, his chest and feet were bare, and his long hair flowed down his back. I stared.

"I told you I was glamoured. Here I look as I should, not constricted to the rules of human society." He turned and walked off. "Come, let us not keep the queen waiting."

Thirty-Five

My body ached all over. They'd stolen the last bit of energy I had left. I lay on the cot and waited for death.

Warren would come for me, but what would he find? A shell? The body, but not the life within. He would tear the entire city down once he saw what they'd left of me.

I no longer had the strength to care about what he'd do. For the first time in my life, I had to think about breathing. My chest burned with every rise and fall. I couldn't even cry. I was at the end of everything and I felt nothing. No remorse. No sorrow for those left behind. Not even joy at knowing the pain would soon end.

My mother's image flashed in my head, and the last words I'd spoken to her haunted me. Growing up, we'd had our differences, but deep down, I knew she cared. I knew she'd tried her hardest with the tools she'd had. But still, she'd lied about who my father was, who I was.

An unfamiliar face popped into my mind. He was smiling and tossing a little kid into the air. The girl giggled and squealed. The little girl was me. Laughter filled the dank room, and I was no longer in the cold cell.

My childhood living room surrounded me, complete with the red-brown carpet and the brown and tan couch. My mother sat in the recliner and watched as my father played with me on the floor. I couldn't be more than a year old. He laid me down on my back and flicked his wrist. Stars burst through the room. Little me clapped her hands and squealed again. My tiny hand waved around, trying to capture the lights. My father laughed and picked me up. He held me so tight I could hear his heart beat.

The musty room surrounded me as I pulled out of the memory and shivered. The images of my father endured, yet I couldn't fathom why I couldn't remember his presence in my life. I craved more—I wanted more—but my time was up.

I reached out with my mind and searched for Warren, then my brother, but silence surrounded me. They were gone. I rolled onto my back and clutched my arms to my chest. My body shook with grief.

I was utterly alone.

A chill ran down my spine. I closed my eyes tight and blocked out all thoughts. My heart broke into a thousand pieces. Rocky was gone. Warren was gone. My father was gone. And soon I would join him in whatever lied beyond this realm.

Whispers broke the silence.

"Won't you people even let me die in peace?" I whispered into the darkness.

The voices continued. I focused on the sounds, but nothing came in clearly. A hundred voices all clambered together. Not the voices of my captors, I finally realized.

Slowly, I opened my eyes, the effort feeling as monumental as lifting a mountain. A dull, relentless ache radiated through every fiber of my being, as if even my bones protested the mere act of waking. My eyelids felt heavy, gritty with exhaustion, and even the faintest light sent sharp twinges of pain through my skull. As my vision began to clear, shapes emerged from the haze—blurry, indistinct at first, but sharpening with each agonizing blink. It was then that I realized I wasn't alone. The subtle sound of breathing, the faint shuffle of movement, and the unmistakable weight of someone else's presence crept into my awareness. My pulse quickened, instinct urging me to stay still, to assess, as my aching body screamed in protest. Who was here? Friend or foe? My muscles tensed, ready to react despite their soreness, as I forced myself to focus on the dim, shadowy surroundings.

The entire room was full of non-corporeal forms floating around and through each other. Not a single one of them noticed me. I tried to move back against the wall, but I could barely lift my arm.

One voice spoke out above the rest. "Josie," it whispered my name. "Josie, you are stronger than them." The voice grew louder.

"Stronger than who? Who are you?" I begged.

The form pushed through the crowd. I gasped. My father—or what remained of my father—stood before me. He appeared young; younger than he should have been.

"Than those that hold you," he said. "You are a Lost Wolsteincroft, remember? You hold the key to their experiments. They won't let you die, but you must find the magic within you."

"Wh-what do you mean? H-how can I even see you?" I shook as I sat up.

"You take after me, my child. You can see and speak to the dead and you can use us to help you."

"Who are all these people?"

"They are victims of the doctors' crimes."

"They... they're..." I glanced around. Every form was that of a child. Tears burst through the opened floodgate of my sorrow. "Children," I whispered.

My father nodded. "They are. And they have lost their way and are afraid. They need you. You have a strong connection with children. Your strong connection with children drew you to education. You can use that talent to help guide these souls."

Slowly, I pulled my knees to my chest and wrapped my arms around them, squeezing as tightly as I could to keep from falling apart. "No. I will join them soon. I can't help anyone."

"I told you. You will not die. Do you hear me, Josefina?" He leaned closer, looking me in the eye. "You are my daughter. Ancient magic flows within you. You are a healer and one of the most powerful mediums I've ever seen. With your help, you can guide them to form an undying army."

I closed my eyes and attempted to melt into the wall. I didn't have the strength or skill to do what he thought I could. The icy grip of death was enveloping me, and nothing could prevent it.

"No... no. I can't." I slumped over to my side and blocked out the sounds. My eyes stayed closed until all the noise stopped. I opened one eye. The spirits were all gone, save for my father.

"You can and you must." He faded.

"But Rocky, he's gone. Warren will be too if he tries to save me; what's the point?"

My father smiled and faded away in a wisp of smoke. I was alone again. I steeled myself for what I knew was coming. There was no way I was going to die in this hellhole.

'Rocky?' I called out to my brother.

'We won't die, sister.' He agreed with my thoughts.

'Rocky?' I breathed a sigh of relief. 'I thought you were dead. I couldn't find you earlier.'

'Sorry, the good doctor just got done with me, and I was taking a bit of a nap. They are getting closer. Have you heard from your match?' he asked.

'Not in a while.' I tried not to think of why.

'Try again.'

I closed my eyes and thought of Warren. His face came in crisp and his worry flooded me. He was somewhere strange. It resembled a forest, yet it didn't.

'Warren.' I whispered to him.

He stopped walking. 'Josie?' I felt his heart race. 'I'm coming, my love.'

'Where are you?' I asked.

'Gathering allies.'

'Hurry!' I begged. 'Rocky and I can't take much more.'

Warren paused. I felt the confusion in his mind. 'She's... she's dead. Jemisha's dead. Have they not found her yet?'

'She's what? Do you really think they'd tell me if they did? But I'm sure even if they did, the doctor wouldn't care. She's just as crazy as their queen.'

'Hold on, Josie. Hold on a little while longer.' He wrapped me in his magic, filling me with hope. 'I will find you, my match!'

'I love you, Warren! Please hurry.'

'I will, my love, I will.'

I pulled out of his head and back to my tiny cell. The lost souls were back and all looking at me. I reached deep within myself, finding the pit of magic. It felt dark and light at the same time. Tame and wild. Something that could instill both fear and admiration. It flowed freely to the tips of my fingers.

Every inch of my body stitched back together and healed itself. I stood, feeling stronger than I had in months. The souls watched me move through them. I stood in the middle of the room and looked each of them in the eyes.

"Others are coming. We must prepare."

Thirty-Six

Josie

The cold stone sent a chill up my spine as I sat cross-legged on the dark cell's floor. Time had lost all meaning. Days, weeks—it didn't matter. Isolation pressed in, gnawing at me, but the oppressive silence was worse. It wasn't empty. It was crowded.

The voices surrounded me, an endless static hum. It wasn't the silence pressing against my ears but the cacophony of whispers that overlapped and clashed, creating a relentless storm in my mind. They were here. They had always been here. Watching. Waiting.

But I needed them to be more than noise.

"Focus," I muttered to myself, closing my eyes and taking a deep, steadying breath. My heart thudded in my chest—a metronome to center me. "You have to sort them out. You can do this."

The static swirled, a thousand voices all at once—pleading, demanding, warning. My mind strained to separate them, to make sense of the chaos. It was like trying to tune a broken radio. Every channel bled into the next. The cold air prickled against my skin as their energy pulsed in waves around me.

"Please," I whispered, my voice trembling but firm. "I know you're there. I need your help."

The storm didn't cease, but it shifted. The static grew sharper, the voices more insistent, as though they were aware I was reaching out. It wasn't clarity—not yet—but it was something. I clung to it like a lifeline.

"Listen to me!" My voice cracked, and I took another deep breath, forcing calm into my words. "I'm not your enemy. I'm here to fight for us. For you. But I can't do it alone."

The whispers ebbed and flowed, fragments of words breaking through. *Help. Hurt. Stop her.* A thousand emotions slammed into me at once—fear, anger, sorrow—but beneath it all, a thread of hope.

I focused on that hope, reaching for it. "You've been hurt. I know what she's done. Jemisha didn't just trap me here; she trapped you, too. She used you, fed on your pain. But she's not invincible. Together, we can stop her."

The air around me thickened, the voices growing louder but more distinct. I began to pick them apart, one by one, isolating them from the static. A young woman's sob, a child's plea, a man's growl of fury. They weren't just noise. They were people—spirits—with stories, with power.

"I hear you," I said, my voice steady now. "I see you. I'm not asking you to trust me blindly, but if we work together, we can end this. No one else has to suffer the way we have."

The shadows seemed to shift; the temperature dropping further. Their energy was coalescing, and I felt a flicker of connection—a hesitant thread weaving between us.

A voice, clearer than the rest, cut through the noise. "Why should we trust you?" It was sharp, filled with suspicion and pain.

I didn't flinch. "Because I am where you were. Trapped. Helpless. But I'm not giving up, and neither should you. I'm not asking you to follow me. I'm asking you to stand with me."

More voices joined the first, rising and falling in a chaotic symphony. Accusations, questions, desperate cries. I stayed grounded, my focus unyielding, pulling the threads tighter.

"She's hurt you all," I continued, addressing them as one. "She's fed on your fear, your anger, your despair. But those emotions? They're your strength. If we turn them against her, she can't win. Together, we're stronger than she'd ever imagined."

The storm around me shifted again, less chaotic, more purposeful. The whispers began to harmonize, their energy aligning. I could feel their power: raw, untapped, overwhelming. It wasn't just theirs. It was ours.

"I'm not leaving this cell without you," I said, my voice resolute. "But I need you to meet me halfway. Focus. Lend me your strength, and I'll lend you mine. Together, we'll make her pay for everything she's done."

A wave of cold washed over me, and I felt them—truly felt them—for the first time. They were no longer just whispers or static. They were allies, bound by pain, but united by purpose.

"What do we do?" another voice asked, softer this time. It wasn't doubt; it was determination.

I opened my eyes, the darkness of the cell now alive with the faint shimmer of their presence. "We fight."

The air crackled with energy, the static gone, replaced by a focused, pulsing force. The ghosts surrounded me, not as fragmented echoes but as a united front. We weren't alone anymore.

Jemisha wouldn't win. Not again.

Thirty-Seven

Warren

We stepped to the edge of a glade. The tree canopy high above kept the area in the shade. Wild flowers sprang up from everywhere. Rabbits and squirrels skittered about. Soft melodies wafted in the air. The fae danced around to the music. Not a care existed in the world.

"Take off your shoes." Lance spoke without looking at me.

"Excuse me?"

"Would you walk into a synagogue or temple carrying in the filth from the city streets?" He glanced back at me and waited. I begrudgingly removed my shoes and socks and set them aside. The feel of grass on my soles sent a shiver up my spine, but I was in his realm now. He turned back to the glade. "This place is no less holy, probably more holy, than those places of worship on Earth."

He walked forward with the gentle grace of a deer. I followed like a floundering fawn. Every blade of grass itched the soles of my feet. Every twig stabbed at me, threatening to take me down.

"How in hell can you walk so perfectly here without shoes?" I hissed.

"By learning a long time ago that your feet are another sense. Use them to guide your steps."

"What the frack else are feet for?" I grumbled to myself and lumbered on. We walked—Lance weaved; I shoved—through the crowd to the center of the glade. A petite woman lay in the grass, arms crossed behind her head and her eyes closed. I stood over her, watching the tiny movements of her eyes. Her golden hair fanned out around her.

"You are standing in my light." She spoke with an airy voice.

Lance pulled me back a step and bowed low. "Apologizes, my queen." He nudged me in the ribs, and I bowed with him. "He has never been to the seelie realm."

She didn't move. "I know very well of your friend. Do you not think I allowed him entrance? Most warlocks who have attempted to travel to the Seelie's realm have died tragically, but none before held the title Mage." She opened one eye and peered up at me. She grinned and closed her eye again. "This one may stay. Speak your peace."

I waited for Lance to respond when I glanced over and noticed he was already waiting for me. I cleared my throat. "Your Majesty—"

"Sit. I can hardly hear you way down here," she said. Lance nodded in response to my gaze, and I took a seat. "Closer."

I held back the grumble I felt in my gut and edged closer. My knees brushed the edge of her dress before she spoke again.

"Better. Continue."

"Your Majesty, I come to you for aid." Her hand moved lazily through the air before she rested it upon my thigh. I took a deep breath and attempted to ignore her caress.

"Please, Majesty. War is brewing and we need your help to prevent it. Jemisha kidnapped my match and several others, using them for experiments to create a hybrid super soldier. I believe she is dead, but she was working with the Corps de l'Ombre. We need to destroy the lab and wipe out her clan before they get ahold of her research." Her hand traveled up my leg toward my hip. I gripped her wrist, stopping her from going higher. "Please."

Her eyes snapped open, and she was inches from my face in a blink. "Why should I help you?" She watched my lips as I responded.

"We need to prevent this war."

"But you, Mage, helped Vlad destroy my people so many centuries ago. Why in any realm would I help you?"

My insides twisted, and fire burned through my veins. Electricity sparked from my fingertips and I ached to wrap them around her neck, but that wouldn't get me what I needed. The thought of dying here, leaving Josie to her fate, was the only thing keeping me from killing her.

"Please," I almost whimpered. "She is my match. I have waited for generations to find her. She doesn't have much time. If I... If she..." I wiped the tears from my face. "I can't let her die."

"Dear boy, love is hardly a reason to help." Her hand gripped my hair and pulled my face to hers. Her lips assaulted mine, but I pulled away quickly. "You can find love anywhere. Why is she so special?" The queen flopped back down to the grass.

"What about the others? Jemisha's been taking children. Figli Del Mito children," I said, hoping to appeal to her need to protect her realm.

She shrugged. "Not any of mine. My children don't venture into the human realm."

"There were fae children." I remembered seeing the pictures. Ears that weren't quite right. Skin that was far too pale, even in death. They were fae. I hoped she'd have compassion.

"Those must be of another queen. Again, mine would never be so foolish, and if they were, so be it. It was probably a better fate than they would have gotten from me," she said coldly.

I stood quickly, readying for a fight. My heart pounded in my ears. "How can you be so callous?" I said slowly through gritted teeth. "The Figli Del Mito needs your help. You are more than capable, yet you lie there in the sun without a care in the world?" I stood toe to toe with her. Lance gripped me by the wrist, pulling me back. He might look thin, but his hold made my hand numb. "Please, I am begging." I dropped to my knees. "She is my only match. If she dies, you might as well kill me."

The queen sat up on her elbow and watched me. "What is it about this one woman that can make you act this way? In all my years, I have never seen a more pathetic warlock. She cannot be a simple human, not even a normal warlock." She cocked her head.

"She is... she is Josefina Wolsteincroft," I gasped out.

The queen's face hardened. She jumped to her feet and snapped her fingers. Two guards stood at her side in an instant. "Well, you should have led with that," she said, her voice brimming with sudden enthusiasm. A grin spread across her face, sharp and hungry, like a predator catching the scent of its prey. Her entire demeanor shifted, her body leaning forward as if barely able to contain her readiness for action. Her eyes sparkled with an eager determination, a fire igniting within them that promised she was more than prepared for the battle ahead. She turned sharply to her guards, her tone commanding and filled with purpose. "Prepare the warriors. We're off to slay some monsters." That grin stayed fixed, fierce and resolute—a warrior ready to charge into the fray.

An hour later, we were at the gateway with a thousand of the Queen's soldiers. She stood between them and the shimmering pool of light. Thick leather armor had replaced the thin, flowing dress, and two long swords crossed over her back. Her small build and fierce attitude bordered on comical, yet I understood well enough that dynamite often came in small packages.

"My dear Fae, it has been far too long since we have seen actual combat," she spoke. I watched the troops dance from foot to foot, anxiously awaiting the fight to come. "Tonight, we will taste blood again." A cheer erupted from the crowd.

A deep guilt settled in my gut. What was I unleashing on the human realm? Would they kill everything in sight? Once we neutralized the threat, would they go home? As long as they helped save my Josie first, I would deal with them later.

The queen stepped forward into the gateway and vanished. Lance and I joined her. We stood back in the enclosure at the zoo, only the sun was now setting. How long had we actually been there?

"Time moves differently in the seelie realm." Lance answered my own thoughts.

"Would have been nice to know beforehand. How much time have we wasted?"

"Only the day. We should contact the others and meet them closer to the factory. If we are going to do this, we need to do it tonight."

I stepped aside as the others passed through the gate and pulled out my phone. Five missed calls from Sam and three from Clinton. I dialed Sam first.

He answered on the first ring. "Thank the gods! Where have you been?"

"Seelie realm, apparently time moves slower there..."

"Are they on board? I have spoken to some other vampire clans. When I heard nothing from you, I called the wolves too. We are ready when you are. Have you talked to the detective?"

"He's next on my list. I am with the queen's army. We will meet you on 12th Street by the old rail yard after full dark. We need to make a plan together."

"Sounds good. See you there, old friend." He hung up without another word.

I dialed Clinton's number. "My wife tried to convince me you were fine. Wasn't sure she was right. Glad to be wrong."

"I have the fae queen and her warriors. Sam will meet us at the old train yard after dark. What else has happened?" I asked.

"Tanner has gathered some warlocks and the other officers that are... what you call them... like you all?"

"Figli Del Mito?"

"Yeah, them. We're all preparing. Now that we have a time and location, though, I'll call Tanner and give him an update," Clinton said.

"Good. Then we are all set to take the factory tonight?" I asked.

"Sounds like it."

"Clinton," I paused, "thanks. Thanks for believing Josie when no one else would, and thanks for helping me. I know there's a history..."

"No history, not like that, anyway. I love my wife and Jo has become like a little sister to me. I'd do anything for her, and now for you. You never have to ask."

No human had ever put that kind of faith in me, especially after they knew what I was. I was speechless. "Th-thanks," I uttered.

"See you soon," Clinton said before he hung up.

I turned around to see the army behind me. We were finally going after her. My heart stopped and raced all at the same time. My brain froze. I couldn't breathe, let alone think. What if we were too late? What if I died while trying to save her? So many what ifs.

Lance walked up and placed a hand on my shoulder. "She is still alive. You'd know it if she wasn't. We will find her." He gave me a reassuring smile. I finally took a breath.

Together, we moved toward the exit. The zoo was closed for the day. The animals all watched us in silent reverence. Night slowly crept upon us, engulfing us in darkness.

We walked with inhuman speed toward our destination. No sounds other than the beating of our hearts penetrated the night.

I rounded the last corner and saw the army that waited for us. Thousands of Figli Del Mito all stood before me, eyeing each other cautiously. Tanner stood next to Sam, holding on tight to his hand. A group of warlocks positioned themselves next to the vampires. They all bowed their heads as I approached.

Clinton and his wife stood next to Tanner. He was watching the crowd, but Nessa stood tall.

"Couldn't convince her to stay home?" I asked him when I got closer.

"Wild horses couldn't drag her away."

She rolled her eyes at her husband. "I have wondered all my life if there was something more to this world. You think I'm going to stand aside and do nothing when my best friend needs me? And besides, I can handle myself." I finally took her all in. She had two handguns and extra mags strapped to her hips and a shotgun slung around her back. She shook a glass bottle before strapping it back to her belt. "Grabbed some holy water from the Catholic church and soaked the ammo in it. Figured that'd do the trick."

"Okay then. Where's the rest?" I asked.

"The wolves didn't feel comfortable meeting with the rest of us, but they assured me they've been waiting to take Jemisha down," Sam said.

I nodded and turned toward the factory. To my match. My magic tingled on the edge of my skin.

'We're coming Josie.' Hold on, I am coming for you. I prayed she knew.

'We are ready.' Her voice rang out strong and clear in my mind.

Thirty-Eight

Warren

The hush of the street overwhelmed me. No one ventured out in the darkness. No noise from inside houses seeped into the night. Complete and utter silence filled the air.

Between the fae and the other warlocks, they covered our massive group in a veil. The army walked, invisible to the world, toward a war no one knew was boiling over.

Magic sparked all around me, sending the tiny hairs on my neck on end. I lit my hands in flames just to brush away the chill. *I will find her.* Over and over, I said the same thing to myself.

We marched down the road stretching from side to side and row after row. We were an army armed with our magic and strength. Only the fae and the two humans carried weapons. My magic pulsed within me, begging to be unleashed.

I clenched and unclenched my fists as we neared 9th Street. The rest of the block was dark, but the factory was lit up like the Fourth of July. No one stood on guard at the door Sam had told us to use. Something wasn't right. No scent of blood or vampires lingered in the air.

Sam stepped up next to me. "Where are the guards? Why are all the lights on?" His voice trembled enough for me to hear his fear.

I tried to connect with Josie, but something was blocking me.

"I... I don't know, Sam. Regardless, I'm going after her. No matter what." I turned to Tanner. "Where are the wolves?"

He shrugged. "I'm not sure? They said they'd be here."

"I'll go check it out." I took a deep breath and stepped out from the crowd. My magic pulled away from the collective and wrapped me in a shield. I walked around the side, down an alley. Peering through a window, I saw nothing. The concrete floor was empty save for dust and debris. I squinted, examining the building, and saw nothing. I even walked around vicinity, and nothing. It was a ghost town.

"Are you sure this is the right location?" I asked Sam when I came back around.

"Positive. I was here this morning. I know it's the right one." He stared at the building.

"Maybe they found Jemisha's body and fled?" I asked.

"I'm not sure. Maybe?"

"So what are we doing here, boys? If the place is empty?" the faerie queen asked.

"We should still search it, just in case." I glanced at Clinton and his wife. "You guys hang back. I don't want you getting hurt, so I don't want you coming in unless we need you. Do you understand?" Clinton nodded, but Nessa was as white as a sheet. "What is it?"

"It's... something. I can feel her. She's there, but everything's muddy." Nessa spoke through a haze.

"She's in there?" I moved without thinking. I burst through the front door and ran into the abandoned factory. Feet shuffled in behind me, and I knew the other Figli Del

Mito had followed. I moved deeper into the building, heading for the stairs Sam had told us led to their lair.

The door slammed shut behind me and the lights flicked off. My heart pounded in my chest so hard it hurt. I snapped my fingers and flames emerged in my palms.

My eyes adjusted to the darkness. Every last one of my army now stood in the old factory, surrounded. We were at least three thousand strong. What surrounded us was not as many, but stronger.

The monsters were at least seven feet tall and twice as thick as a normal human. There were a range of creatures staring at us. Some were half wolf standing on two hind legs with twisted, snarling faces, while the others had long, protruding fangs that dripped with blood. There were closer to a thousand of them, but a wild hunger burned in their eyes. Howls echoed around the massive space. Swords being unsheathed rang out. The buzz of magic filled the room. We all stood on edge, waiting for the first shot.

My eyes scanned the room. I had to fight my way to the stairs and to my Josie. She was all that mattered. A tiny spark of magic slipped from one warlock and chaos ensued.

All at once, the hybrids charged, their monstrous forms surging forward like a tidal wave of chaos. The wolves, massive and unyielding, slammed their front paws against the ground with a thunderous impact before launching at the attackers, their snarls echoing through the cavernous space. Her vampires were blurs of motion, their preternatural speed slicing through the dark like shadows wielding blades. The clash of bodies and the sickening thud of impacts filled the air, but it was the screams—raw, desperate, and unrelenting—that froze me in place.

I stood there, rooted to the spot, my limbs betraying me as I watched the tide of battle churn. One by one, they fell—my allies, her warriors—cut down in a frenzy of blood and fury. My eyes darted through the melee, searching for her, my match, desperate to find her, but she was nowhere in sight.

I couldn't lead them. Not again. My chest tightened, the weight of past failures crashing down on me. I couldn't let the Mage's power take hold, couldn't risk becoming the monster I'd fought so hard to suppress. But the battle roared around me, and every fiber of my being screamed to act, to fight, to protect her. Instead, I stood there, trembling, the war unfolding before me like a nightmare I couldn't wake from.

'Help is coming. You must fight.' Josie's voice echoed in my head a moment before I saw them. A ghost, an actual ghost, floated through the floor. Hundreds of them. My army halted before they realized they were fighting for us.

The shadowy figures darted through the monsters with an eerie grace, their delicate forms moving with a quiet determination. Each touch seemed to unravel the creatures, leaving them to crumple to the floor in silence. Still, the path to the stairs was crowded with hundreds more of the looming threats, their presence a daunting obstacle that filled the air with tension.

I shot fireball after fireball at the creatures. They brushed it off like they hadn't felt a thing. I dug deeper. I pulled on the magic in the air and combined it, drawing it within me.

"Sam!" I shouted. My entire being vibrated with the magic. "Run. Get them all behind me."

Sam shouted to the others and shuffled around, but I was blind to their movements. I could only hope they were safe when I let the magic loose. I focused on the stairs and created a path to them. Fire and ice. Lightning and rain. I was a jumble of magic, and I couldn't sort each ability out. I had never taken in so much all at once and had no idea what would happen next.

I dropped to the ground and let go of the hold I had over the magic. Fire erupted from my being, scorching out a path in front of me. The monsters dropped one by one as my flames engulfed them. With another push of the magic within me, I called a storm down, dousing the flames. My vision blurred, and I fought to stay awake.

"Go!" I shouted again to Sam. "Save her." The magic burned inside me, threatening to suffocate me. Tears welled up in my eyes, blurring my vision. "Please, Sam, save her." I watched as the others ran for escape. My friend locked eyes with me and nodded before he followed. I felt my strength wane. The surrounding magic died down and the blackened remains of the monsters Jemisha had created were all that remained. The stench surrounded me. I choked and sputtered as I collapsed to the ground.

My breaths grew shallow. I lay on my back, heartbroken I'd never see her face again. One ghost floated to my side. I'd join them soon.

"Not yet, Mage. You have my daughter to care for."

I blinked, observing the ghost. His appearance resembled the image I had seen of Rocky.

"Rocky?" I whispered.

"He is my son. Just like Josefina is my daughter. She held on for you. Now you must hold on for her."

But I couldn't. My eyes drifted closed, and all was black.

Thirty-Nine

Sam

I ran to the stairs, pausing just long enough to see my oldest friend collapse to the ground. I knew Jo would be the only one who could save him. I jumped down to the next level.

More vampires had hidden themselves away down here. Our army pushed through Jemisha's. Bursts of magic shot all around me. Vampires opened veins of other vampires. Blood soaked the concrete floor, making it slick.

Jemisha's bedroom door loomed ahead, its ornate frame standing out against the dim corridor. The stretch of space between me and it was narrow, just wide enough for me to use my speed without colliding with anything. I focused, feeling the tension in the air around me, and in a blink, I propelled myself forward, closing the distance in an instant. The moment I opened my eyes, a hulking figure emerged from the shadows—a goon of Jemisha's—and lunged at me with surprising speed.

"'Bout time your traitorous self came back," he said. "Did you think we wouldn't know? We want your blood now more than ever."

They knew. My eyes flicked to her door. *They found her body, and that is why they are fighting so hard.* I reached for the handle and, before he could stop me, vanished inside. I ran for the wall of weapons and pulled down a long sword just in time to block the massive vampire's blow.

He howled in pain as I sliced through his hand. It fell to the floor with a dull thud. Losing his hand didn't take the fight out of him. He came at me harder with the other. His long, claw-like fingers scratched out. I dodged, but he grazed my cheek. Blood dripped down my face.

I stumbled backward. My back slammed against the wall. His hand gripped my throat and squeezed. I gasped for air. My feet dangled as he lifted me higher. I kicked and scratched at him, to no avail. My vision blurred, and I would not last long. But if I spirited, I'd just take him with me.

The vampire's eyes went wide. He loosened his grip and dropped to the ground. I hit my knees, heaving in breaths, then jerked at the hand on my shoulder.

"Relax… It's me." Tanner's smile greeted me before his lips pressed into mine in a quick kiss.

"T-thanks." I tore my eyes away from the vampire that lay flat on his face. A hole burned straight through his body where his heart once was. I pulled Tanner back to me, kissing him deeply, running my fingers through his hair. Magic sparked between our lips, tingling me all over. "Whoa," I said, pulling away.

Tanner grinned and helped me to my feet. "We need to get to their lab. There's no way we can fight through this crowd in time. They'll kill all the kids before we can get to them."

The sounds of fighting raged on beyond the walls of my former lover's room. I searched for a way out but found nothing. Getting to Josefina and the others was the only thing that mattered.

"I can't spirit us both that far... hell, I don't think I could spirit that far myself." My heart was pumping faster.

"Can you show me where it's at? I might be able to get—" A loud growl pulled our attention to the hall. We watched from the doorway as massive wolves descended the stairs. They tore through the enemy vampires like sharks in water. Bones splintered and blood flooded the floor. My stomach churned at the carnage.

I stepped out into the hall to meet the leader of the wolves. He bowed slightly to me. I bowed back.

"We need to get to the lab." I brandished the sword out in front of me and lead the way. We had started with thousands.

We dashed down the corridors, making sharp turns. The few vampires who peeked out from their rooms to see what the noise was would never see again.

I rounded the last corner and stopped dead. Jemisha stood between me and the door to the lab.

"But... but I..." I stuttered for the words.

"Stabbed me in the chest? Yes, I know. Good thing I had already injected myself with that little girl's serum. She is an excellent healer." Jemisha brushed her fingers to her chest where the dagger once was. "It still hurt, though, so I will have to repay you the favor." She hissed and charged.

I raised my sword just in time to block her. Her hands gripped the blade and tried to pull it away. We spun around.

"Where's my old Samuel? The one who enjoyed the hunt? All those bodies we left behind. What the frack happened to you, my Samuel?"

"You. You happened to me." I pushed her off me with ease. The wolves growled behind me. "No, she's my responsibility. I created her; I'll deal with her," I told them without looking away from Jemisha.

"You what?" Tanner asked.

"Yes, I turned her. She's my responsibility, so I'll handle her."

She laughed. "You? Handle me? I think not!"

I closed my eyes and took a deep breath. Before opening my eyes, I heard her move. I spun around faster than she could recover. She slammed into Tanner, who stood watching. He shoved her back toward me.

"I don't want to do this, Jemisha. I killed you once and I will do what I must." I refused to let the tears I felt fall.

"You're a fool to think killing me will end this."

I paused. "I know, but I must stop you. We'll deal with the others later."

"You can't stop this war. It's already begun."

"It doesn't matter. I won't allow you to create your monsters and we will stop the others from rising."

"We could still rule this world together." Her voice hitched, but her face hardened.

"Once, I loved you. Your thirst for blood became too much." Glancing past her to Tanner, I continued, "I've discovered a new life, filled with beauty and joy. Blood alone cannot sustain me. I craved more from life, and you never comprehended that."

"I love you!" she screamed. "We could be great together again!" She was the only one to know what I was truly capable of. Her trembling hands showed me she remembered.

"I'm sorry, my love. You know this is wrong." I raised my hands to my sides. "Your warriors are dead. Your monsters are burnt to a crisp. It is over."

She screamed through her teeth and charged once more. Before I could move, Tanner's sword plunged into her back, piercing straight through her heart and out of her chest. I caught her as her body dropped to the floor.

"P-p-please," she whispered. I sat with her dying body and took her hand. Tears leaked down her cheeks. "I'm sorry." Her voice was barely audible.

"I will always love you, Jemisha." She smiled and took her final breath.

The metallic tang of blood filled the air, thick and suffocating. My eyes locked on the crumpled form of Jemisha on the cold floor. Tanner stood over her, his chest heaving, his blade slick with her blood. I couldn't bring myself to speak, the weight of what had just happened pressing down on me like a vice. Jemisha had been my tormentor, my captor—but she had also been a part of my life for far too long. And now she was gone, by Tanner's hand.

I forced myself to turn away, but my thoughts were a storm. Did I hate her? Did I pity her? Did I mourn her? I didn't know. What I did know was that Tanner had stepped into the role I hadn't been able to fill, made the decision I hadn't been able to make. He'd saved me, but at what cost? The lines between heroism and vengeance blurred in my mind.

"You okay?" Tanner's voice broke through the haze, low and strained, his face as unreadable as ever.

I didn't answer. Instead, I nodded and started moving through the chaos. Around us, the fight still raged—vampires clashing with hybrids, blood and shadows mingling in the dim light. Every scream, every clang of metal, was a reminder of how far things had spiraled. But I couldn't focus on that. I had to find Jo.

"Stick close," Tanner said, his tone brokering no argument.

I bit back a retort. He'd just killed for me—how could I argue with him now? But every step I took felt heavier, like the weight of Jemisha's death clung to me. My chest burned with the strain of holding it all in. I had to stay focused. I had to find her.

"She's here somewhere," Tanner muttered, his eyes scanning the chaos.

I nodded again, keeping my eyes peeled, my instincts sharp. Jemisha's death had shifted something in the air, and I couldn't tell if it was for better or worse. All I knew was that Jo was out there, somewhere in this mess, and I couldn't afford to lose her, too.

Forty

Josie

Round 386 was about to begin. A nurse dragged me from my cell and roughly strapped me into the chair in the surgical suit. She was about to inject me with another vile liquid when chaos erupted down the hall. Screams and cries penetrated the door.

The door flung open and a bodybuilder type man stepped inside. The flash of his fangs as he spoke reminded me he was not a man at all.

"They're here. Get to safety!" he ordered, and without another look back, the two of them ran out the door. They hurriedly left without bothering to shut the door behind them, leaving me still strapped to the table.

A day ago—hell, a few hours ago—I wouldn't have been strong enough to use my magic, but I felt him. Warren was here... and in trouble. I summoned every ounce of energy as I could. A nearly unbearable heat crawled up my arms, yet it never burned me.

The flames melted through the thick leather on my wrists. I quickly undid the buckle at my throat and moved on to those on my ankles. My bare feet hit the floor the second they were free. A cool breeze washed through the hospital gown.

"Crap." I grabbed the back of the robe. "How the frack can I fight my way out like this?" I asked myself.

As soon as the thought crossed my mind, a shadowy figure stepped into the room. I ducked behind the chair and peered around. It was the twisted sadist doctor. She slammed the door closed, locked it tight, and pressed her back to the metal. Her fear radiated off her like crashing waves against a rocky shore, making me smile, knowing Warren had come for me. Her entire body trembled. She turned around and backed away from the door, never taking her eyes off it.

I stepped around the chair and waited. She backed right into me. I reached around and grasped her throat in my hand. The good doctor wiggled in my hold.

"Where's your guard?" I asked her.

"D-dead," she said. "P-please, help me."

Every needle poke flashed through my mind. The liquid she had injected into me that pushed me to the edge of death burned into my memory. Her treatment of me as if I were a rat demolished any ounce of sympathy I might have held for the pleading woman, and my rage boiled over. My magic took hold and followed my emotions. My hand ignited in the same flames that freed me. The vampire in its grasp screamed, but I didn't relent. She was guilty of so much more than torturing me.

I thought of all the kids she had used and discarded like trash on the street. All of those parents who would never see their children again. Their faces flashed in my mind, making the fire burn brighter. She took me; she took Rocky, and God knows how many others she still had here. I had to end this now.

"P-p-p..." she tried once more, then went silent. When her body stilled, I dropped her to the floor and walked towards the door.

The fire licked up my arms and down my body, igniting every inch of me. My footsteps burned the floor as I walked. The fighting echoed outside the lab, but I passed no one on my way to the exit.

My shaky hand ripped the door open and my heart sank for a moment when the face that greeted me was not my match.

"Josefina?" Sam spoke.

"Sam? Where is he?" I begged.

"Jo, you need to snap out of it first. You are safe. They are all gone or dead. Release your magic." He dropped the sword he held and walked gently toward me. "Please, Jo, you'll burn the place down like that."

I glanced down, remembering that I was a human fireball.

"Oh... sorry." I closed my eyes and focused on one thing: Warren's face. His pain tore through me, instantly dropping me to the ground. I screamed through gritted teeth as the fire burn hotter.

"Jo, he needs you, but you need to stay focused. Push past his pain. Find something happy. Think of that." I heard Sam's voice through the hiss of the flames.

Warren was standing on the balcony of his bar, watching me. Looking back, I felt it: the pull he had felt that night. It drew us together even though I hadn't known it then. I had resisted every step of the way to that bar that night, but Nessa knew. She knew I needed to be there to meet him.

I focused on the first time he'd touched me. An icy chill ran down my spine. The pain slowly retreated, taking my fire with it. I lay on the floor gasping for breath. Sam was quick on my side, kneeling beside me.

"Jo, are you okay?" he asked.

"Y-yeah." I sat up. "I need to get to him. Will you help me?" Sam nodded and helped me to my feet. Officer Tanner walked up to the other side of me, taking my arm.

"You might want a little more help. Do you mind?" I shook my head. His magic washed over me, giving me strength.

"Thank you." I stood on my own, then turned to Sam. "Now, lead the way."

We walked through the dead and those still living. Warlocks rushed from one injured person to the next, healing what they could. Others were dragging the bodies against one wall. Everyone was so busy with their task they didn't notice us pass.

Sam stopped and pointed down the hall to a set of stairs. "Last I saw him, he was up there." I started forward, but his hand stopped me. "I'm not sure what you will find, Jo."

I glared at him. "He's alive, I can feel it, but he's in pain. Let. Go." He released me and I ran, taking the stairs two at a time. The only part of the floor that wasn't charred led me straight to him.

He lay in a heap, shaking, massive piles of ash surrounded his form. I ran to him, dropping to my knees. He lay there curled up, smoldering like a dying ember. My hands hovered above him, terrified to touch.

"Warren," I whispered.

His eyes fluttered open. "Josie? My Josefina?" His voice was weak.

"What... what happened?"

"I came to save you." He smiled.

"Now I think I need to save you. What can I do?"

"I-I'm not sure." He rolled over and groaned. "It... an overload of magic. I can't... release it all. It will destroy the city if I do."

"It will destroy you, jackass, if you don't!" The tears flowed down my cheeks, searing trails like molten rivers carving paths through a fragile mountainside.

"I'm... I'm sorry, Josie." His hand trembled as he reached for my face.

"Don't. Don't you dare give up. Not now." I begged him.

"I can help." Nessa's voice nearly broke me. My friend knelt beside me and held my hand. My fear vanished at her touch. A cloud lifted from my stressed mind, and I could think clearly. I grabbed Warren's hand with my free one and pulled it to my chest.

"I can take it from you." I breathed out.

"No, Josie, you—" He arched his back and gasped as I tugged on the magic inside him. Beside me, I felt Nessa tense and whine in pain. My focus was so intent on Warren that I didn't worry about why I didn't feel any pain. I closed my eyes and pushed on, absorbing as much of the excess magic as I could until I felt the familiar tingle of his magic. It was like my favorite hoodie on a cold winter's night. His magic wrapped around me in a warm embrace before returning to his body.

Warren and Nessa both eased their tension, returning to normal breathing. I opened my eyes and turned to my friend. "What are you doing here?" I asked.

"We have a lot to talk about, but later." She eyed Warren laying on the floor. "I need to find Clint." She leaned in and kissed me on the temple before standing and walking away.

I watched Warren's chest rise and fall. He was alive. That was all that mattered. I waited until his breathing slowed to lie beside him. He dropped his arm, letting my head rest on it, before wrapping me up in his embrace. He hissed slightly as I touched his side.

"I-I'm sorry." His arm tightened as I tried to pull away.

"Don't be. You saved my life." He didn't look up as he spoke.

"But I couldn't heal you. Not all the way, at least." Guilt settled in my gut.

"I'm alive, and you are lying next to me. How bad could it really be?"

I propped myself up on my elbow, examining the tattered remains of his clothes. My fingers followed the scar that stretched across his torso, from his hip to his neck and around the edge of his jaw on the right side, resembling lightning etched into his skin.

"It's..." I paused, searching for the right word. "Incredible." I chuckled.

Warren finally opened his eyes, meeting mine. I grinned so widely it was almost painful. He drew me into him, eliciting a giggle from me. His arms held me close to his chest, and he gently guided my face with his hand as his fingers ran through my hair.

The kiss was slow and soft. Time stopped, and it was just us in the ruins of the old factory. He was here. I was here. We were alive and in each other's arms.

"Ahem." Sam's voice from behind broke us apart. "I am happy you two have survived, but... the children?"

Forty-One

Josie

My mind connected with Rocky's the moment Sam mentioned the kids. I wasn't sure what to expect, but I mentally braced for no response. The sounds of his heart beating echoed in my ears, calming me.

'Rocky! Where are you? The other kids? We are safe now, but we need to find you.' I projected my thoughts as clearly as I could.

'We're here. We're all together. I'm not sure where, though?'

'Did she take you to the surgery room? Walk us through where you went from there.'

I stood and was moving toward the stairs before Warren had time to stand. Only when a buzz like an all-night bender hit me in the gut did I pause. The nausea washed over me in waves. I gripped the cold metal railing and doubled over. When my stomach settled a bit, I glanced back at my match. He was leaning against Sam for support and appeared as green as I felt.

"What is this? Why do I feel so sick?" I asked.

"Because I do," Warren said plainly. "We are bonded now. Whatever you did to save me has connected us together. We can sense each other's emotions and pain. I'm sorry, my love, that you feel as terrible as I do right now."

Something fluttered in the pit of my stomach. But it wasn't the nausea, it was pure love for this man. Goosebumps ran across my arms, and I smiled.

"I love you too, my Josie," he said. I ran to his side, taking some of his weight, and wrapped my arm around his waist.

"I didn't speak those words." I laughed.

"No, but I felt it. You can't deny it now."

I let my hand slip under his shirt, brushing his tender flesh beneath.

'Later, my love.' I felt the burning desire of his need course through me, and I gripped him tighter.

"If you two are done making gooey eyes at each other, I'd prefer getting these kids outta here before sunrise," Sam finally spoke.

I couldn't see my face, but I knew I must have blushed. Sam took a step forward, forcing Warren and me to follow. With each step we took, what little strength I had drained out of me, but finally we made it to the stairs.

Warren and I were huffing for air like we'd ran a mile. His skin was slick with sweat and his heart beat so hard it vibrated against my hand on his chest.

"We need a break," I said to Sam, leaning against the railing.

"Mind if I help?" Tanner walked up the steps to where we stood. "I can help you heal him," he said to me.

Warren sighed, but nodded. Tanner placed his hands on my shoulders as I turned to face Warren, placing both hands on his chest. I closed my eyes and pushed out with my magic, looking for any injury. It was as if I were a human CAT scan. In my mind, I saw all the organs in his chest. His heart pumped a little faster, but otherwise normal.

Everything else appeared normal. I mean normal for what a high school gym teacher would understand as normal. Except for his lungs... something was definitely not right with one of them.

"I'm no medical expert, but I think your lung is punctured," I told him without opening my eyes.

"Well... that... explains... why... it... hurts... to... breathe..."

"Relax. I think I can fix it."

I searched out the hole. He had a broken rib that had nicked the lung. I ignored his gasp when my magic pushed the bone back into place and welded it back to the rest. The tissue of the lung stitched back together and the air slowly re-inflated it. His breathing slowed to a more normal pace.

"I-I... Thank you," he said.

When I opened my eyes, they were all staring at me.

I bunched my eyebrows together. "What?"

Sam spoke. "Most healers would have taken a day or more to heal something that bad. You did it in a matter of moments."

"Well, I am one of the Lost Wolsteincroft's." I shrugged and headed down the stairs.

'That was a little more than normal. Even for us.' I heard Rocky's voice in my mind, but brushed it aside. My stomach was a mess, and I wanted out of this place. I'd worry about what I was when we were safe.

As we walked through the halls, we could see people cleaning up the mess. But this time, they moved to let us pass. I heard Sam talking to a few, asking for help once we found the kids.

I moved as quickly as possible to the place where I'd been held and reached out to Rocky.

The moment I connected with him, a map laid out clearly in my head. It showed me exactly how to get to where Rocky was.

'That wasn't me, Jo,' Rocky said, and a shiver ran down my spine.

We followed the path to another set of stairs leading us further underground. The stench hit me before we reached the bottom. I could only assume it was that of feces and urine and the general stink of unwashed flesh. I nearly gagged as I opened the door to the subbasement.

'Jo! Behind you!' Rocky warned at the last moment.

Something hard hit the back of my head, and everything went black.

I woke up with a pounding headache, and my wrists bound behind my back. My vision slowly returned. Warren lay in a cage not twenty feet away. *Great. I just patched him up too!* And Sam was in a cage next to him.

"I'm sorry, sister. I didn't know he was there." I searched for Rocky.

"Him? Him who?" It was so dark I only saw row after row of cages with shadowy figures inside. But as I turned, I saw the "him" he was talking about. Even in the absence of light, I knew exactly who he was. "Caleb!" I spat.

I struggled to my feet and faced him. He was the reason I was here in the first place. He was the reason I'd only now come into my true self. Rage burned deep within the pit of my stomach. I'd let it simmer there a little while longer before I unleashed it.

"Oh my, Josefina, how I have missed you! But I will have you back now." He almost purred.

"I know what you are now. Even more, I know who I am, and you can never again manipulate me into doing your will." I had to rein in the rage.

"I think not. You might know your name and lineage, but you don't have a clue what you are."

I could no longer contain the building anger. It spilled over onto my skin. The heat melted the plastic ties around my wrists, but I didn't move.

He stepped closer, falling right into my trap. His icy finger grazed my cheek. The moment he touched my burning flesh, he knew his mistake. I snapped my hand around and grasped him by the throat.

Death wouldn't suit this man. He had done far too much to me to have earned a quick death. No, I'd send him back to where he came from and let them deal with him.

I pictured every image of Hell I'd ever seen in Sunday school or the movies and tightened my grip. He squirmed and whined but didn't break free. I thought of the lesson Warren had given me on how to move things through space, and I shoved Caleb. I shoved him through the space between us and Hell. One second, he was here in my grasp, the next, he was gone.

I held onto the image of him falling on the hard floor of Hell, begging for mercy from the demons that reigned there, and smiled.

Forty-Two

Josie

The sun had long set, leaving Warren's bar bathed in twilight. The only light came from the circle of softly glowing candles and the faint shimmer of magic that swirled between us. The air smelled of petrichor and pine, carrying a quiet sense of reverence. It had only been a few weeks since he'd rescued me and shut down the operations at the warehouse, but standing here with him and our friends, it felt like an ancient memory.

We stood in the center of a circle in the middle of his bar. My fingers were laced with Warren's, our hands illuminated by gold and silver threads of magic weaving between them. My heart pounded, not with nerves, but with certainty. This moment, this bond, felt as natural as breathing.

Warren held my gaze, his blue eyes steady and filled with something deep and unshakable. Rocky, Sam, Tanner, Clint, and Nessa stood just beyond the circle, silent witnesses to what we were about to do. Rocky watched with quiet approval, Tanner elbowed Clint, who was clearly trying not to tear up, and Sam smirked, arms crossed over his chest.

A soft gust of warm air swirled through the circle, carrying the pulse of magic higher. Nessa must have whispered something under her breath, but I barely noticed. All I could focus on was Warren.

"I vow," he said, his voice low and firm, thick with emotion, "to love you, protect you, and stand beside you for as long as I live. My magic is yours, my strength is yours, and my heart will never waver."

The golden threads of magic brightened, wrapping around my hands, waiting. I took a steadying breath.

"I vow to love you, to protect you, and to walk this path with you, no matter what comes. My magic is yours, my soul is yours, and I will never turn away."

The moment the words left my lips, the magic surged, wrapping around us in a brilliant, spiraling weave. A warmth spread through my veins, sinking into my skin, into my bones, sealing the vow in something far deeper than flesh. I gasped softly as it settled.

Warren let out a breath, a slow smile breaking across his face. "It's done," he murmured.

I smiled back. "It's done."

Tanner whooped, clapping Warren on the back, while Clint wiped at his eyes. Rocky gave a small nod of approval, and Sam smirked as he nudged my shoulder. "You're stuck with him now."

I laughed, squeezing Warren's hands. "Wouldn't have it any other way."

Warren pulled me close, pressing his forehead against mine as the last flickers of magic faded into the night.

I ROLLED OVER AND REACHED OUT A HAND TO WHERE Warren lay in my bed, only feeling the sheets. I shot open my eyes and searched for him. My heart stopped. It was real. I was a warlock and Warren was my match and we had gone through the tying ceremony last night. Right? *My ex is gone, and the doctor is dead. Vampires and werewolves are real.* I had to repeat this mantra to myself at least five times a day since Warren had freed me. But he wasn't here, so could it all have been a dream?

I jolted when the bedroom door creaked open. Inside the doorway stood all six feet five of my Warren, garbed in only an apron around his waist, carrying a tray of breakfast. His lightning bolt scar ran down his entire right side, peeked under the fabric, and continued down to his knee. I sat up and took him all in. His muscles flexed as he walked closer, careful not to spill the two mugs of coffee.

"What?" He finally glanced up.

His hair, which is normally neat, fell around his eyes and became disheveled.

"What?" he asked again when I didn't answer.

"Not hungry." My voice sounded husky even to me. I sat up on my knees on the edge of the bed. He was close enough I grazed my finger down his scar, stopping at the rope of the apron. "But I am a little... thirsty." I grinned. My hand slipped beneath the cloth and cupped the tender flesh he'd been hiding.

"Josie..." he gasped. "Food..." I pulled away from him long enough to let him set the tray down. The second his hands were free, I pulled him onto the bed. He laid flat on his back beside me as I continued to caress him.

"I thought we were supposed to be relaxing today so you could get back to work in the morning?" Warren teased.

"Screw that." I flipped over, straddling him.

Now that we were connected, I felt everything he felt as well. The depths of his love for me. The ache that remained in his scar. My skin on his skin. I felt it all. His magic coursed through me, sending lightning bolts rippling over my flesh in a tidal wave of pleasure.

THE DAY HAD WORN ON AND WE HAD YET TO LEAVE THE BED. We'd devoured the breakfast he had made up after warming it back up. Other responsibilities had called to us, but we were content to lie there in each other's arms all day.

"You know you don't have to go back to work, right? I have enough money, and now that you're a warlock..." Warren had been trying to win this argument since the warehouse.

"I know I don't have to, but never again will I allow another man to put me in the position of subordinate. I can take care of myself."

"Yes, I know you can. I'm just saying—"

"I know exactly what you're saying. But I enjoy my work." I sat up, looking at him. "Okay, how about this? Let me work and stop complaining about it and I will let you spoil me over the breaks."

"It's not even that. You've been through a lot, and I want to make sure you're ready?" His fear and concern radiated off him.

"I am fine. I promise. Now, do we have a deal?" I put out my hand for him to shake. "Rocky has asked if we'd come visit him in Europe?"

His frown slowly turned up. "Fine. But we will spend the entire summer overseas?"

I nodded. He batted my hand away and pulled me closer. "Oh, my Josie. You might be the death of me yet," he whispered in my ear before kissing me softly.

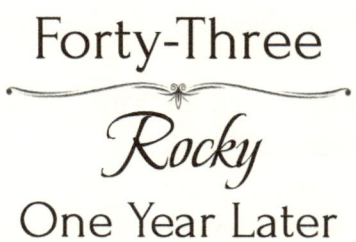

Forty-Three

Rocky

One Year Later

The purple and pink haze of the setting sun filled the sky over my favorite city. I stood, sipping whiskey on my penthouse balcony, watching patrons leaving the Louvre and wondering what it would feel like to be an ordinary human with average worries.

Instead, my gut churned at the war I knew was brewing, and I knew the only way to stop the destruction of humanity was to unite the Figli Del Mito of the world.

Although I was young compared to Warren or Sam, my name held weight. And for those who didn't believe me, they would quickly learn I was the only male heir to the lost Wolsteincroft's.

A knock on the glass door pulled me from my musings.

"Rockefeller, sir. They're here," Asher said. He'd been the first warlock to join my cause when I first came to Paris.

"Thanks." I handed him my glass and walked inside. My family had money, so I hadn't been concerned at the price tag of a loft in the heart of the city. I knew I'd need the space, so I'd splurged.

Six Figli Del Mito leaders sat at the teak table in the middle of my formal dining room, all sneering at one another. Their glares turned to me when I approached.

"Thank you all for joining me tonight. I have asked you here to give a warning and a proposition."

"And who the hell are you to call us here?" One of the two fae queens snapped.

"I told you in my fire message. I am Rockefeller Wolsteincroft." I straightened.

The queen stood and circled me. "You look like a sapling. Nothing but a twig to be broken." The metal twang of her removing a blade behind me hit my ears, and I reacted.

My body transformed seamlessly into that of a massive wolf and my jaws clamped around her neck, tossing her to the floor before she'd blinked. With a twist of my maw, I snapped her neck. I was back in my human form before anyone had left their seats.

"If you walked in here doubting my origins, I hope that is no longer the case." The few who were half out of their chairs sat back down, never fully looking me in the face but also not looking away. "Good. Now to business. Roughly twelve months ago, a vampire clan kidnapped me and conducted experiments on children. They weren't acting alone. They were part of a group calling themselves Corps de l'Ombre. I've been gathering information about them ever since my sister and her match rescued me from that nightmare. Then a few months ago something happened in the New England area. Some are calling it the Flash because there was a burst of green light only the Figli Del Mito could see." No one reacted. "Now, magic is slowly leaking back into the world."

A long moment passed before one warlock spoke. "So? Isn't that a good thing for us?" he asked.

"I'm sure many of you know the name the Mage?" They all stiffened. "He is my sister's match. Long ago, someone gave him a prophecy of this war. Magic will rip this world to shreds and destroy everything we have built, as both humanity and the Figli Del Mito. This war will split alliances, but I propose we create a new alliance here and now. I have asked you all here because you represent the strongest leaders of your people in this area, and I wish to unite all Figli Del Mito under one rule."

The other fae queen kicked over her chair. "And why in the goddess's name would we do that? The fae would never stand with the warlocks or any other monster."

"Then you will lie on the floor with the other fae. Our world is splitting apart and the only way to save it is to unite against the Corps de l'Ombre. There is magic out there, and soon the humans will discover our existence. We might be stronger than them, but they outnumber us a thousand to one. If you want to go up against those odds, then be my guest." I stepped aside, pointing to the way out. "There's the door. I won't stop you." No one moved. "But if you want to stop this war, we must unite before it is too late."

One by one, they all agreed and signed a blood oath with me and the other Figli Del Mito before departing into the night.

My phone rang the moment I was alone again.

"Jo," I answered. "Perfect timing. You guys on your way yet?"

"Yeah, Warren chartered a private jet, so we're boarding now." My sister's voice was light, so I did my best to match her tone.

"Great! I'll meet you at the airport. We have a lot to talk about."

"See you soon!"

"Safe flight, Jo." I hung up before the worry seeped into my voice. I just became the leader of a powerful society and had to convince my sister it was the right decision.

Afterword

Thank you for reading the first book of the Lost Wolsteincroft Series, Almost Tragic Magic. If you enjoyed it, please leave a review on Goodreads, Storygraph, Anywhere books are sold.

Almost Tragic Alliance, A novella (book 1.5) will be released Summer 2025 and Anything for Magic, Book 2 will be released by the end of 2025. If you are interested in keeping up with the progress, please follow me on TikTok, Instagram, or Facebook.

If you want sneak peaks, sign up for my newsletter.

If you want to read more while you wait, check out the rest of my books on my website.

Acknowledgments

The past two years have been the hardest of my life and I didn't think I'd ever get this book done but here we are. I've put my heart and soul into this story and I hope you loved it as much as I do.

First and foremost I have to thank Jamie for seeing the potential in this story when I was ready to quit. Because of you Josie grew into the woman I knew she could be. Words cannot express how grateful I am to you for giving me hope.

As always I have to thank my critique partners, Julia, Liahona, Amanda, and Marissa. Your advice and support over the years have been invaluable.

Thank you to my editor, Sage Santiago for shaping and molding this story into what it is today. And for her patients when I chose to change three scenes after starting the line edits!

About the Author

Kari Robins has always preferred the written word to the spoken word. She has been writing flash fiction since she was in middle school. She would write stories instead of taking notes in class.

Kari is a working mom and wife.

A high school teacher encouraged her to become a writer but feared her grammar wasn't good enough. But now she pays an editor for that!

She recently graduated from college tobecome a teacher for Technology and Engineering but the COVID-19 pandemic changed her plans and she started writing again.

She started off writing new adult paranormal romance but has recently discovered the paranormal woman's fiction genre and has fallen in love with older main characters.